THE WHITBREAD STORIES *1*

The first collection of stories chosen from the entries for the Whitbread Prize for the best short story by a writer aged between 16 and 25 displays a remarkable range of talent and theme. Here are stories set in Greece and in Liverpool, during the First World War and at a disastrous coffee morning; there is a strangely touching look into the future, there is a searing portrayal of madness, there is the hilarious diary of an outspoken girl who is not at all like Adrian Mole. Tragedy, drama, fantasy, humour, they are all present in this exciting collection.

THE WHITBREAD STORIES *1*

HAMISH HAMILTON
London

First published in Great Britain 1985
by Hamish Hamilton Ltd
Garden House 57—59 Long Acre London WC2E 9JZ

British Library Cataloguing in Publication Data

The Whitbread stories 1.
823'.01'08 [FS] PR1309.S5
ISBN 0-241-11544-2

Filmset by Pioneer
Printed and bound in Great Britain by
Richard Clay (The Chaucer Press) Ltd, Bungay, Suffolk

CONTENTS

Introduction vii

The Face of the Horned Magdalene 1
by Vanessa F. Brunning

A Man of the Body 16
by Nicholas Butt

Good Intentions 42
by Leonard Dean-King

Mad Brother 55
by Tim Etchells

Borneo 69
by Patrick Gale

Down the Light-Well 85
by R. M. Hale

Ghost Writing 101
by D. A. Herling

Loomis 114
by Mark Illis

Thiepval 128
by Ruth McCracken

Madness 142
by David Rogers

Tomorrow is our Permanent Address 156
by Diane Rowe

A Freeborn Man 169
by Philippa Tyson

INTRODUCTION

There is a distinct prejudice against the form of the short story. On many occasions I have been shocked to hear critics and writers speak disparagingly of it on the grounds that a short story cannot develop character or plot, simply because it *is* short. I mutter balefully, and with growing aggression, names like Maupassant and Colette, Frank O'Connor and William Trevor, V. S. Pritchett and Graham Greene, Katherine Mansfield and Chekhov (and I am not even allowed to get on to the Americans), but the prejudice remains undiminished.

It is, therefore, particularly satisfying that Whitbreads have instituted a new prize, awarded for the first time in 1985, specifically for the best unpublished short story by a writer aged between sixteen and twenty-five. Twelve stories have been selected from the 149 entries and now appear in this first collection of Whitbread Stories.

When Martin Amis and I read the stories we had no idea of the ages of the writers. This was entirely appropriate so that we were not tempted to favour those nearer sixteen than twenty-five. As it transpired, the ages of the selected writers range from seventeen to twenty-four. The range of subject matter is, of course, far wider. Certain recurring themes did emerge. There were a great many stories concerned with the unfairness of parents, the unfairness of school-teachers, the unfairness of life itself. There were a number of attempts – almost all unsuccessful – at what can loosely be called genre stories: fantasy, science fiction, the ghost story. There was not much humour, there were rather too many stories heavily influenced by either James Joyce or Virginia Woolf. There was a deep fascination with madness.

The theme of madness does indeed appear in this collection, most obviously and remarkably in David Rogers' story, but also highly originally in Tim Etchells' 'Mad Brother'. There is fantasy in Vanessa Brunning's sinister tale of peculiar goings-on in an old people's home, and there is a glimpse of the extra-terrestrial in Leonard Dean-King's 'Good Intentions', which manages the difficult task of making science fiction both comic and touching. Richard Hale's 'Down the Light-Well' also has its comic element, though it is essentially a study in disintegration. Patrick Gale's 'Borneo' is a sharply-observed piece of social comedy with a tragic core which will appeal to admirers of Alan Ayckbourn's plays.

Nicholas Butt's 'A Man of the Body' is the longest story in the collection, indeed it is two stories in one; it is also an extraordinarily vivid evocation of the age-old enmity between Greek and Turk, and of the power of God to overcome the results of that enmity. D. A. Herling's 'Ghost Writing' is perhaps the most consciously 'literary' of all the stories, in that it concerns the involvement of the writer with his characters and with the plot which he weaves around them. Mark Illis and Philippa Tyson both present portraits of loners, though the two stories are totally different in atmosphere and approach: Loomis is a master of illusion and sleight-of-hand, so that he even fights like a dancer; Miss Tyson's down-and-nearly-out Irishman in Liverpool with his disastrous sentimental memories is something else again. Ruth McCracken's characters are also Irish, two brothers caught up in the holocaust of trench warfare at Thiepval and their parents waiting for those inevitable telegrams. Finally, there is Diane Rowe's very funny and often gloriously rude diary kept by a girl who may seem, at first glance, to be a down-market female Adrian Mole but who turns out to be completely different.

These, then, are the stories in the first collection of Whitbread Stories, the first, I hope, of many such annual collections.

Christopher Sinclair-Stevenson

THE FACE OF THE HORNED MAGDALENE

Vanessa F. Brunning

Agatha Scritchwallow was a small woman with grey skin and wild eyes. She gave the impression that her life lay in the direct path of an express train and that from the moment of her birth she must always be running from it, always on the look-out lest it should catch her off her guard and run her down. For this reason she was beginning to go bald at forty and what patches of hair she still had hung in clumps like couch-grass or the fur of an old and misused teddy bear over her terrified magnolia eyes.

Major Scritchwallow's eyes were a deep pink in colour. He had once contracted some hideous skin disease whilst serving in India. He had been an officer out there for many years and had killed lots of men but his eyes had never recovered their natural shade and they gave his face an uncharitable air even in his more pensive moments. They were smiling now, however, a little vermilion smile of welcome, while his dry, prune-brown, thin, lizard lips echoed the sentiment joyously. 'Welcome, my dear Mrs. Bruise. Welcome, welcome to our humble home. Welcome to Placculent House.' His angular limbs were straining forward over the balcony in the effort of effulgence like some gigantic asymmetrical spider.

'Well, here we are then, mother.'

Behind the wheelchair where Mrs. Bruise sat, small and damp and woollen, was a tall, nervous young man with thin hair, smoking a pipe that was much too large for him. He wheeled his mother noiselessly over the threshold. 'I hope you'll be happy here.'

'I'm sure she will, sir. I'm sure she will. We shall do our utmost.' And Major and Mrs. Scritchwallow received Mrs. Bruise with open arms.

Her fine-haired son stayed for a respectable length of time, then he kissed his mother's bluish cheeks and left very quickly in an old Morris Minor.

'Welcome to Placculent House, Mrs. Bruise!' repeated the Major. 'Welcome, welcome, welcome!'

'Such a lovely view,' Mrs. Bruise said.

'Yes, Mrs. Bruise, it is a lovely view, isn't it. Would you like to take your coat off? May I help you?'

'Thank you.'

'Not at all, not at all. Let me introduce you to someone, Mrs. Bruise. Through here, there we are. Am I wheeling you too fast, Mrs Bruise? No? That's good. Mrs. Bruise, this is Alistair. Our oldest guest. Our only guest in fact. But now that you've come we shall be much more cheerful, shan't we?'

In one corner of the room sat a peach-coloured old man, wrapped in innumerable blankets, clutching in one hand a crumpled souvenir guide to the Cheddar Gorge. He was learning how to integrate 1tanze with respect to x, in black and white, but found time to nod at Mrs. Bruise.

'That's right, Mrs. Bruise. Much more cheerful. Would you care to see your room? It's upstairs. Next to Alistair's, in fact. Lovely view. You can walk a little, can't you, Mrs. Bruise?'

'A little, but it tires me.'

'That's good. Up we go then.'

The first thing Mrs. Bruise noticed about her room was the wall. She had been staring at it for quite some time before it really began to make her uneasy. It was completely bare except for a small, yellow-tiled fireplace that held an electric heater where there should have been a fire. The wall itself might once have been yellow or even white but was now smeared with a uniform, sickly grey. What it was about the thing which distressed her so much Mrs. Bruise could not begin to describe. She sat on the edge of the bed huddled in her tiny pink cardigan, with her damp little hands clenched together, staring at it till the nurse came to take her away for supper.

Mrs. Bruise could not stop thinking about her wall all evening. It coloured her conversation so that it seemed to her that she answered a disproportionate number of implausible questions about walls and to all Major Scritchwallow's polite enquiries replied with unfaltering regularity, 'Greyness.'

Alistair was silent throughout the meal. It was only when they brought in the semolina that he was prompted to ask if Mrs. Bruise had ever been to the Cheddar Gorge. Mrs. Bruise replied rather tremulously that she had not.

'Mrs. Peg had been to Cheddar. She'd been there lots of times. Did you say you'd ever been to Cheddar, Mrs. Boose? I forget whether you said you had or not.' Mrs. Bruise shook her head again.

'Oh,' said Alistair and he was moodily silent again for a few minutes before continuing with, 'Mrs. Peg and I used to talk about the Cheddar Gorge a lot. Almost all the time. She'd been there, you see, and she used to knock on my door first thing in the morning and I'd say, 'Who is it?' and she'd say, 'It's me, Mrs. Peg, can I come in?' and then she'd come in and we'd have a little chat. Of course she was in that same room you've got now. The one next to mine, number four.'

Mrs. Scritchwallow looked as if she saw the express train coming for her. 'Not in the room next to yours, Alistair, that wasn't where Mrs. Peg lived. It was the one opposite, don't you remember?'

'Oh yes,' said Alistair, and wheezed.

'How old would you say Alistair was, Mrs. Bruise?' the Major asked suddenly.

'Really,' offered Mrs. Bruise, 'you don't look a day over . . .'

'Eighty-nine,' said Alistair triumphantly. 'I'll be ninety next June. Course, I can't get around like I used to. Artificial hips. But Mrs. Peg, now she was good at walking. Nothing artificial about her, she was all real. Even died standing up, you know. Went to the lavatory one day and when she didn't come back they found her dead with her hand on the door.'

After this unusually long speech, Alistair was stricken by a paroxysm of wheezing and relapsed into peachy silence for the rest of the evening.

'Oh,' said Mrs. Bruise after a pause. Then she added, 'I'm not old either, you know.'

'And don't look it, Mrs. Bruise, don't look it!'

'Only sixty grey,' Mrs. Bruise said. Then she became conscious of having made a mistake and was confused.

'I think I should like to go upstairs now.'

'Of course, Mrs. Bruise, you must be tired. How thoughtless of us. Why not use the chairlift, yes, use the chairlift, we have a chairlift you know!' said the Major.

She was escorted up to her room by Mrs. Scritchwallow and the express train while Major Scritchwallow stood at the bottom of the stairs and shouted, 'Horlicks, Mrs. Bruise? Horlicks for you? And a ginger biscuit perhaps, if you're not too tired. Are you too tired to eat a ginger biscuit, Mrs. Bruise?'

At last Mrs. Bruise was sitting on her bed again. Staring at the wall through the gaps between her little pink fingers, she could now discern the source of her uneasiness, it was so obvious she could not imagine how she had come to miss it before. In the top right-hand corner of the wall, quite close to the ceiling, was a face. It was not a large face, about the size of a man's hand perhaps, and it was drawn without any great degree of skill, in thick black ink. It was clearly intended to be the face of a woman for it had long hair arranged in ringlets through which protruded ears of unusual size and shape, and on top of the head, where the hair was thickest, rose a pair of fine curling horns. The lips were quite obviously feminine, as were the large black eyes that seemed to follow one about the room. They were staring towards the bed now and at Mrs. Bruise sitting bolt upright with her limp pink cardigan clutched to her face.

After a while Nurse appeared with a mug of grey, over-sweet Horlicks and a single ginger biscuit on a pale blue plate.

Mrs. Bruise would have liked to tell her about the dreadful face but somehow the words seemed to stick in her throat. Had she been able to utter them they would in any case have been of little use with this huge clean large-handed woman with her wide, friendly bloodless face and thick pale lips. She left Mrs. Bruise with a garish blue copy of the New Testament in its newest form, and then turned out the light.

Mrs. Bruise drifted off to sleep that night to pink and white tablets and the sound of barking dogs.

At half-past eight the next morning, Major Scritchwallow appeared at the door in a pair of stained khaki trousers and an odd dark-coloured jumper that was much too small for him. The clothes gave his body a curiously misshapen air and he glided into the room with a gait more suited to the pelvic girdle of a dinosaur brought to life than to any human being. He was carrying a steel tray with breakfast things on it and carrying it so that his tiny pink eyes were on a level with the spout of the willow pattern teapot.

'Good morning, Mrs. Bruise, lovely day.'

Mrs. Bruise clutched the bedclothes about her. 'It's raining,' she said.

'Oh, Mrs. Bruise, you haven't drunk up your Horlicks! Or eaten your ginger biscuit for that matter!'

'I didn't like the colour,' said Mrs. Bruise. She was afraid she had been rude but, if she had, Major Scritchwallow did not seem to have noticed it. He was putting the tray onto a small, peeling gold table by her bed and whistling to himself. Then he sat down on the edge of the quilt and looked at her without blinking until his eyes watered.

'Do you, ah, do you like the table, Mrs. Bruise?' He seemed to be under the impression that Mrs. Bruise was deaf for he raised his voice to a ridiculous level when speaking to her and pronounced each word with horrible distinction. 'Yes, I brought it back with me from India. Served out there for quite a while in my younger days. Nice piece, isn't it, Mrs. Bruise. Probably quite valuable.'

Mrs. Bruise had a vague idea that it was probably one of the nastiest and least expensive 'pieces' she had seen since her days at the vicarage but she only clenched her little hands together and, smiling, tried not to look at his eyes. There was a pause. 'Well, I won't keep you then,' Major Scritchwallow said. He got to his feet and Mrs. Bruise noticed he was wearing odd slippers, one purple velvet and one a bamboo-coloured cork-matting affair, both filthy.

'Oh, one moment, Major.'

He turned in the doorway to find Mrs. Bruise pointing with one trembling pink hand at the corner of the wall.

'Who did that?'

'What, Mrs. Bruise? Who did what?'

'The drawing.'

'Oh, you mean the face.' The Major let out a short, sharp, audible sigh which was his usual substitute for a laugh. 'That little thing? Why, that was Mrs. Peg's invention. She said it made the wall look a little less bare. It's supposed to be the Magdalene, I think, you know, Mary Magdalene? Staunch R.C. was Mrs. Peg, big strapping woman, too, but you can tell that by looking at the picture. See how high up it is! Way above my head.'

'But what about the beard?' Mrs. Bruise insisted. 'The beard on the face, it wasn't there yesterday.'

'What was that, Mrs. Bruise?' Another loud sigh. 'Yes, a remarkable woman was Mrs. Peg. Marvellous red hair she had, down to her waist it was, yes indeed. Not real of course, she was quite bald underneath, but don't you go telling that to Alistair, will you! No. I'm sure you won't, Mrs. Bruise.'

'The beard.' Mrs. Bruise had a very small voice even when she wasn't terrified and probably the Major did not hear her.

'Anyway, I'll be getting on now. Nurse'll be here in a little while to help you dress.' He winked at her once and then he and his thin scarlet eyes slid soundlessly out of the room. Looking at herself in the mirror after he'd gone Mrs. Bruise noticed something rather alarming. She decided to go downstairs after breakfast to find Mrs. Scritchwallow and ask her advice.

Mrs. Scritchwallow and Nurse were sitting in front of a scabby-looking Indian screen listening to Radio 4. Nurse was knitting something small and knotted in purple wool and Mrs. Scritchwallow was eating marzipan with a teaspoon from a huge five-pound block. There was a distinct smell of diesel fumes about her.

'Mrs. Scritchwallow,' said Mrs. Bruise.

'Yes, dear?'

Mrs. Bruise came a little closer.

'What is it, lovey?'

And closer still until she could just whisper in Mrs. Scritchwallow's rather yellowish ear.

'Why yes, my dear, I think you are.' Mrs. Scritchwallow said loudly. 'Just a bit of a one.'

'What's that?' Nurse had a deep husky baritone voice rather like a bloodhound's.

'Mrs. Bruise thinks she's growing a beard,' Mrs. Scritchwallow informed her.

'A beard? Well, well, whatever next! We shall have to be buying you an electric razor soon, shan't we, Mrs. Bruise! Never mind, ducks, soon sort you out with a few hormones. Just leave it to Nurse.'

In the next room Alistair was sitting in front of the television being fed Biblical Allegory by a well-spoken young man in horn-rimmed glasses. Alistair smiled at Mrs. Bruise as she came in and waved the Cheddar Gorge pamphlet at her. 'You should take a look at this, Mrs. Boose. Very interesting place is the Cheddar Gorge. My son works there, you know, in the caves. Mrs. Peg told me she'd actually seen him there once. Just fancy! It's such a small world, isn't it'.

'Yes,' said Mrs. Bruise.

'Of course, you haven't been to Cheddar Gorge, have you. But take a look at this anyway, you might find it interesting.'

Mrs. Bruise took the guide and thanked him. 'Were you . . .' she hesitated, 'were you good friends with Mrs. Peg?'

'Oh, she was a good woman was Mrs. Peg, a good woman. Very religious, mind you, always careful to remember to cross herself and not to tread on insects. A very good woman.'

The thought occurred to Mrs. Bruise that it was a strange kind of good woman who drew horns on the Magdalene, but she said nothing and as if in reply to her thoughts the well-spoken young man on the television said, 'Figural Allegory.'

'Ah, Figural Allegory, figural allegory,' murmured Alistair.

Mrs. Bruise tried again. 'Did Mrs. Peg . . .'

'Mrs. Bruise, Mrs. Bruise.' She jumped at a light bony touch on her shoulder. 'Not letting the ghost of Mrs. Peg trouble us again, are we?'

He advanced blinking into the room. The Major had a curious habit of preparing himself, whenever he entered a room, with a series of rapid blinks. He was then free to converse for the next four or five minutes without so much as a flicker.

'Of course not, Major,' said Mrs. Bruise, and the Major smiled at her.

She spent the rest of the day in solitude, staring passively at the face until it seemed to be grinning at her from beneath that thick Russian beard.

It rained very heavily that night. When Mrs. Bruise opened her eyes she could scarcely believe it was morning. Three melancholic crows were sitting on a large blue chimney opposite her window, croaking the semblance of a dawn chorus, and the sky was a deep, dying brown. Several tiles had blown off during the night and the holes they left were like small dark mouths or eyes in the livid glistening of the rooftops. Major Scritchwallow was outside trying to retrieve some of the less damaged ones, treading the wet, brown grass in his odd slippers. He happened to look up as Mrs. Bruise came to the window and waved at her. 'Good morning, Mrs. Bruise, lovely day.'

Mrs. Bruise sat down in one of the bald green armchairs and stared once more at the face. Yesterday she had made Nurse turn all the furniture round so that she should never have to sit with her back to it and feel those ink-black eyes piercing into her soul. Today the face had grown a beauty spot. A small heart-shaped mole near the left-hand corner of the mouth. The grin she thought she had discerned yesterday was gone and in its place was a discreet coquettish smirk. The ears had grown too, so long that they had begun to entwine themselves around the horns like some stunted fleshy birdweed from tropical parts. 'It must be Nurse,' Mrs. Bruise thought. 'She must creep in here at night and do all this just to frighten me. She's the only one tall enough to reach. It must be her.'

As she came downstairs there were two skinny young men in black cheesecloth carrying a piano across the hall. A bleary-eyed Mrs. Scritchwallow stood in one of the adjoining doorways watching the proceedings and peeling a tomato with nervous fingers. She smiled at Mrs. Bruise and there were bits of tomato skin stuck to her teeth. There was a terrible noise of dogs.

'Ah, Mrs. Bruise,' the Major emerged startlingly behind her. He had his arms full of wet tiles and was soaked to the skin. Not for the first time, Mrs. Bruise was struck by the amphibian-like nature of his countenance. Now, with his wet grey hair clinging to and accentuating the curious, angular shape of his skull, she realised afresh that Major Scritchwallow was not a real person at all but a gigantic newt.

'The shed's started to leak, Mrs. Bruise,' he shouted, 'so I decided to bring the piano indoors! It'll be something to do of an evening anyway and maybe encourage you to come down a bit more, Mrs. Bruise! You really should, you know, it's no good staying up in that cold old lonely room of yours all the time. Do you play? No, neither do I. But there's the good thing about the pianola. No skill required in the playing of. Absolutely none! Just pedal away and the old pedals, ye—es.' He gave one of his habitual abrupt sighs. 'Drat those dogs! Where's the noise coming from?'

He poked his head around the nearest door, 'Settle down now! Settle down,' and then retreated with a shrug. 'Not in there, can't imagine where it's coming from. Didn't know we had dogs as a matter of fact. Must be Nurse's. By the way, I hear you're growing a beard, Mrs. Bruise.'

The two young men looked round.

'Have to watch out, Mrs. Bruise. In the old days they'd have burned you for a witch!'

Mrs. Bruise did not come down in the evenings. She stayed in her room and watched the face. She could hear the pianola downstairs being played with tuneless rapidity and the wild, muffled thuds that meant that Nurse was dancing. Mrs. Bruise stood up slowly and went over to the small scaley wash-basin that occupied the darkest corner of the room. There was an old dishcloth on top of the fireplace with which Mrs. Scritchwallow had recently been pretending to dust. Mrs. Bruise picked it up and a large spider scuttled across the tiles and disappeared in the semi-miraculous way unique to its race. Mrs. Bruise whimpered a little and dropping the cloth into the basin, turned on the hot tap as hard as she could so as to both boil and drown any companion monsters. It was a slow progress to drag one of the chairs over to the wall and then stand on it, all the while in constant terror that Nurse should hear the noise. Standing on the chair and stretching her frail blue body to its utmost, Mrs. Bruise could just reach with one ancient hand to wipe away the face of the hateful Magdalene. She scrubbed until her hand ached and her little birdlike heart was painful. It happened, of course, as she had expected it would. Not a line of the saint's face could be washed away except for the small birthmark on the left cheek. Mrs. Bruise's legs crumpled beneath her, she sank to her knees, then toppled and fell with a soft thud to the floor.

Downstairs, the music and dancing stopped and a few seconds later Nurse appeared, red in the face with her hands full of hormones and tiny pink tablets, closely followed by Mrs. Scritchwallow and the express train.

'Oh, Mrs. Bruise,' said Nurse. 'Oh, Mrs. Bruise, what a silly thing to do!' She took the ancient bundle of clothes in her huge clean hands and attempted to bring it to its feet, but then leapt back with a yell. 'Oh, Mrs. Bruise! What a naughty girl you are! Such sharp teeth!'

The following morning Mrs. Bruise was sitting looking at her picture as usual when the doorbell rang. She was no longer as terrified as she had been the night before. Nurse and the pink tablets had reduced her fear to a vague uneasiness, the texture of porridge or mild migraine. Even the discovery of a small mole on her left cheek did not distress her to any great degree.

The doorbell rang again and the dogs began to bark. There was a sound of the front door being opened and someone said, 'Mrs. Bruise in?'

'Certainly!' this from Major Scritchwallow.

'Arnold Bruise. Just popped along to see . . .'

'Mr. Bruise, come in, come in! Your mother's upstairs. I'll fetch her for you, come on in!'

Mrs. Bruise dressed herself as best she could, which was not very well, without any fine regard for detail, and hurried downstairs as fast as her trembling, emerald legs would carry her.

'Lucky Mrs. Bruise,' the Major was saying as she reached the landing, 'to have such charming visitors. Mr. and . . . Mrs. Bruise, is it?'

Hand in hand with Mr. Bruise was a large-boned, ugly woman with straight brown hair. She could have been any age from thirty to fifty but was probably about twenty-five. She was wearing a rectangular nylon costume in a colour that was not navy blue but produced the same effect, and her skin was very red. It went even redder as Major Scritchwallow said, 'Mrs. Bruise.'

Mr. Bruise coughed and said, 'This is Fiona.'

'Pleased to meet you. How d'you do!' shouted the Major and leaned forward at a dangerously acute angle.

Arnold Bruise stood back to let his companion enter. His hair and beard seemed thinner than on his last visit and in the cold morning light there was an ephemeral air to his appearance. The young woman shook hands with Major Scritchwallow as if she was the vicar and then followed him into the house. Arnold came after her with his head bent, wiping his feet very carefully on the mat. When he looked up Mrs. Bruise was standing quite close to him with a bright tearful smile on her usually flaccid face. He noticed with some distaste that she had smeared dark pink lipstick in a thick, clownlike ring round her mouth.

'Hello, mother,' he said.

At that moment the dogs stopped their barking and Nurse appeared.

'Ah, Nurse! You've met Mr. Bruise, haven't you? Our Mrs. Bruise's son. And this is . . . I'm sorry I don't know your surname.'

'Scott,' said Miss Scott.

Nurse smiled broadly and shook their hands. Miss Scott again pretended to be the vicar.

'Ah, through here, I think. This is our . . . our sitting room. We've just bought a pianola as you can see,' crossing over to the instrument and lifting the lid. 'My wife and I enjoy a little music-making of an evening. So does Nurse come to that. In fact Nurse is quite a performer, aren't you, Nurse?'

'Well, I wouldn't go as far as to say that, Major.'

The Major gave another of his abrupt sighs. 'Haven't persuaded your mother to take a turn yet though, have we, Mrs. Bruise!' He laughed again and then there was a long silence in which Mr. Bruise and Miss Scott smiled at each other. 'Well then, I'll, ah, leave you to chat,' said the Major, clapping his hands together. 'Perhaps you'd like something to drink? Tea, coffee, vodka?'

'Tea would be lovely, thanks,' said Mr. Bruise. 'No milk or sugar.'

'Fine, fine, and what about you, Miss Scott?'

'Nothing for me, thank you,' said Miss Scott. 'It's Ash Wednesday today and I'm fasting.'

'Right,' said the Major. He drew the word out into one of his sighs, and repeated it several times to himself, under his breath.

'Tea for you and Nurse, Mrs. Bruise?'

'Please.'

He disappeared and the four of them were left in silence. It was desperately important to Mrs. Bruise that Nurse should leave the room but she was spread like a stone over most of the sofa and showed no signs that she would ever get up again.

Arnold Bruise coughed. 'Well, how are you, mother?'

'I'm very well, thank you, dear. How are you?'

'Fine, fine,' said Arnold, unconsciously echoing the tones of the Major.

'You look very pale,' Mrs. Bruise said. 'Are you quite sure you're not ill?'

'Never been better, mother.'

There was another very long pause and then Mr. Bruise and Miss Scott made simultaneously incoherent beginnings.

'You first,' said Miss Scott.

'Well,' said Arnold. 'Ah, it's like this. What we actually came to tell you about, mother, Fiona and I, that is, is that . . .'

Just then Nurse unexpectedly rose and left the room.

'Well, thank goodness for that,' said Mr. Bruise, and they both laughed.

Mrs. Bruise suddenly realised that this was the worst thing that could have happened. For now Nurse would be able to slip up to her room and wipe off the face from the wall. To be sure, she herself had not been able to, but Nurse with her huge scrubbing muscles and strong detergents would be able to remove all trace of it without any trouble at all. It became of overwhelming importance to Mrs. Bruise that she should get Arnold up to her room before Nurse had a chance to spoil the evidence.

'Arnold,' she said, 'would you like to see my room?'

Mr. Bruise smiled at his mother without really paying attention. 'I've already seen it, mother. I came round to inspect the place before we put you here. Do you remember? You don't imagine I'd dump my own mother just anywhere surely?'

'But there's something I want to show you,' insisted Mrs. Bruise.

'What, right now?'

'It's very, very important.'

'Well, of course, mother, if it's important', smiling at Miss Scott, 'lead the way.'

When they reached Mrs. Bruise's room, to her immense relief there was no sign of Nurse. Moreover, the picture was still in its usual place, more hideous than ever. The birthmark had recently been replaced and the horns extended so that they curved in a wide arc over the top of the head and under the chin where they branched into two like the tongue of a serpent. In addition to this the whites of the eyes had been blacked out so that they now resembled the gaping orbits of a skull.

'It's horrible!' exclaimed Arnold. He crossed himself.

Fiona frowned at him. 'What is it?' she asked Mrs. Bruise.

'Every day she adds a little bit more,' Mrs. Bruise said. 'Sometimes twice a day. I dislike her.'

'You mean Nurse? Surely not. I would have said it'd be more likely to be that batty woman without any hair, what's her name, Mrs. Scritchwallow. The one that smells of petrol.'

Mrs. Bruise shook her head. 'Can't you take me away from here, Arnold? Can't I come home with you?'

'You know I'd love to have you, mother, but it's simply not possible. You know what a small house I have and now . . .'

'Oh yes,' said Mrs. Bruise, and then there was another long pause.

'Is it only the picture that's upsetting you, mother? Surely we can just rub it off.'

'It won't rub off,' said Mrs. Bruise. She stared at the ground and then at Miss Scott's broad, methodist shoes and her son's shabby, leather sandals.

'I'll get a cloth,' Miss Scott said quietly.

She returned in a little while with a large bottle of detergent and after a few minutes of scrubbing with those competent, brick-red hands the picture was gone. It might never have been there at all except for two small patches of grey where the eyes had been and where the ink had been laid on so thickly as to have permeated the paintwork and made it impossible to remove entirely.

'Thank you,' said Mrs. Bruise unhappily.

Miss Scott only smiled and said, 'Bless you, dear.'

'Well, that's all settled then,' said Arnold. He stood up. 'Perhaps we'd better be going then.'

'Not yet!'

' 'Fraid so, mother. But we'll come and see you again soon. You know that.'

Mrs. Bruise walked down the stairs much more slowly than she needed to and held onto her son's arm all the way. When they reached the door, she knew it was her last chance.

'I'm growing a beard,' she said.

Arnold laughed rather uncomfortably and kissed her very lightly on the forehead, then turned away to brush the powder from his lips. Miss Scott kissed her too but stoically did not wipe her lips.

'Oh, I almost forgot,' she said and produced a large bar of milk chocolate from her handbag. 'For you, dear.'

'I'm growing a beard,' said Mrs. Bruise. 'And so is the picture.'

'And so am I,' said Arnold.

'Anyway, the picture's gone now, dear,' said Miss Scott. 'I cleaned it off for you, remember?'

'You don't understand,' said Mrs. Bruise.

Mr. Bruise climbed into his Morris Minor rather more quickly than he had done on his previous visit. As they drove round the corner with Miss Scott alternately dabbing at her lips with a tissue and waving, Mrs. Bruise stood on the doorstep and cried, 'I can feel lumps on my forehead! Lumps!'

As soon as she closed the front door, the dogs started barking again, even more loudly than before. Mrs. Bruise listened for a while, trying to detect where the noise was coming from. It proved quite impossible. She remembered which door the Major had opened last time and walked over to it slowly. The noise was definitely louder here. It was the door to the kitchen, Mrs. Bruise had never been in there before. Slowly she tried the handle and opened the door a crack. Instantly the noise intensified. Mrs. Bruise pushed it open the whole way and said in a soft voice, 'Quieten down, dogs, quieten down.'

On the kitchen floor, on hands and knees with her tongue hanging halfway out of her huge mouth, was Nurse, barking at the top of her voice.

Probably Mrs. Bruise was not looking where she was going as she ran upstairs; her poor old limbs were certainly too frail to take the strain and Major Scritchwallow had made the sad mistake of leaving a large stack of roof tiles on the stairway that morning. Mrs. Bruise's ancient frame on coming into collision with them in midflight was sent tumbling down the stairs to the very bottom where she died even before the expression of astonishment had had a chance to leave her face.

'And we hope you will be happy with us, Miss Apricot,' the Major concluded, 'This is your room, next to Alistair's. Used to belong to a nice old lady called Mrs. Bruise. Such a surprise to us when she went. Such a stout hardy old person she was. Went to the lavatory in rather a hurry one day and never came back. We found her hours later with one hand on the door. But Alistair will tell you all about that. One more thing, don't be alarmed by the pictures on the wall. Just a little whim of our Mrs. Bruise's, quite an artist she was. I think they're supposed to represent the two Marys or something like that.' He blinked rapidly. 'Anyway, I'll leave you now. Nurse will be up in a few minutes.'

A MAN OF THE BODY

Nicholas Butt

They'll be coming for me soon. They'll come, but I won't go with them. No, not even to dance and eat lamb I won't. They'll ask me why, and ask me if I'm quite well, and what the devil has got into me, but I won't go with them. They don't need me, and they'll get on just as well without me. Would it have held them back if I'd been killed? No, they'd dance and eat lamb, and drink the new wine till dawn like they always have done. Look how many of us didn't come back. They drink to the living and they drink to the dead, and they dance and eat lamb, and soon they don't know who's living and who's dead.

My old father, there's one that didn't come back. When they told me he was dead I went out with my knife to some infidels we'd caught and made sure there'd be no fathers among them. We didn't want them raping our girls, either, see. There was a lot of that going on, and worse things too.

They said it'd make a man of me, not knowing I was a man already. When I said goodbye to my mother and my sisters, weeping for me among all the other mothers and the other sisters, and their mothers, and their sisters, they said, 'Stavros, you'll come back a man!' My old father leaned on his stick and punched me (hard for a man getting on), shouting with the other fathers, and wanting to join me in the struggle. The other boys slapped me on the back and embraced me, and I embraced them, and we all shouted and music played, and there was dancing and the smell of lamb roasting on the spit. I never want to smell that smell again. We left the village, and they ran alongside us dancing and laughing, and the old women crying and praying, and the church bell clanging down the valley, and the goatherd, on an outcrop above us, playing a tune on his pipe, and his dog standing and barking beside him.

That was five years ago, maybe more. We're free now of course. Freedom. It doesn't mean much to me, this freedom they speak of. I was free when I was fighting them, I was free then. I decided what to do, and where to go, and what mercy there would be, what little there was of it. There weren't many of us, but we knew what we were about. And we were fair for all that. We wouldn't roast a Turk, despite everything they did to us. An insult to good lamb to roast a Turk. Never let me smell that smell again, that smell of lamb roasting. We made a few eunuchs here and there, but not once did we turn a Turk on the spit, God help me.

Take an example. There was a time we'd been walking all day, and had settled down in a cave for the night, and they came on us of a sudden – slit the throat of the guard before he could breathe his last, twenty of them, and us barely ten with the boy. But we fought as we knew best in the half-light of the fire, and I took care of six, and then we were down to four and the boy. And they took our boy and ran down into the cover of the olive groves, where no man nor beast is seen, and we chased them and lost them, and went back bleeding. I can hear his cries now as they carried him off, like a young kid in the jaws of wolves. We had to listen to them till dawn, no matter how we searched. Do you know what it's like to hear the voice of a child of yours screaming where you can't see, like pain in the darkness? With the rising of the sun the mist seemed to smother the sound, and he was quiet. We found him by the smoke, and he was well done.

I don't know how many I killed in that war, more than the olives on the trees. I used to think death was something you got when you were old or unlucky, and I used to stand with my friends and laugh when they brought out the corpse of an old woman, bloated and ridiculous in death, like a pig they'd killed and left out too long. War changed all that. I courted death, and married death, and death was with me always, in my bed, on my lips, in my heart, death nagging me like an unwed daughter.

It's dark in here, and I don't want it light. They'll come for me, and I'll not go. I can hear them outside, listen. Music, singing, shouting, children. That'll be Costopoulos on bouzouki – he only plays like that when he's had too much wine.

'Papadimitriou! Are you in there, stupid!'

They're trying to get in. It's my brother and his two friends, opening the door, letting in the night.

'You m'laka! Why are you in here? There's still some wine left if you're quick.'

'I don't feel well. Don't worry about me, I'll be out later.'

'Now!' His friend, Yannis, whose girl I had, and he was too stupid to know it. 'All right, lads. Let's show him the way as he's apparently gone blind.' Out into the night, but I can't struggle any more. I've done too much struggling. So much light, fires all over, and the noise, and people moving and dancing, and shouting, and Costopoulos on his back still strumming bouzouki. They're roasting lamb and I'm going to be sick. I feel like I'm trapped inside the corpse turning on the spit, and this smell is my flesh peeling, and these people are revelling around me, and waiting for me to be quite done.

'What's this, Stavros?'

A calm man with a square grey beard, and his hair tied up because he never cuts it. One who will shout at no man nor dog, nor the devil himself, they say.

'It's a feeling, like I'm roasting, like a lamb on feast day turning on a fire. I'm afraid of the night, my head aches, and I feel sick. Surely they told you how I fell down when they were celebrating, and how my sisters feared for me.'

He looks me in the eyes, and the wind blows his garment, and he pauses a little before he speaks. 'Afraid of the night? You, who would fight thirty infidels and still find time to sleep before sunrise, afraid of the night? What delusion is this, Stavros?'

'All the shutters must be closed and the door as best it will, though it doesn't shut tight, or else I sit trembling on the floor like a dog without a master.'

'What manner of sin have you committed, that the Lord should punish you in this way?' He's watching the snow on the mountains melting, and the rocks grow.

'Priest, don't speak of sin to me. Five years a fighter and you speak to me of sin! When has a day passed free from sin?'

'Perhaps you are blessed among men. This may be a sign, Stavros.'

'Are you serious? I fear the setting of the sun, and all day I think how I can stop it going down. If there were a way to keep it in the sky I would have found it.'

The priest is smiling a little at my foolishness. 'Leave God to worry about the sun, Stavros. You recollect your sins, and ask that they be forgiven. Then I think you'll find this affliction will leave you.'

'But my sins are all spent. I can't go looking for them now. It's impossible!'

'All things are possible. Be sure to recollect them, and be sure to repent.'

The stench hangs in my nostrils, the stench of my own flesh burning. I can hear the flames crackling, and underneath every layer of skin that peels from me is a new layer, and so it goes on through the dark hours.

'How is it to repent? I know how it is to sin, but to repent is a new thing.' He puts his arm around my shoulder, and his black garment hangs over me, smelling of priest.

'Tell me, Stavros, if your dear father were alive now, and he asked you to go with him to the next village, supposing you wanted to be with your friends in the square drinking ouzo, or maybe you had a girl who was waiting for you . . . what would you say?'

'I would make some excuse, and maybe he would go alone; but if he particularly wanted me with him I would go with him.'

'And what if he did go by himself, and on his way was set upon by brigands and beaten, and even killed, how would you feel then?'

'I would regret not going with him, and feel bad that I was not there when he needed me.' The priest slaps me on the back and draws away.

'So! That is how it is to repent, Stavros, that feeling, only much more so, for there you repent of only one sin, but before God you should repent of all your sins.' I am beginning to understand him. 'And can't you see? The Lord is like your father, and is asking you to go with Him. But in your heart you would rather be with your friends and enjoying yourself, and the Lord goes alone without you. So you feel bad, because your soul is crying out for the Lord, and tormenting you. Go to Him, Stavros, ask His forgiveness, follow

Him while you are still able. Then I promise you your suffering will end, and you will be at peace.'

I told the priest I couldn't repent. I'm proud of what I did. I hate the infidels, and I wanted to avenge the death of my father, and the deaths of my friends, and I wanted to make people free. Look what they did in the villages, what they did to our boy. The priest speaks of forgiveness, but I'll not forgive, nor will I repent. Now he wants me to go to a place where they know how it is to repent, where he thinks they could help me. He wants me to go with him part of the way, and to take a letter to a friend of his. I wouldn't go, except that now it's worse than it ever was, and they talk about me in the village as though I were dead already, and they say I've got the devil in me, and the women are laying out the black clothing, and the old men curse me. Even the girls are afraid and won't be seen near me, and their mothers beat them if they so much as greet me when I go by. I've heard they fear for their crops, and they want me to leave, and if I don't they want to kill me and be rid of the spirit that way. What I want to know is who would dare attempt it, when they know who I am, and what I did, and how I fought for them, and saved them.

I slept well last night. I told the priest as we rose, and he said, 'Lord have mercy on you, Stavros. Did you pray?'

I didn't pray. I was afraid of what it would lead to. We were a week following the coast east to Itea, and two days through the Amfissa olive groves, that spread like the Corinthian Sea, grove after grove, and barely a man left to tend them.

'God be with you, Stavros, and the Lord Jesus Christ have mercy on your soul, that you may find peace through His love.' I hear talk of the soul, but I know only the body, and the only love I feel is a love of woman, and a love of the men I fought with, and those that died. 'Tell them in the village, those who wanted me dead, that one day I'll be back, and they won't know it until they see me at their doors, and tell them to be ready for me. Tell them only this.'

'Don't be angry, Stavros. They're ignorant, these people. They don't understand.' We embrace, and he leaves me, and his mule clatters down the rock path to the olive groves, and I watch him go.

* * *

What would you say, priest, if I told you that after you left me I killed a man and made love to his woman, and abandoned my mule for his own? He was an infidel, and she was a pretty girl, and led me across the wide plain of Thessaly. Last night we were together for the last time, and the air was strong and put out the fire. The hills climbed above us into the night, but while I was with her I felt no fear of it, and the vision that has haunted me was gone.

Salonica, a noisy angry city, with starving children and whores I would rather kill than call Greek. Stenches I'd forgotten, and houses built of stone. Where is the Lord, priest, in this forsaken place?

My mule carried me part of the way across Chalkidiki, but it was weak and I slaughtered it and roasted it and ate it, and shared it with a traveller who let me ride his mule, and together we entered the gateway to the Holy Mountain. It's a calm day, good for a passage. Six hours they tell me, and two gone already. My companions are a monk who speaks Greek with a foreign tongue, and the brother of one who is dying. They ask me who I am and from where I come, and I tell them I am Stavros Papadimitriou and I come from the Peloponnese.

They call this place Athos after a mountain you can't see. The hills fall into the water and tell you nothing. Only the cloud communicates, layer on layer of it, rolling up to you and wrapping itself round you, and taking you further and further into its confidence to the exclusion of everything else. Even the people address themselves more to the cloud than to one another. We gave up our foreign friend to a strange place with high walls and fortifications, and steep roofs with onions made of gold on top, and rooms hanging on the outside of the walls. It was like a king's palace, but they said only monks live there, and he went in alone. Then they brought the boat to another landing place and told us the sea was too rough. So now we walk, and in three days we will reach the monastery they call Lavra, where Father Pavlos lives. We walk along narrow pavements through the forest, with the mist dripping from the branches, and the sound of the sea outside us.

We climb up and we climb down, and we cross fast-flowing streams, and all the time we say nothing, and the cloud answers us.

Sometimes there are dwelling-places, small huts built into the ravines, and the long drop to the sea. They give us hospitality, a measure of ouzo and a lozenge of loukoumi, and they carve little crosses by day, and at night they pray. They are strange humourless people. They build walled towns and small villages, but there are no women, and the only children are boys, whom they dress in black like themselves. The nights are worse here, and I see the faces of those roasting me, the faces of dead Turks. Once the man whose brother monk is dying — or dead by now, who knows? — came to me, and muttered a prayer, and when I was calm he spoke to me.

'Is it always like this, every night?'

'Since the day I returned from the war to my village. They were afraid, and made me leave again.'

'Maybe you are lucky. God may have chosen you. It happens, you know.'

'If God has chosen me, why does He torture me like this?'

'Ask Father Pavlos. He'll tell you.'

Lavra, like a Turkish ship on a sea of land riding out the forest. Something about it frightens me, I have seen nothing to compare with it. Down there it looks so vast, yet we are still two hours away, and the way is steep. If God had a Kingdom on Earth I would say I had found it, and it was a secret no longer.

'How many live there?'

'Two thousand.'

'And they all believe?'

Athanasias came here first, and they keep his bones in a glass case with the hand of John the Baptist and pieces of the True Cross, and they say he protects them, and that is why they have survived. Inside it's like a city, once you've passed through the double gates, and the inner gates, and are standing in the main square waiting, with buildings all round you, and a tree in the middle the girth of fifty men.

'Father Pavlos, I have a letter for you from the priest. You know him, I think.' A small man in brown with a white beard and no eyes.

'Welcome! Welcome! What a day this is!' He pushes the letter, unopened, into a pocket. 'Come, you are tired. Take my arm, and we'll find you some ouzaki.'

We are sitting in a room high up in the fortress. There is a fire, and a lamp, and outside it is dark.

'They read me the letter, Stavros. I pity you for what you suffer, and I want to help you, but I am only an old man, and know nothing of the world outside, so you must help me too.'

'I didn't want to come here, you know. I had decided not to. I could have stayed in Salonica, where no one would question me, or be afraid of me.'

'So you changed your mind. That's good. It was a long way to come for one so young. What made you change your mind?'

'I don't know. I hated Salonica.'

'I hated Salonica once. I grew up there.'

'Is that where you went blind?'

'No. This is where I went blind. The Lord is my eyes now. I see more clearly that way. These old things sometimes used to play tricks on me.'

'I'm glad I can still see. I don't like the night.'

'To me the night doesn't exist. There's no day, and there's no night. He gives me all the light I need. You needn't be afraid, Stavros.'

Here I am alone and in my cell. They took my clothes and gave me this rough brown thing, and I have a table and a rug on the floor for a bed. There's a small window, but it's high up and lets in no light. The smell is worse than Salonica. I despair sometimes. There are so many men and no women. I go screaming to my floor for a woman. Even when we were fighting there were always women nearby to appease us. But here there are only men, and I know they turn to each other, because they have nothing else. What kind of a place is this, where they breathe God during the day, and love one another at night?

'I want you to think hard today, Stavros, and tell me honestly and without justification the worst things you have done in your life. Tell me who you have tortured or killed, who you have loved, though you are not married, who you have betrayed or lied to. I want to know everything.'

'It will take more than one day, Father.'

'We can begin today.'

I began. I told him what I could remember, though there was much I had forgotten. When I told him about the death of my father he flinched, but otherwise he was silent, and showed no emotion.

It is later and I have finished. Pavlos is sitting on his straw chair staring empty-eyed at the wall. 'Am I to understand you killed a man on your journey to this place, and several times made love to his mistress, and stole his mule, and you had received the blessing of my friend the priest?'

'That's right.'

'And you don't regret it?'

'I regret something.'

'What?'

'I regret I don't have his mistress with me now.'

'Are you still suffering at night?'

'I have the same dreams, and the same pain.'

'Without relief?'

'Only when I wake up, but then it seems real.'

'Stavros, I believe you are in danger. If you think as you do now you will continue to suffer every night of your life, and it will become worse, and worse, until you are in agony. Then you will die, and the torments reserved for you in Hell will surpass all that you have endured on Earth.'

He speaks with conviction. Because there are no eyes you feel it's more than a person speaking to you, something beyond the person. You can't catch his attention in the same way. You have to listen, and his voice grips you, so that whereas you would laugh at another man with this one you are serious, and you begin to believe the nonsense he's telling you. 'But it needn't be like this. There is another way. The Lord loves you. You are blessed among men. He is calling you. He is saying, "Come to me, come to me." There are many men, who have done more evil than you, who go through life without pain, because they will never know the Lord. But you are chosen. The more you defy Him the more He weeps, and the more pain you feel in your soul. For it is your soul they are turning on the spit. Your body is strong, but your soul is dying. It craves the Lord.'

'Why should I be chosen? Of all the sinners in the world why has he got to choose me?'

'He knows, Stavros; and if you think deeply, and allow Him to speak to you, you will too. Empty your mind of gross thoughts, thoughts of violence, thoughts of passion, and the Lord will enter your soul, and with His true love, the only love, cleanse it.'

I thought. I thought in the room where we eat, not that we have very much to eat. That room always makes me think. It's more like a church than a room, long, cold, few windows, a high ceiling made of wood, painted all over. The walls are painted with pictures of men larger than men. They were painted in the days when men believed in miracles, and all things were possible. Father Pavlos told me once who they were. He said when the Day of Judgement comes, those who have repented will go to Heaven, and the rest will go to Hell, there to suffer tortures unknown even to the infidels. I can see them on the walls being dragged down by demons, and the others climbing up a staircase assisted by angels to Heaven. Saints look down at us from all sides while we eat, and not one of them smiling. Not much laughter in this place. They eat at marble tables shaped like horseshoes, the monks on that side, the postulants on this. The abbot sits at one end and rings bells. This bell means begin. That bell means end. The other bell means depart. The only words are the words of the monk reading by the light of two candles up there in the wooden box. I never listen to him, and I don't suppose anybody else does either. One bell and he stops, and snuffs out the candles, and then what little light we had is gone. They serve us fish, with bread and a little wine. No lamb here. Sometimes you get an apple but unless you eat quickly you never get round to the apple because the abbot rings his bell and dong, it's all over. We stand up, they come round with a stale loaf to kiss, someone sprinkles us with holy water, and the abbot goes out singing, followed by the monks, the postulants, and me. I'm always last. This particular day I sat down to my fish and thought. I saw the pictures on the wall of the people being pulled down by demons, and thought, can this really be true? Is there really such a place as that they call Hell?

The bell rang, the reading began, and I tucked in.

'Tell me,' said Pavlos, fingering a hole in his brown habit, 'what it is like to die.' I was still feeling hungry, despite the meal. 'I don't know. How should I know? I'm not dead yet.'

'Ah, but you have been close to death. You have seen death staring you in the eyes, and you have seen death in others, in your family, in friends, in whole villages. What is that like?'

'In the end you get used to it.'

'But surely you cannot get used to something as terrible — as final — as death. For me it's different. I'm old, and I'm expecting death, but you're young. It must seem worse to you.'

I walked over to the window. I could see the forest falling away to the sea, and a little boat fishing out there.

'Look,' I said, 'to me death was something I saw whatever I did, wherever I went. It was as common as the olive trees. I got used to it. When your life is taken up with killing your enemies and burying your friends you have to get used to it. There's no other way.'

He stood up. 'There is another way. I'm certain there is.' I looked round at him. He was weeping, a blind man weeping. 'There is another way!' He sat down again on his straw chair. Something stirred inside me and I asked him to explain. The light from the window was streaming over his face making the dead eyes glisten, but how could he know it when daylight meant nothing to him?

'We are all men, Stavros, no matter where we happen to be born. We all have bodies, and we all have needs, and we all have families, and friends we love and who love us. Isn't that so?' I nodded. 'Whether we are Greeks or Turks, isn't it the same?'

'The Turks are infidels.'

'But aren't they men like yourself, with families they love and want to protect? Are they really any different from you, except in some of their traditions, and in what they believe?'

'They're not men. They don't behave like men. Look what they did. I killed more than I can remember, and I'm proud of it too.'

'Don't be proud, Stavros. The Lord weeps when you say that. He asks you not to kill, not to be proud that you kill.'

'Why not? I hate the Turks. They killed my father, and made us slaves. Now we've fought them and beaten them, and I'm proud, and my family is proud.'

'And you love your family.'

'Of course I love my family.'

'Then you must think of the Turks as your family and love them too, for the Lord would have it this way.'

'What are you saying, priest?'

'Now I have made you angry. Listen to me, Stavros. Who are you to say this man is my enemy, therefore he must die? Are you God? And all those other things you have done – the suffering you have inflicted, the sins you have committed – are they things to be proud of? I think not. It wearies me, Stavros, when I hear of young men like yourself doing these things, bringing suffering and torment down upon your enemies, and upon yourselves. Think what you have done each time you killed someone, think of their families, their wives, their parents, and their children. Think how it grieves the Lord, who gave you life, to see you so wantonly take it away. He suffers most of all to see His children so engaged – hating, and fighting, and killing, and all for what?'

'Freedom.' Father Pavlos turned his head, so that the empty eyes were fixed on me, and staring at me, and the voice sounded more terrible than usual. 'What is this freedom? Is a mother free when they tell her she no longer has a son? Is a wife free who has lost her husband? Are the little children free when they have no one to support them? Is a man free when you take his manhood away from him? Is a girl free after you have set upon her? Is a village free when there is nothing left of it except ashes and smoke, and its people are all gone? Are you free because you can kill somebody, yet escape death yourself? What is this freedom you speak of, Stavros? We are all slaves, and the Lord is our Master. We may pretend we are free because our hands are not tied together, and we may fight for something we call freedom, but ultimately we never can be free nor should we. God made us to obey Him, to do His will. There is no freedom except fool's freedom!'

'You are wrong! The Greeks are a free people. Why, we have been feasting and celebrating. We shall never be slaves again. Never!'

'You are young. Things seem simple to you. But I tell you again – you are not free, nor will you ever be. You may continue to assert your idea of freedom, and destroy those who threaten it, but one day you yourself will die, and where will freedom be then?'

'I don't care! Would you have us a servile people once more, with barbarians for masters?'

'We are one people, Stavros, all Mankind. And there is only one Master. Why do you pick and choose? Do you remember in this land there used to be Spartans, and Thebans, and Athenians, and many other people, all fighting amongst themselves to be free? Now look at us – we are one people, and proud to be so, if we are to believe what you say. If we are at peace with one another, why can't we be at peace with the Turks, and with all men?'

'We will never be at peace with the Turks. Can't you understand that? How can you say there is no freedom after what we have done? Don't you know what it is to fight to be free, to throw off the yoke and set it alight? Don't you know even that?'

He sat motionless in his straw chair and said nothing.

'Don't you? What do you have to say?'

He raised his head as I stood over him, and I felt my cheeks burning.

'There is nothing,' he said, and turned away from me.

I am sitting in the panelled room once again, with the smell of woodsmoke soothing me, the logs crackling and spitting in the stove in the wall. There is a lamp on the desk flinging shadows across the ceiling. It's dark outside, no noise, only the roaring of the logs, the smell of woodsmoke.

Father Pavlos is praying.

'I wanted to see you sooner, but there are many things. Listen to me. This morning you became angry with me because I said there is no such thing as that you call freedom. And I said we are all the same – Greeks and Turks – all one. Are you still angry with me?' How fragile he looks, a little brown bundle of skin and bone, so frail, yet so self-assured. 'No, Father, I am not angry with you now.

I have thought about what you said, but I am not angry with you any more.'

'This is what I asked for. Now, I have something to tell you. I want you to know something of my own history, and how I came to choose this way. I was younger than you then, but in some ways similar.'

Him? Like me? Him! The lamplight is shining half-yellow on his face.

He looks ill.

'I am from Salonica. I have a brother who lives there still, though I've not seen him for many years. We were a very poor family, always hungry. I had to beg on the streets, approach the wealthy people for a little money; but often they would beat me, or their servants would beat me, and if I came home at night empty-handed my father would beat me. I was not a happy child, Stavros.

'One day I decided to leave my family, to run away with a friend of mine, and beg only for myself. In the beginning I felt free, like you say you feel, for I had only myself to feed, and no family to beat me. But after many days tramping the streets of the city, with no place to sleep, and only the clothes I was wearing, I became very miserable. I quarrelled with my friend, and we parted. I was all alone. Suddenly I was plunged into deep despair, tired, hungry, dirty, and cold. I fell weeping in the gutter, and the people kicked me as they passed, and shouted at me to get out of the way. I was very frightened. The noise, and the people, and the horses crashing by all made me feel ill, and the smell of the street. And I thought, I have no one, and nothing. I have lost even the little I once had, and now I am going to die here and no one will care. I was only a small boy then, and these things meant much to my poor troubled mind. What price to be free, Stavros!

'An older boy saw me weeping there and asked what the matter was. When I told him he laughed. "You little fool," he said, "of course you'll starve if you expect people to give you food." I asked him how else I could survive. "Take it, of course!" he said, "Take it." He ran away and I never saw him again, but he had sown a seed, an evil seed, and it began to grow inside me. I stopped weeping and considered his advice. It seemed so obvious I don't know why it hadn't occurred to me before. Yes, I thought, they won't miss a little food or money. So, you see, I began stealing. At first I was very afraid, and often spotted, and had to run quickly to escape. But slowly, slowly I became cleverer, picking my victim more carefully, taking his money with more skill. As the months turned to years people didn't notice me, and I was able to steal enough not only to survive, but to flourish. For the first time in my life I no longer felt hungry. I was able to buy new clothes, to go to the bars and the cafeneions, and to gamble and drink; and I made many friends. I met thieves more experienced than myself, and more ruthless. They became my constant companions, and together we robbed whole carriages, and carried pistols, and did very well.'

I can hear rain outside, and the sea on the rocks below. The logs are crackling, and the stove is glowing red through the half-light. The lamp is flickering and may go out. If he were any other man I would have called him liar by now.

'We are talking about seven years of this kind of life. In the end it was high summer. The streets were baked, the shutters closed on all the windows, the walls glaring and hot. Dust filled the air, blown into frenzies by the boiling wind. No one moved. They were all taking siesta. A calm had fallen over the city that was almost deathlike. Stray dogs lay curled up under the plane trees in the squares, and the great sailing ships bobbed idly up and down on the flat listless sea. We were on the quay, because there was a delivery of gold that day and we wanted some of it. We knew where it would be, stored in a wooden crate in the harbourmaster's house. The door was open and we walked in. The office was in a terrible state, piles of papers, invoices, customs duties, newsheets. A clock with a huge glass face ticked slowly on the wall. I won't forget the time. It was three o'clock. There was a model ship in a glass case, and there, in the corner under more papers, was the crate. It had iron locks, impossible to force. The only way was to use the pistol, but we knew it would make a terrible noise, and wake the whole street. Still, we had taken risks before, and this time the rewards seemed very great indeed. So my companion glanced out of the door to tell our guard what we were going to do. He came to help, there being little point in his staying outside. I held my pistol to the crate, and my companion took the other lock, and at the count of three we both fired. My dear, the noise was deafening. Splinters of wood flew away, one embedding itself in my friend's face. He dropped his pistol and put his hands to where the blood was flowing, whimpering like a dog. There were stirrings upstairs, where the harbourmaster had been sleeping, and we heard shouting and footsteps outside. "Quickly!" I shouted, "Gregore, quickly!"

'The two of us grabbed what ingots we could from the shattered crate, and ran out into the street. The third was still moaning, and he was the first to be caught. We ran in opposite directions along the harbour, meeting people on all sides. They were still sleepy, and very confused. They shouted and cursed, but they didn't know what was happening, and I easily passed them. Even so I dropped all but one of the ingots in my haste. Several men gave chase, seeing that I was shedding gold bars; but some of them stopped to pick up the gold for themselves. I was desperate now, and my steps rang through the deserted streets ahead of me, with those of my pursuers hammering close behind. The dust choked me, and the heat pulled at my lungs, and strangled my heart, and my legs screamed out to me in pain, and my head span, and still I ran. Through the sweat that was blurring my vision I saw a theatre and ran in hoping that the others would lose me. It was a grand place, with tiers of marble seats climbing high into the polished sky. I stopped briefly at the bottom, looking round furiously at row upon row of gleaming empty marble; then I started to climb up the steps to the top. It was a dreadful mistake. One man had seen me go in, and now appeared himself in the orchestra, and watched me going up in front of him. "You can't escape!" he shouted, but I ignored him. I reached the final tier, beyond which there was a ghastly drop to the street, enough to kill a man. The little houses of Salonica stretched away from me on all sides, their red-tiled roofs radiating heat, the sea tranquil in front, with the tall sailing ships moored in the harbour. I could see the White Tower gleaming in the sunlight by the edge of the sea, and cypress trees around it, dark and pointed like spears. I didn't know what to do. I stood there, alone on the marble, my heart pounding mercilessly, and this man climbing up slowly towards me.

'He was tall with a noble smooth face and a bronzed complexion beneath matted black hair. A fine athlete, no doubt, for he seemed little short of breath, despite chasing me for so long. He was dressed in loose-fitting white clothes that caught the sun's glare.

'"Stop there!" I shouted. "Don't come any higher."

'He stopped and looked up at me, and the sun shone full in his face, so that he had to squint to see me silhouetted against the sky.

' "Throw down the gold!" trailed up to me. "And I'll go."

'Isn't that typical, Stavros! "Gold!" I shouted. "What gold? I've got no gold!"

'"Liar!"

'"I tell you I dropped it all in the street back there." I knew there was a bulge in my pocket, and the top of the ingot was shining out like a blazing torch for him to see. "I've got a pistol!" I shouted, and held it up for the sun to catch. He came a step closer, and there were seven tiers between us. "No closer!" He stopped, then advanced one more step, standing with his arms to his sides like the statue of an ancient god, and there were six tiers between us. "I tell you I've got a pistol!" I said again. It was unloaded but I had ball and powder in my pocket.

'"I know it's empty," he said, and climbed onto the next tier. His eyes were fixed not on my pistol, but on the bar of gold he could see shimmering in my pocket. There were five tiers between us.

'I fumbled with the ball and powder, and made a show of loading the pistol. He watched me curiously, his head tilted to one side.

'"You see!" My voice resounded around the empty theatre. He advanced one more step and there were four between us. I pointed the pistol.

'"One more, and I'll shoot."

'He was silent. The sunshine played upon his face, and his eyes sparkled. The breeze flapped his white clothes, and tousled his black hair. A murmur arose from the sea, a murmur for . . .

'"The gold," he said, and stretched out his right hand. Mine went to my pocket, and I felt the warm metal moisten my trembling palm. The other kept the pistol pointed at him. I gulped. My throat was dry. I felt a passion for some water, any water. And yet there was water dampening my clothes, and running in rivulets down my face and down my chest. The sun was roasting the back of my head, boring into my skull.

'He was calm, and he was not sweating, nor any mark on his bleached clothes. His hand remained palm-up, and I detected a movement, the slightest muscular contraction of a leg.

'"Don't!" I yelled, a fever bursting open my brow. "Don't or I'll shoot. I'll shoot!"

'He smiled at me. I was all caught up, trapped by that face, from which it seemed all things must come, as though nothing, not theatre, nor houses, nor ships, nor sea existed but by virtue of it; and as though the sun drew its light from him, and the exchange was on his side, and it was alight with fire.

'He took a step forward and I shot him.

'The crack of the pistol rang out in all directions, swirling down the marble steps and along each row, so that suddenly the empty spaces were filled with a rowdy clamouring audience of sound. A thin plume of smoke twisted in and out of my vision, as my gaze stayed on his face. The smile had gone. So had the face.

'His body crumpled away from me, and the hand that was stretched out flailed upwards and backwards, and he turned over on his back, and rolled down some steps where he ended up, with the marble spattered, and his white clothes soaked. He was a hunk of meat slumped in a shapeless heap, and the blood was trickling away from him and dripping onto the stone beneath. I pressed the gold, and felt the warm metal in my pocket. People were shouting and the theatre was filling. I could see them scurrying about at the bottom.'

'What did you do?'

'Jumped. At least I don't remember jumping, but that's what I must have done, because when I woke up my bones were all broken, and I was in a room, and there were three girls watching me.'

I laugh.

'It wasn't funny. It was embarrassing. They told me I had fallen from the theatre, and they had taken me in out of pity, for fear I should die in the street. What I had left behind returned suddenly like the Furies, and the horror of it persecuted me, and there was nothing they could do to quieten me. Eventually I told them what I had done, and begged them not to tell anyone. I was too weak to argue with them. They looked after me well, and when my strength was restored I . . . obliged them.'

I laugh loudly, and rain beats against the window of the flickering room.

'There was really nothing else I could do. I didn't want them to give me up, and what money I had they had taken from me in the beginning. All this time I was having nightmares, reliving over and again that smiling face, and the moment after I had shot it. The girls tried to comfort me, but I was too disturbed, and I lashed out at them and wanted them gone. Sometimes they came and I took them, and afterwards I would feel guilty, that I was debasing myself through them, and had become a depraved and abominable creature. My poor mind struggled with these things, and the nightmares and the girls persisted, and I thought of that poor young man whose life I had taken for the sake of a thing so trivial as a bar of gold. I buried my head in my hands and wept, no longer concerned with my own safety, but dwelling for long hours on him I had shot; seeing his body somersaulting away from me down the marble steps, with the blood saturating his white clothes.

'Now I could no longer face the girls, and when they came I turned them away saying I was ill. But I was not ill, Stavros, I was quite well. I had recovered from the fall that should have killed me. I wanted to leave them, and one day I told them so, and asked for my belongings back. They wouldn't have it, and begged me to stay; but I was firm, and said I had met their conditions, and they had no more right to keep me. They accused me of being false to them, and threatened to deliver me up. They came to me one by one imploring me to remain there with them, but I refused. So they grew angry with me, and beat me, and dug their nails into my skin. I threw them to the ground saying, "I have already killed one person: it is not beyond me to kill more." They wept, and clung to one another like whelps, whimpering on the dusty floor, with their clothes torn and their hair in tangles. The eldest sister pulled herself to her feet and left the room. She came back with my things. "Take them," she said. "Take them, and go." I took them. The pistol must have fallen in the theatre; of the gold there was no sign. "The gold," I said. "Give me the gold." "There was no gold." She was lying, as she would not look directly into my face, but turned to address her sisters with words intended for me. I was trembling, and I seized her by the arm. "The gold," I said, and again. She twisted, eyes blazing, trying to free herself from my grip. "There is no gold!" My hands went for her throat, and her face turned pale, and her eyes grew wild with rage and fear. One of the sisters cried out for me to let her go, and said she would fetch my gold. She handed it over in a small canvas bag, and I snatched it, and I left.

'I made my way to the sea-front, and there I sat down and paused to think. It was a pleasant place, with tall ships in the bay, and little fishing boats far out at sea, and below me a group of children bathing, and lying in the sun. I sat beneath a palm tree, where there was a little shade, wondering what they would think if they knew what fate had befallen me since I was their age. I felt a terrible loneliness, the loneliness of a life wasted and spent, and wished I could wipe it clean, and begin again, and become a child like the ones on the beach in front of me. I was only seventeen then, Stavros, but I felt like an old man, waiting for death to release me from life's chains.'

The lamp goes out and the darkness is tempered only by the red glow from the stove. He doesn't realise it, and we sit for some moments alone. Then he gets up, and I see his shadow fumble to a wall cupboard, and there take out a bottle of oil. I go to assist him, but he waves me back, and manages to refill the lamp on his own, and the dull sticky smell of lamp oil is carried through the darkened room. The rain beats repeatedly on the window, as though trying to escape from the wind and the sea. He opens the stove door. A red profusion of light floods out, and the room goes wild, with the shadows of the furniture dancing madly around the walls, and a surge of heat, and the sight of flaring logs deep in the stone wall melting away to ash. The oil spurts, the wick glows, and a new amber brightness combines with the red and intensifies it, and restores the shapes to their original forms, and pushes back the margins of the room.

'So you came here.'

'Ah, I can see I am wearying you with my story. There is more to tell, but it can wait. Time is something we have plenty of here.'

'No, go on. I didn't mean that.'

'It's late now, Stavros, and I have to pray. Tomorrow, if you come early, we'll go for a walk. I'll tell you the rest then.'

Last night I lay on the rug on the floor of my cell staring up at the wooden ceiling, listening to the noise of wind and sea outside engaged in some tremendous battle. I thought about my battles, and what Pavlos had said about them. If it was true that there was no freedom it would have been all for nothing, all wasted. Our people would have died needlessly, and so would theirs. The whole struggle would have been in vain. I didn't come here to be told that. I didn't come here to be told all I had fought for was valueless, that it didn't exist, nor could it. I didn't come here for that. This priest is a mystery to me. Today he is old and frail and blind, and wrapped in a brown rag, as vulnerable as the leaves on the trees; and yet he speaks with authority, and he tells you how he killed a man for a bar of gold. He says we who are free are not free, and though he has no eyes he says he can see more clearly than he could when he had eyes. I am as confused as the wind and the sea, which now as a new day begins persist in their struggle, each trying in its own way to win supremacy over the other.

'Did you pray last night, Stavros?'

I never pray. To pray is to submit.

We have come to a clearing, which looks out to sea. Aghio Lavra, the great monastery, is set at the foot of the forest. A stone tower guards the approach from the sea. Up here the wind stirs the trees, and the birds never cease. The sea is grey with specks of white. Above us is the mountain in communion with the cloud. There is always cloud concealing the mountain, and it rolls down in sheets and sweeps across the forest.

'Tell me the rest of your story, Father, so I may question you afterwards.'

We begin walking again, his arm in mine, down steeply towards the sea.

'Did I tell you about the bar of gold, and what it came to mean to me?'

'I think so.'

'I began to think more and more that there was no value in living. Every time I felt the gold there in my pocket I remembered what I had done to keep it. I could no sooner dispose of it than I could restore to life the man I had killed. It had become a part of me, a symbol of my depravity. To sell it would have been to sell my conscience. Just as the gold would never tarnish or fade, so too the memory of the crime. Stealing was one thing, but to steal life itself was the gravest thing of all.

'As the days went by I grew weaker. I wasn't eating very much, and the constant heat exhausted me. I only ever shuffled up and down the sea-front with my hand in my pocket, and I must have become a familiar sight. At last the morning came when I woke up on the beach and knew in my whole being that I was going to die. The sun hadn't risen, and the chill of the night remained. The sea washed gently against the pebbles, and the city was silent, and the shutters of the houses closed. For the first time I felt calm, a stillness coming across the water and settling me. I was long ready for death. In everything I did there was ritual, because it was going to be for the last time. I stood up, my tired limbs aching, and prepared to enter the water. It was warm, warmer than the air, and swirled around my legs, and climbed up to my waist. It was so clear I could see little fishes swimming round my ankles. I jumped up in the air and dived full length . . . The water rushed up to meet me, bursting over my head, and running down my back. I swam some little way, feeling the pulse of the tide against my body; then lay on my back floating, staring up at the light blue sky. The sun rose suddenly between two purple hills and turned both sea and sky pink. I felt happy. This was my last day in the world and I was enjoying it. I bobbed up and down, the city still asleep in front of me, alone with the sea, drifting. I forgot my troubles, my hunger, and the bar of gold. I sensed only the rippling water, and the swish, swish, swish of the tide pushing past me.

'As the pink turned to gold, and dark shadows filled the waves, and the sky deepened and hardened, some boys came running along the shore, and dived one after another into the water I called my own. They were cursing and laughing, jumping one upon the other, and raising great fountains of sea-water. Their sleek forms caught the sunlight, and glistened with a vitality I had long lost. But I stepped out invigorated by my swim, captivated by the sunrise, and strengthened by the energy of the boys. Today I shall not die after all, I thought, as I went back to my clothes and saw there glinting my bar of gold.'

We have come to a stone bridge across a stream. The water tumbles down from a great height, and sends bundles of spray into the air, and dashes the black rocks, and rushes beneath the bridge, and races down and away into the depths. The air is moist and sweet, and the branches of the trees form an arch above us, and drops of rainwater spill over them and drip onto the smooth pavement at our feet.

'There was a church on the sea-front called Aghio Dimitriou, with a red-tiled dome, and a stork's nest on top. The storks were standing in the nest, keeping a long sentinel. I had walked past it countless times, but never once had I ventured inside. Now, in my new elation, I was curious, and walked through the great arch and pushed open the door. Inside it was like being cased in gold, like a fly caught in amber. There was gold everywhere, everywhere the sight of gold. Gold paintings on the walls and the ceiling, and gold crucifixes, and gold icons, and a wheel of gold hanging down from the dome, with gold candleholders at every spoke, and gold chains beneath. It was a great shock to me, not being familiar with what churches were like inside, for it seemed like a judgement on my crime – magnified and intensified by so much gold. My sudden optimism, so newly arrived, drained away from me, and I sank grief-stricken to my knees, guilt welling up inconsolably inside me, gnawing me, and binding me to the stone floor.

'I don't know how long I remained in that state, not daring to open my eyes for fear of the glimmering and glinting; but gradually sounds became known to me, sounds of singing, and sounds of prayer. I lifted back my head and listened, and they drifted out from some hidden place.

'A strange melancholy replaced the despair, and as I listened I grew calm, and it was as if someone was whispering sweet thoughts in my ear. The sounds grew louder and a peculiar hypnotic smell reached me, gripping me more tightly. There were three dark figures before me, and they swung gold in my face, and the incense swirled around it, and the candlelight flickered at their dark hollow faces.

'Stavros, they blessed me! I had never been blessed before, only cursed. This was a taking-up of my troubles to scatter them: they were ashes, and then they were gone. A part of me did die that day, but only the thing that had been choking me, only the canker. The rest of me revived, and there was nothing I could not do. It was a calling, and I was drawn by it like a dog to its master. Now the Lord was my gold, and in all gold I saw Him. And so I came here to do His will. It was not easy and it was slow and it was painful. It took many years to find some kind of peace, for I was still struggling with my conscience, and remembering the young man I had killed. But the Brothers here helped me, and showed me how to reach the Lord through prayer, and find grace through Him. And I know I have been forgiven, and that is the greatest of all gifts.'

We have come out onto the sea-shore, where slabs of rock slant diagonally into the water, and gulls wheel and dive in the wind, crying hungrily. The noise of the waves resounds, and sparks of spray spatter the air. The forest hugs the shore, and a stream runs out of the wilderness into the open like a child that was lost and has found its way home.

'There is only one more thing I have to say to you, Stavros.' We stand side by side by the sea, and I watch it, and he imagines. 'God has sent you to me, because He sees in you what I used to be, and He wants me to help you. Every day I pray for guidance and for strength, and the Lord comes to me and speaks through me. If I cannot help you it will be because the Lord would have it so. We are both in His hands.'

'Father, I don't see that there is any similarity between us. You only killed one man, and you killed him because you had to. Your guilt hounded you like a pack of wolves and drove you to this place. Look at me, I don't know how many men I've killed, and I don't care, and I killed them because I hated them and I wanted to kill them. It didn't make me guilty, it made me proud. You killed for yourself, but I killed for my people. You killed for gold, and I killed for freedom. We are entirely different.'

'Stavros, Stavros, isn't it enough to say that we have both taken another's life? Do you think it matters why we did it? Is that important to you?'

'Of course it is. How else do you justify it?'

'But you don't justify it! You can't justify it. Before God it is the deed that counts, not the justification for the deed. Oh, Stavros!' He turns away, away from me. He takes some steps, and he stops, and he turns, and his voice matches the cries of the waves. 'And tell me this. Why do you suffer? Why do you not sleep at night? Why do they turn you on a spit and roast you? Don't they haunt you as he haunted me?'

'What are you saying, priest!' I watch him shamble back into the forest, fumbling and feeling his way, and the darkness swallows him up. Behind me the waves yell at me, like open mouths jeering, and spit at me.

I see only a body, and feel only what a body feels. There is nothing else.

'Leaving?' I have caught him as our paths cross in front of the ancient tree. 'Can it be so?'

'Tomorrow. I'm going tomorrow.' He sets down the wooden pail.

'Forgive me. We must arrange a guide to take you back, because the boat won't come down this far with the sea so rough.'

'Don't you want me to stay?' The wrinkles smile. The eyes don't.

'You forget, Stavros, that I too have felt the need to go when those around me would have me stay. There is nothing I can do to prevent you. The Lord wishes it. I hope you have not been unhappy here.'

'No, not unhappy.'

'Good, good. But come, I have something for you. I may not see you before you go: there is a sick brother I must visit the other side of the mountain.' He hurries me inside, and up to the stone corridor that leads to his room.

'Here you are.'

A bar of gold.

'Take it, Stavros, and remember me by it.' He pushes it into my hand, and his face tosses and turns like the sea. 'Please.'

The boat pushed away from the jetty at Daphne, the harbour where I first set foot on Mount Athos. The waves bobbed it like an apple in a barrel, and we clung to the sides with the water slopping over us. The wind stung us like a whiplash, and the clouds across the sky fighting against the mountainside tore themselves to shreds. The little stone buildings of Daphne grew smaller as the sea lengthened the gap between us, and I watched the coastline emerge from out of the bay, and the mountain ridge spread itself along the peninsula. The tiny port shrank into the backdrop, until the forest had taken it. It was steep and it was olive-green, and it was beset by the layers of cloud.

There were some honourable men on that peninsula, and some brave men. I thought of Pavlos, of his struggle to win me, and of his graciousness in defeat. I thought of his suffering, of the bar of gold I could feel in my pocket, that same bar of gold which meant so many things to him. I thought of his tears, and I thought of his prayers.

A great rift opened up for the first time the summit of the mountain. A remote snow-face peered out against a halo of blue sky. I marvelled for the moment it took the boat to mount one wave and drop into the trough of another. Drenched with spray I looked again, and the tip of Athos had gone. I clutched the side of the boat more tightly, as new thoughts came to mind: thoughts of feasting and dancing and wine; thoughts of family and friends and of people with an account with me; thoughts of the sunshine, the vines, and the olive-trees of the Peloponnese. And then they were driven out by one final thought which occupied me for the remainder of the passage, and kept me warm.

GOOD INTENTIONS

Leonard Dean-King

Have you ever been scared? I mean, really scared? A stark white-faced horror that creeps upwards on your body until every small hair from your toes to your scalp is rigid with fear? Never? I thought not.

Oh, yeah, you've probably been frightened. At the cinema, right? I remember when I was about twenty (getting on for fifty years ago now, but it's funny how you remember things at times like this) there was a whole rash of films with an axe-wielding weirdo chasing a half-naked girl; they scared me too. But it was a funny-scared, remember, no real harm done. We saw 'em all. This scare though, the one that got old Chaz, and the one that'll have me soon (but not before I finish this) is all too real. With real harm done.

Chaz and me go way back, right back to the Seventies and Eighties. Neither of us married (though we both came close) and we just kinda stuck together. We saw each other's friends pass on, mutual friends; Bill, Gary and others, but somehow we both just shuffled along together. So it wasn't surprising when Chaz called me straight after that alien-fella landed and presented himself on Chaz's doorstep. He sounded real excited over the phone and I couldn't get no more out of him other than that I was to get my backside over to his place. Naturally, such a request, demand, was not to be ignored, so I put down the King novel I was reading for the umpteenth time (I'm an avid reader and writer), locked up my place and clunkered around to his house in my heap of a car. As I left my car, remembering to lock it up, I noticed again how isolated Chaz's house seemed. I mean, he had neighbours, yes, but there was a house width between his house and theirs. He had had some money at one time, bought three houses and a fair patch of land at the back. He knocked down the two outside houses and customized the middle. He was younger then.

As I paused for a moment, looking at his home, something caught my eye. The roof was smoking. Or appeared to be. Thin wisps of grey-blue smoke curled their way lazily into the night sky, seen clearly against the sparkling blanket of stars. I took off my spectacles, cleaned them on my shirt-tails, and looked again. I was mistaken. The smoke was coming up from behind the house, but I was at such an angle to the roof that it appeared to be smouldering. I shook my head in dismay, wondering what Chaz had been up to now. (At that time, I recalled the year he'd tried to make his own fireworks, and given everybody a boxful, guaranteeing success; that little gift had cost Gary two fingers of his left hand.) So it was with some trepidation that I limped up to his front-door (I didn't know of the alien yet). I rattled the letter-box flap and waited. Not for long though. The door was flung wide open and Chaz's wiry form was framed in the doorway.

'Len!' he stated.

'No. A strait-jacket salesman.' Sarcasm was a great thing between us. 'What you done, Chaz?'

He wasn't listening to me, but he ushered me into the lighted hall-way and closed the door, noticing the pained expression on my face.

'Ankle acting up again?' he asked.

'Yup,' I answered, shifting my weight to my good left foot.

'I told you to get it fixed at the time.'

'Yeah, I know, but it didn't feel busted then.'

'I told you it would hurt when your bones got old and started giving up.'

We began moving down the hall to his modest kitchen as I countered his good-natured jibe, being careful not to put too much pressure on my aching right ankle.

'Who're you calling old? You're older than me, Old Man!'

'By four months!'

'See he admits . . . it.' My voice trailed off to a whisper and the sharp pain in my foot was relegated to secondary concern as we entered his kitchen.

Standing, or seated, it was hard to tell, in the exact centre of Chaz's kitchen (he'd had to move his dining table, obviously) was the alien. The first thing I noticed was its three legs, apparent even under its skirt-like form of dress. It seemed to use its extra leg as a form of prop on which it could rest, as it could obviously not sit down. Before I realised I was staring (gawping, more like) I noticed it had just two arms, with three fingers and a thumb to each hand, and a Terran like upper body and head, with only two eyes and tiny, unobtrusive ears. The only curious features about it were that it was covered in a fine layer of fur or hair, and its whole body gave off what I can only describe as a glow. A subdued shimmering. A cosmic sheen.

Then I realised I was staring.

'Uh. Oh. Sorry.' I looked away.

'Don't worry, Len. I didn't mind.' With astonishment I realised it was the alien speaking and I was hearing English. (When I say hearing, I'm not too sure. When it spoke, you felt a pleasant buzzing sensation inside your ears and around the back of your head; I expect machinery was involved somewhere along the way, but I never thought to ask.)

Anyhow, in absolute surprise, I sent a piercing glare at the place where Chaz was standing. But he'd moved. I looked at the alien once again, it was smiling (smiling, dammit) and good ol' Chaz had his arm drooped over the alien's bare shoulders, and I noticed then how that peculiar glow was interrupted and seemed to travel some way up Chaz's arm. He never noticed though. (Good-intentioned Chaz: once he gets an idea he's blind to everything.)

'See, Len, intelligence!' He was smiling too, false teeth beaming away. 'He says his name is Tarque, and he needs help.' I had to sit down so I did so, my eyes never leaving the two standing there, grinning away like madmen. 'I said we'd help him, Len.'

I silently nodded my agreement, my attention once more being dragged back to my aching ankle. It hadn't hurt this bad in ages. The ache made it a great storm-predictor; but an alien-predictor, nah. Couldn't have been, could it?

Perhaps I should pause a moment to explain something. I do have the time, I believe.

Maybe reading this, you're wondering why both Chaz and I so readily accepted the alien, who was, after all, three-legged, hairy and glowing. Well, we had a sort of pact, me and Chaz. All of us really, all growing up on the *Star Wars* series and other outer space adventures, that if we were ever to meet an alien (an Extra-terrestrial; an E.T.) we would do our level best to be good-intentioned towards it/him/her.

So we were. If you would have reacted any differently, then maybe you wouldn't have had to write this, as I have. So who would be right? You or us? We felt right.

Anyhow, to cut a long story short, and not go into tedious details of how Tarque (the alien; it was his name, for Chrissakes) got to merry old Earth, other than to say his ship (a small one, he said) had been forced to put down in Chaz's substantially overgrown garden. For me, that explained the smoke I'd seen. I'd visions of atomic-powered thrusters burning and cutting their way through our tentative atmosphere and then turning Chaz's garden into ash. Fortunately, my imagination was over-active, but I did suggest Chaz got Tarque to burn down the lawn while he was here.

Chaz appreciated the wry humour but Tarque himself failed to respond. No sense of humour? I dunno.

One of the thingamajigs in Tarque's little ship had cracked up and he needed help.

And that's where me and Chaz came in.

'You see, Len,' Chaz said from his position next to Tarque, a while after I sat down on one of his dining chairs, 'Tarque reckons he can temporarily fix his ship with what I've got in my den.'

I looked at them both sceptically. 'Great, Chaz. Through hyperspace on a lawn-mower, powered by ever-ready batteries.'

Chaz took his arm from around Tarque's shoulders and came over to sit next to me. He put his elbows on his bony knees and leaned in intently. Once again, I noticed the cosmic sheen but it was on Chaz's arm this time. I blinked and it vanished abruptly.

'Len,' Chaz was not really enjoying my jokes any more (jokes, what jokes?), 'he needs help.' Remember what I said about Chaz when he gets an idea? Talk about the plank in the eye.

'Okay, okay. Don't get all sincere and pious on me, Chaz.' I put my hand on his face and pushed him away, like you would an over-eager dog, playfully. I looked once more at the alien, who was regarding our behaviour with what I took to be pleasant curiosity. At least there was an expressive twinkle in his eyes. 'How can we help you, Tarque?'

The alien cast aside his amused expression and immediately his brow furrowed in instant concentration. As he spoke, he moved closer to where Chaz and I were sitting, his skirt-like affair making his walk seem a glide. 'As I understand it, Len, Chaz here has a den full of bits and pieces from television, radios and videos. He says he builds compilation devices consisting of parts taken from standard models.'

'He tries. Nothing he makes ever works.' I looked at Chaz. 'What a waste of cash.'

'We've always wasted money,' retorted Chaz, 'remember video-games and slot-machines?'

'Now, that's years ago!' I pointed a finger at Chaz. 'More years than you or I care to remember. This is different.'

'It's not too different.' He put his hand to his wrinkled brow and feigned a woeful expression, 'And besides,' he moaned, 'what's a man to do in the autumn years of his life?'

I had to laugh. 'Okay, okay. You get the Oscar, Chaz.'

'How kind.' He dropped his hand back to his knee, and during the course of the motion I saw that the tips of his fingers were glowing, shining. I blinked, but the luminescence remained.

The alien spoke again. 'If I could just look among the parts? The repair I need to effect is minor, but essential. I would not require much.' There was an almost pleading quality to his voice.

'Hey, Tarque, my man,' said Chaz, waving his arms and indicating expansively, 'take all you want. Len, take him to the den, will you?'

At that moment, I looked at my friend. He looked old, really old. His hair seemed a lot greyer than I had previously noted, and I caught a peculiar quality, a strained edge, to his otherwise steady voice.

I hesitated before standing. Chaz noticed the hesitation and his eyes caught and held mine for an infinitesimal period. Then I stood. But knew, by God I knew, something was very wrong.

Tarque had noticed nothing. Which was proper in his position. Here he was, stuck on a strange planet, getting help from two of the weirdest characters he'd ever experienced. And all he was concerned with was getting home. Looking back (everything is so easy in hindsight), even if he had noticed something was going on between me and Chaz, he couldn't have done anything. And so I could hardly blame him for Chaz's death or my predicament.

It's just one of those things, really.

I showed Tarque out of the kitchen and along the hall. A door under the main staircase opened onto Chaz's den; a living-room-sized cellar, dug out in the course of Chaz's customizations. A descent of a dozen steps took us to floor-level. I flicked a switch and the interior was bathed in a muted yellow glow from conventionally powered lights (no nuclear stuff for Chaz. Or me). The lights revealed a mass of modern technology; televisions with exposed backs, gutted radios and ripped-out video equipment. There was also a rack of batteries and power-packs of all types, plus a varied selection of tools, from an unsubtle mallet to the most delicate pair of pincers.

'It's all here, Tarque,' I indicated unnecessarily, 'the choice is yours.'

Tarque seemed positively enraptured, his eyes caressing the (to me) scrap parts and pieces.

'Thank you,' he breathed.

''Sokay. Look, I'll just be in the way here, so I'll go up and wait with Chaz.' I didn't wait for a reply, and quickly but politely made my way back to the kitchen as fast as my aching ankle would allow.

Chaz was where we'd left him. I realise now that he daren't move. His elbows were on his knees and he was rubbing his fingers with startling violence for an old man with arthritis.

'Chaz?'

He didn't look up, but he did say something. Something he called me that I hadn't heard for over fifty years, and it made me sit down abruptly.

'I'm really scared, Kid.'

'Kid'. A term of affection that had arisen in our late teens and continued on into our twenties. But, like I say, neither of us had used it for years. It made me wonder at the time and now, as I tell you of it, it brings a lump to my throat.

He raised his chin to look at me, and then I realised just how scared he was. His face was drained of colour and his eyes had become sunken, dark orbs.

He was at the edge of the type of scared I told you about. Remember that? It's an edge I'm fast approaching.

'Have you touched Tarque yet?'

It was a curious question, and so I was startled into answering it before I'd got used to Chaz's appearance.

'N-no. Why?'

'Don't. And don't touch me, either.' Suddenly, he clenched both fists and brought his knees to his chest, his eyes squeezed shut. I reached out to him as his eyes strained open.

'Don't . . . touch . . . me,' he managed to say. You cannot believe the incredible effort it took to speak during a spasm. I know from experience that every muscle in your body seems to contract, your heart hurts and your lungs burn but you have no choice but to go with the flow, as they used to say. But the flow, this time, is like acid.

I waited. And, after the eternity that was a few seconds, Chaz relaxed as much as he could.

'Jee-zuss. I . . . I hurt, Len,' he panted. I wondered if his heart would last. Then he must have noticed my far-from-cheerful expression. He smiled, actually smiled.

'Come on, Kid. We always said we'd accept the end, right? We don't care as long as it's quick, right?' He began rubbing his finger-tips furiously again, even scraping them along the table-top. It reminded me of Lady Macbeth, a character in a play I once studied.

'Chaz?' I said again, helplessly. I was pitiful, like a bad actor in an even worse movie. Chaz was dying here, and there was nothing I could do but sit and try not to break down.

He looked at me again, and, being careful not to touch my skin, pushed my slipped spectacles back up my nose.

'It's Tarque, see? He must be carrying some kind of disease peculiar to his home, something so common it's overlooked. Maybe it's even a social asset.'

Again, Chaz's body was hit by a spasm. Only this time he couldn't talk through it. I watched, and waited. And then I thought of the glow, the sheen, that surrounded Tarque's body.

Chaz relaxed again, returning once more to chafing his finger-tips.

'Probably doesn't even realise it's a fatality to us, poor guy. Can't blame him. I must have got it when I touched him, somehow.'

And I pictured Chaz with his arm slung around the alien's bare shoulders, interrupting the peculiar sheen. That must be it, I thought at the time.

That is it, I know now.

'Don't blame Tarque, Len. Please.'

I shook my head. 'No. Okay, Chaz.' And then I asked a stupid question; yunno, when somebody gets hurt you go and ask if they're all right, that type of question.

'How do you feel?'

'Oh, I'm in fantastic health, Kid, can't you see?'

'Sorry,' I hung my head, averting my eyes from his.

'Hey, Len. Len?' I looked up. 'Don't feel sorry for me, right? I hurt something rotten, that I can take. So far. I'm gonna die. That I can also accept.' Then his voice dropped to a whisper, 'I'm just so bleedin' scared. I want to scream and shout, pound something to death. But I daren't move unless I have to. Something tells me more is going to happen to me. And I can't accept the waiting.' He curled up again, but voluntarily this time, and glanced fearfully about himself. His eyes only seemed relaxed when they settled on me. 'I'm glad you're here, 'cos I'm hanging on to you. You're keeping me sane. I'm scared of everything, Len. Must be part of the disease.'

His eyes locked on to mine, and I was held by their helpless gaze. Then he groaned in agony and slammed his right hand palm-upwards onto the table. He held his wrist tight with his left hand and his eyes had to leave mine as he looked at his outstretched hand.

I looked too, and was horrified.

His right hand and fingers were flexing convulsively, but I could see clearly the same sheen I'd observed earlier. Chaz was speaking.

'Oh, Christ! Oh, Jesus!! No!!' His terror was obvious when you know he was absolutely aware of what he was about to undergo. And I realise he must have remained sentient and lucid throughout his ordeal.

Suddenly, almost immediately after they had begun, the convulsions in his hand stopped. His hand formed an upturned claw, and I saw it begin.

His finger-tips cracked, and skin peeled backwards down his fingers, revealing inner liquids and tissues that somehow remained in position. I recall glancing away from this abomination to look at Chaz's strained features. His entire face was bright red, and sweat stood out from his brow. Blood speckled his lips from the clenching of his false teeth, rupturing and tearing his gums. I looked back to his hand, drawn by the primitive blood-lust residing within us all (the part that wants to see a car crash in a race, that wants to see what the accident victim looks like; we all have it). The peeling had extended to his wrist now, and I noticed with a grimace that the veins and such-like had begun to fall away, following the skin in its journey along Chaz's hand. But still it did not haemorrhage and bleed. The cosmic sheen was preceding the shedding of the skin by a fraction of an inch, and was now upon Chaz's forearm.

I looked to Chaz again, revulsion bringing bile into my throat, and noticed something more than a sparkle of sweat on his forehead. A glow was present, a cosmic sheen.

I shook my head slowly, denying the inevitable. I did not want this to happen, his hand was one thing, but his face!

I moved back. (This was the first time I'd ever been afraid of Chaz in our entire friendship. We'd never argued, exchanged blows or anything, and now I was scared of him.) As I moved, my chair scraped noisily on the floor. Chaz's eyes snapped open and once more caught mine. Then the skin above his eyes dropped down like a curtain and he was momentarily blinded. He began to shiver with the pain, trying to shake off its effects, I presume. In that moment, I left my chair and dashed out into the hallway, closing the door carefully behind me. I grasped the handle and held it firmly shut.

I really hate myself for doing that to Chaz. Not that it matters now.

They say that a drowning man sees his whole life flash before him in the moments before his death. Well, I had much the same experience in the time I hung onto that door-handle scared to Hell and back in case Chaz tried to follow me, except it wasn't my life as such, but memories of Chaz, going way back.

I remembered him as a quiet kid in a new school; smiling the first time he saw his favourite rock-group; drinking bottles of alcohol on his twenty-first. I remembered him almost married (boy, that was close; what a mess she was) and I've seen him almost die in a car accident.

I guess I almost grew to love that guy, in a way, over the years. We did a hell of a lot together.

Seems we're dying together, too.

All this went through my mind (in a secret place behind my eyes) in a single moment whilst I hung onto the door-handle. It was a long time since this old man had cried, but I came very close to crying then. Until I was distracted.

By Tarque.

Forgotten about the alien, hadn't you? Yeah, I had too. As I was staring at the kitchen door I felt that buzzing inside my ears and then heard his voice.

'Is there something wrong, Len?'

I turned quickly, startled, suddenly aware of the cold sweat on my hands and face. Jerkily, I brushed my palms on my trousers and ran a sleeve across my forehead. Then I took my glasses off and polished the lenses on my shirt-tails, not looking at the alien. Because I didn't want to look at him, not just yet. I was seeing Chaz, in pain, but saying to me:

'Don't blame him, Len.'

And I was doing my best to comply with Chaz's wishes.

Replacing my glasses, I looked up at Tarque, and tried not to hate him. He stood in the hallway, a confused but benign visitor from another world. In his hand he held an object around the same size and shape as a video-cartridge, with a couple of wires sticking out of one corner. Other than that, it was sealed perfectly, and a light-absorbing black in colour.

'Is . . . is that it?' I pointed at the box, ignoring his enquiry.

The alien moved the box in his hand with a smooth, delicate turn of the wrist. 'Yes,' he said, 'with this the repair will be made.' And then he looked directly at me and I swear he looked sad (and also, also, something told me he was sorry).

I wonder if he knew.

'I'll leave now,' he said.

Curiously, now I think of it, Tarque didn't move until I did. In fact, up until the moment he left, he never came any closer to me than he had to, and I regarded his glowing body in a new way.

I turned my back to Tarque and slowly pushed open the kitchen-door which I'd so fiercely held closed a few moments ago. Looking through a head-sized gap, I expected the worst, but nothing was amiss. Only Chaz was gone. The chair he'd been seated on when I ran out was on its back, like he'd pushed himself away from the table really quickly. He must have gone through into the adjoining sitting-room. To die.

I gestured for Tarque to follow me, and quickly set the chair to rights as he glided into the kitchen. Without looking back, I limped (my ankle, acting up again) towards the outer door which led into the backyard, presuming the alien would follow me.

Tarque did, not questioning the glaring absence of Chaz. As I heard him close the back door quietly, stating that we were both out under the night sky, I turned to face him. The ever-present glow was even more prominent in the darkness, and I said to him, 'Where's your ship, Tarque?' I was tired, scared and upset. I glanced at my watch and with astonishment saw that only a half-hour had passed since Chaz had called me, and was even more shaken by that fact.

Tarque pointed towards the rough, just a few yards away, beyond the well-kept lawn.

'It is among the long grass. Over there.'

He walked over to the spot, and parted the overgrown grass. From my position, and with the help of Tarque's own bodily sheen, I could look and see that the craft was black, and no more than three feet high. I presumed that the alien lay down within it, because, even sitting, he'd be too tall for comfort. As far as I could see, there were no windows, and, though curiosity made me move quite a bit closer, I could discern no engines or exhausts.

'Everything is totally automatic, Len,' I realised Tarque was speaking, 'there is no need for me to suffer a lengthy journey, so I go to sleep. Sometimes for years.'

I looked at him, impressed. 'I see no engines . . . ?'

'No. The ship has a drive-system I cannot explain because,' and he smiled a little, 'I just fly it, I didn't build it.'

I thought for a moment, something tickled my mind and I recalled the curling smoke I had seen. I mentioned it to Tarque.

'That would probably be caused by the outer hull of the ship being extremely hot. After all, I did hit your atmosphere a little hard.'

I nodded agreement and then silence fell between us. A moment passed and then Tarque turned to his ship and bent to the task of fitting the repair he'd constructed into it, leaving me with my thoughts.

Chaz was dead. I was sure. He'd died because he'd wanted to help an extra-ordinary being who needed him. As I watched Tarque working away silently I realised I didn't hate him. Any malice I'd developed towards him seemed to just drain out of me and I understood.

I understood Chaz's desire that I didn't blame Tarque for what had happened. No one was to blame. Hell, the poor guy probably doesn't even know the effect his body has in our atmosphere.

I stepped to within an arm's length of Tarque, forgetting the horror of the evening and recalling all the good we'd done. I saw Tarque finish and straighten up.

'Tarque.' He turned, and I noticed a look of mild surprise sweep over his face, 'will it work?'

'It should do, Len,' he answered quietly. He smiled, 'It wasn't the engines, thank the Gods, it was part of the computer itself. It tells me all systems check out now.'

'I'm glad.' And without thinking (I do not know why I overlooked the danger) I reached out and grasped his hand, shook it firmly.

The glow around Tarque's body was broken, and the sheen crept onto my fingers. My handshake hesitated as I realised just what I had done. I looked at Tarque and saw the confusion in his eyes.

Then my hand gripped his firmly, and I clasped my left hand in a double hand-shake.

'Good luck, Tarque, good luck.'

I stepped back and allowed him to climb into his ship. Even at that time, my fingers had begun to throb and itch, on both hands (it has been a fantastic ordeal to hold this pen, never mind write with it) and I began to feel as scared as Chaz said he was. Even more so, because I had seen what was about to happen.

Tarque's ship rose vertically to a height of about six feet. I saw that it was about ten feet long, and needle-shaped towards one end, and then it seemed to disappear. It didn't appear to fly away, it just vanished; without disturbing a blade of grass or a grey hair on my head.

I turned away from the scene and made my way back into Chaz's kitchen, limping all the while. Searching the drawers I found paper and pen and decided to set down what you have read.

I'm incredibly scared now, and I feel it has to be a by-product of whatever it was Chaz and I caught. I've been under threat from a pen seeming to writhe and twist and wrap about my hand in a crushing action; a simple sheet of paper enlarged itself to giant proportions and covered me, suffocated me. I experienced choking, lack of air, and found myself fighting and destroying a sheet of paper before I checked myself, forcing myself to recognise the hallucinations for the horror-effects they were. Every little thing about me is warped and bent into a nightmare denying its reality, but I have to refuse to accept its existence. The room about me is tiny, tiny, so very small and constricting but I go on writing. I've had two spasms already, and I keep dropping the pen. But I don't regret anything, not really. I'll be dead soon, like Chaz, and we can have our youth together again, if we go to the same place. I suppose we'd do the same again, if we had to.

Just as I'd like you to do. Please help them. If, by any chance, you meet an alien who looks like he glows, or shines, be really friendly to him, say hello and help him out if he needs your help. Please.

But, ah . . . don't shake his hand.

MAD BROTHER

Tim Etchells

It was raining. Those were underwater days. There was man with a mask on walking down the city street. 'You call it your street, & I'll call it mine — that's the way of the world, sunshine, that's the way of the world.'

It was me & Jo again in the rain. Visiting a friends in Leeds on that afternoon (of whom maybe much more later). We'd been in the market (gorgeous ceiling, rabbits hung bloody-sided on the meat stalls, I bought bread & cheese) and then we'd walked down this pedestrian bit. Women were runnin in high heels on wet paving slabs. There was clack clack & you keep expecting to hear a fall. Everyone's face pressed down tryna meet the ground, hiding from the wind. It kissed you wet & bitter cold on your cheeks going red in the daylight outside the shops. Everyone not really looking where they're going because they're shuddered & shuttered & 'scaping under 'brellas & head scarves. That kind of overcast daytime that makes you think about the nighttime. The lights of the shops. People probly buy more then — they go in to get warm & they buy somethin. Somethin for themselves or the kids when they get back home like a bag of sweets or somethin. Anyway. A bloke was shoutin about the papers he had to sell — saying each word separate like a thing in itself — pausing for whole seconds between words so a quick walking shopper might be there & gone & back again before he'd said anything whole or graspable like he went like this:

'Does!'

'Any!'

'body!'

'want!'

't'buy!'
'this!'
'evnins!'
'Star!'
'Does!'
'Any!'
'body!'
'at!'
'all!'

All that & nobody was buying one.

There was something Biblical in the poor drenched bastard, flat cap an all, yelling grimly at his voice's middle point, not desperate like but accepting it all with bitter coal hardness. His hands clutching wet rag of paper half shredded with the pressure: the tiny detail of his newsprint fingers. No eyes under that flat cap. Just holes of frighten & cold. Some prophet. Some empty cynic of street vendor. A cancer of a wind there was too.

The board beside him said:

'Policeman shot dead in Leeds!'

And everyone was walking as fast as their cold feet in little wet shoes could carry them.

Everyone, that is, but the man with the mask on.

See his leisurely pace, brother. Feel that one.

It was then, just then, in the rain on earth that we saw him. Mr. Nutcase himself, or so simply I thought then. He had this Guy Fawkes mask on — a sort of lurid putrid essence of nastiness fluorescent orange & green kind of colour with sick swirlings near the eye holes. Kind of thing that would have cost 25p when I'd have bought it (yrs ago at a joke shop now not closed down — contrary to all gloomy false nostalgic expectation) but Lord knows how much now.

Strange sight this figure in mask strolls ambly in that cursed rain. Like he loved nothing more — no: like he cared not at all. Mask indifferent to all this except what went off between his skull and his radio.

More detail, more detail. He'd ripped the mask off at half mast so his lips showed through — visible face had this thickness to it — a sort of wanting to spit its teeth at yer & all that, with the Orange Line where the mask ended like a knifegash cut to leave his face open — the whole thing enough to make you (simply) look away. We looked away.

He was behind us by then. Jo wasn't looking at him. I wanted to but dared not. I kept sneaking ½ cross shoulder looks at him, secretly fascinated though not wanting him to know. In stories they want to know what Death looks like but they dont want to die. Anyway he kept coming. Like something that the bullets couldn't stop. He carried this slow motion with him so the street appears to stop almost, the raindrops crying down the face of the day, slow slow like slow baby, & splash all broken on the concrete ground. His legs powerful. He has jeans on & black DMs. His crotch isnt zipped up with a fly like normal but crisscrossed with safety pins — an evil-looking mess of sharp steel bits & bulge. Reminds you of pain somehow. Some evil-looking baby nappied up to die. Sex menace — his cock in there. His hair (that which you can see anyhow) is cropped short. All of this contained in his slow-motion amble, lord of the dirty rain.

Jo & I hold hands, we're walking on. No one else will look a look at him. They scurryin on, they purse-clutched. In his hands, the detail *A radio*. See the strength that he turns that dial. The strength in those legs, I mean. He holds it close to his car, twiddling the dial & listenin. Who knows where those eyes (visible only through spot black spots of tiny holes in the mask) are looking. Whose carcass does he rape or looks he at the radio, in search of its music in flight. Yes — music would flee from him — twould run in the rain.

In my mind, but not in the real wet street I hear him speak. Speaks he:

'I was here I mean way back, before they took the trolleys away* — I walked this place before the Queen came round & laid the stone to earth. She buried it here that afternoon with the mayor looking on & the papers. She buried it & all & went away.'

Walking on we leave him behind. A strange ghost who haunts

*'Years before they'd opened supermarkets on the edge of estates. With no cars & not far enough for buses people pushed their trolleys 'ome right piled up with stuff. They'd unload shopping then push the trolleys into the road, there they lie like broken animals abandoned until the council collects them, as "menace", in trucks.'

the streets behind us. With us & not with us. A man in a mask. The shoppers all gone quiet. Safe from him (further down road in the rain) we discuss him, Jo & I. Drowned city. Computer software in the window of every shop.

Slowly, through our conversation I 'learn' the story of him. Its dark. With no regrets. First of all we learn the place he lives — its reminiscent of some place we camped in in the darkness in Spain — Jo & I — some renegade city area — ½ built or tumbledown I cant remember, or will not, there was something unfinished in the air — Styrettes & syringes on the ground — broke needle in arm no longer there — we wrapped up warm in the tent & listened as some kids lit a fire. Hoping that they wouldnt notice us or that they wouldnt say.

It's in a place like that where this masked citizen lived. He's mean I mean Lord he's mean. See the strength that he turns that dial, the strength in those legs I mean.

Through our talk then we learn the place he lived. But then we give him a rest, having other things to do & Jenny to find. Jo leads the way. We circle back on ourselves endlessly in the precincts that we dont know. The rain drips harder. We ask an old woman who's sat on a bench, resting beside the scratched & scrawled names on it, if she knows directions to the place we're going but she doesnt. Shes a 'visitor, to this town'. We carry on, & askin somewhere else just further down the road. The bloke who we ask is pretty drunk. He's the porter at the barrier of the university there — stood in the doorway of his little sentry box/cabin in front of the concrete & glass building before us — far away faces not visible looking out & down, to the paving slabs. Another old bloke is stood with him, the two of them like great outdoor passers of the time of day, like you get over fences & garden gates, resilient, ruddy-cheeked through drink, impervious to the rain with their genial smiles & hands in pockets, their sway slightly in the sharp breeze. 'Yes, yes & yes,' they say to one another, warm eyes marking the cars as they thunder past in the road. Jo goes up to them, their ears prick up.

'Can you tell me . . .'

I drift off a few yards, toying gravel of the road with the end of my shoe (its seen better days) as back there the two bastard weebles begin their routine, their arms waving & eyes narrow to indicate (with precision, at all times, with precision) the direction — the left, the right, the left again, by the car park, by the car park, by the car park, yeah thats yer bes route, I'd reckon yeah I'd reckon, yeah thats the route thats bes for you if you're left then right, then left agen, I'd reckon that'd be bes for yow –

Jo by this time backing off to join me as they begin to repeat the 3rd repeated set of repeated directions (the same ones or different – we could not tell) – so eager were they to pass the time – their alcohol breath forming steam reaching out to Jo in the wet hour – curling on the air its happy mission to drag us in close, make us stand stocky in the rain with them, push our hands deep in pockets to fumble change & push bellies out to warm in heat from non-existent brazier, there'd have been four of us then & they'd have liked that. But we passed on. A truck passed too. Thundered it did & splashed Jo with dirty rain splashed up from the gutter. 'Marathon Health Studios,' it said on the side, 'Be fit NOT fat.' Direct & brutal in the rain on earth. Underneath the slogan a big muscleman embraces a big-breasted girl. He could rub her muscles with his breasts, it's that stupid, the two of them being fit not fat.

We continued up the road, did the obligatory left then right then left again (but only did it once) & then came to the rd. where Jenny lived. Jenny is our friend in Leeds who that day we'd gone to see but no more information's necessary since we missed her, didnt manage to get hold of her. She's the girl not really in this story. She's the one who is the gap which the masked man fills. On arriving at her doorstep – feeling 'thank lord we'll soon be out of the rain', having counted down the street, its odd this side & even that, to her number (its 209) – we descended stonesteps to the basement door. To reach the door (its a green paint peeling) you have to step across a 3ft expanse of water (part rain part drain – all grey & suddsy, with a still stink to it despite the rain reminiscent of nature, trees, etc). I step from the bottom step, foot outstretched to the doorstep – poised across the water grey beneath me & ring the bell – a far off sound you're sure no one would hear even if next to it, a muffled cry & on that particular afternoon sounding particularly weak & ineffectual, we so desperately wanting to get in out of the wet & dry our hair on her towel & our socks above the little gas fire we could glimpse through the slightly patterned kitchen window. Ring, ring. Balanced above the water. My posture and my action seeming more a fools errand every sec. it goes on.

Jenny isnt in. Funny how you know that sometimes even when you first ring the bell or bang on a door. Its echo sounding lonely from the start, doomed to be useless & an isolate. I ring again & again. Shapes of light & dark within appear momentary flickering to be J on her way to answer but always fade. Jo & I mutter 'I don't believe it, dont believe it' but liked or not liked the fact is there, to be believed. We turn aroun. The sound of a bell ring in an empty hall. In an empty house. In a street empty all but for the soddin rain. Disappointed we doubleback. Thats the end of our little plan to see Jenny and now we face a wasted afternoon goin back 'ome. Walking back into town, under overhangs of concrete flat-blocks under which wet footsteps appear on the dry ground we talk about nothing & follow those footsteps religiously — a dark prophet in DMs passed this way. Standing in a shop doorway is where we suddenly see him again. Beside the door (which is the first thing I notice) there's a small child figure made in plastic or some such — figure, blonde girl child holding out a box, she's stiff & eyes wide open, has stood here in wind & etc. holding out box. She has had donations (in aid of child care charity I cannot remember) over turning years since these stones were laid, since the high rise rose up. Since then she's stood in its shadow. Watched the birds die in its lack of earth, watched an old man roll fag on broken bench beside space where they forgot to put the trees in or where the trees forgot to live or where the trees only remembered to die. This plastic figure-ine stands quiet & watched it all. Watched them come & go from 'CLUB video shop — 7 days per week free membership 1,000 of titles in VHS & BETA' just across the rd. tho she couldnt read its name. Blind to its language. She accepted donations of pence, ha-pence, buttons & paper. She accepted a pat on head, accepted real life child who stood beside her confused, she accepted kids & scuff marks & then one day (must be recent: it stands out like worst thing in a dream) she accepts red paint dashed across her tiny face & yellow swiss chocolate box hair — red it runs like broken blood, the blood of brokenness down her face & child skin of nowt but plastic — her blue eyes of birthday card open to see pet dog or something perfect now seem to cry out the blood the blood the blow. And he stands next to her. Mask on still. That radio in his hand. Lord release us.

They're the perfect partnership. The Father. The Daughter. The holy Ghost. Blood on her face. His face he hid. See the strength that he turns that dial. From out of the radio come noises. Interference. Strange voices swirlin from inside a white sound. Germany talks music to France talking talking. A pop song. Something about 'lovin' someone. Something about hurting them. A fractured opera. Taxis calling back to base. Masked Citizen keeps his poison polo dark eye holes on the radio. Lord knows where his eyes are. The bloke on the radio is talking talking. Strange lies. Masked man seems to say (although he doesn't), 'Thats where I get my orders, somewhere in the spaces between the stations there's the message that I only hear.' No plug, no cord. He carries his orders roun with him, speaker pressed to his ear. He has one fingerless glove (black) on his rt. hand. Thats the detail, sunshine, thats the detail.

When did he first get his orders? How did all this come about? Only later, on the bus home did I work it out. When these things drifted thro my mind like ½ asleep.

Just then we walked on past him & left him standing there staring out the sky, the 'Club Video', the world like he was expecting it to bottle out & back away, what with his hair & his cock all scrap ironed in like that. He was a mean one & I mean that it nothin else.

Jo & I just went on home. The rain abated like it do & the town recovered, spread its shoppers out in the lie of sunshine to dry out a bit, unfold. The cafs stopped being crowded & started being empty. We went in one – read a bit of a paper over someones shoulder & rowed about money. What else is there to row about when there's not much else to row about? The tea was expensive. We left the bill thing stuck to the not real formica topped table in this cold wet ring left by someone elses coffee cup. A woman behind us was saying, 'Oh. Oh. She's gottah nerve she as, she's got ah nerve, she's got a bloody gob on er . . .' and the bloke with her was ignoring her, or tryin to, saying occasional salvoes of, 'Shut up goin on about it wont yer then' from his head sunk into the paper.

Outside there was a queue for the bus (glad we got there early 'cos we'd of missed it if we hadn't). We stood in it behind some old dears. They were talking away but I couldnt hear them or couldnt be bothered. Just then he arrives again. His 3rd & final His late & great. A late final (Two mins approx before the bus departs the depot). He's striding again. Radio to his ear. Scary mask still on and his whole face like looking aroun — hes jus dyin for someone to catch his no bloody eyes. An as he comes closer everyone starts looking hard at their papers, or their fingernails, or they start to talk, forced & quiet to their neighbours, in the hushed tones of people who dont want to be interrupted but dont dare to interrupt. In stories people wan to see what death looks like but they dont wan to die. And he rolls along. Those legs, in fact his whole body possessed of a clumsy grace rigidity in Co-op jeans that turns the eyes (quite simply) of those in the bus queue & Finding all eyes turned this lord of Rain inc. turns to the side & surveys the kingdom of scrawled wall, kingdom of bus shelter name writing, before him. A promise was made and Dawn promised never to stop loving Peter Jones & promised also never to pack him in. Peter kissed her here that night & then she left him, wrote 'I love you' on the steamed window of the last bus home (back seat). But now the spaces where eyes of MM should be, or might be take in the messages carved at midnight on the toilet door. His feet turn the pages of ripped up yellow phone book sodden on the ground. Its a strange lie. He walks up to the bench beneath the messages. His movements hint of someone irresponsible once taught him karate and the way he looks — the way he points his head at things, or people (its something to do with his No Eyes) — makes it seem like all this place & people is new to him (and later in some ways I learn that it is). Looks round like its a new strange thing he's found to hate, this world. With his face ripped up & his radio, black boot uneven hair. He sits on the bench & stares out. You'd expect him to be laughing but no, instead there's just the occasional silent tipping back of the head & movement of the jaw, sharp intakes of dirty air — a signal & laughter perhaps.

Then he turn to old lady (clutched poly bag in boned hands her jaw limp & whitey there beneath the messages). Everyone around us is watching in secret as he turn to her then he speak (for real this time), 'Alright luv.'

'Yes thank you.'

'Ar yer waitin ferra bus then? Which one yer waitin fer?'

'The 32, I think, is that it?' her voice doddery but not frightened she motions the bus for which we queue.

'I dont know.' Say he matter of fact, 'I'll find out for yew.' Then he stands up. Like hes stretchin himself — tall/strong — that masked head moving round like interrogator (Hun SS officer in War film torture sequence survey the selection of dental equipment & electrics). He pulls himself up to his fullest height as tho there's a meat hook in his brain — raises hand to mouth, hand to mouth (he's left the radio spewing its slight, battery lifeless voices to the floor by the seat), inserts fingers next them spit yer teeth and whistles. A long whistle the length of the platform that causes heads to turn & them eyes to avert to avoid his none, all but an inspector who's walking towards MM down the length, the grey length. Potential gunsling sequence: wind whips crisp packets & toilet doors slam — jukebox cont. its rackety song from nearby caf, mixed with M.M.s radio — the 2 men silent — M.M. stock still like nothing could make him move cept thunder bolt from sky or stake to heart etc and all the while advancing, seeming casual, unstoppable: The Inspector, fiddles with his scratched black box of timetables at his side, comin up all the way, those fingers moving seemin not to but we're sure he's seen the gunman at the other end. Everyone's bin expectin chaos since M.M. started stalkin roun, his cock all clocked up & that grim bugger face — we got a bit of a surprise when Old Lady incident went off so well, expecting harshness or violence but he turned into some ½ arsed rob. hood & damn well helped her, but now tho, now's the real time, & we're sure there's going to be trouble. Them gunfighters, they approach down the grey length. The whole platform watches (silent & surreptitious).

'Oy!' shouts citizen masked.

No reply the busman he just kept on coming. Yer should have seen him, he like

'Oy!'

He like 'Oy! yew' he like just 'Oy!' he like just ignored him 'Oy! Yew!, bloody 'ell' (that last bit under poison breath) he like just ignored him & carried on his way.

Our guy turns back to the old lady. Sensing his audiences knowing of defeat. He strolls so slowly (see that) roun the front of the bus & looks at it. Again this time his looks like that of a newchild, a child new to things, like he's trying to work this bus thing out, whatever it is, wherever it came from, wherever he go to. All this stuff here around him dont mean nothin to him, no, no, not at all. He prowls back — back rigid & fists clenched up. 'Its a 32,' he says to her. 'Does it go to Sheffield?' 'I dont know love Im sorry,' hes lookin her full in the face with this mask on & his cock an all & she's talking to him like her own Jesus son. Not blinking. 'Im sorry love I cant help yer more,' says he, 'Im sorry but yer know.' 'That's alright duck,' she say, her jaw all limp & whitey, her hand all bone & boney, her eyes all glaze & glassy in bus station depot platform 9. Then turns round the man with mask on. There's a multitude of quietness while he savours the softness he's shown — not a feeling he likes, this one. We in the queue might perhaps he wonder feel safer now he's shown his 'side of human PLC' but he wont therefore let it rest at that. He turns roun. He sends his conscience for a lie down & lets the rot start here.

Spins on an icepick & turnsa roun staring to the queue. He strides in his pocket of slow motion up to the man behind us who's in business now tryin to look like the anonymous man. Staring him blank black hole eyed in the filthy face M.M. speaks the word: 'The proverb for today is . . .' he says 'The PROVERB for TODAY IS . . .' What happens next is a mumble from man behind & bus roar simultaneously from over in the road which makes me miss the proverb. The point, the proverb, the whole point: I miss it. But the citizen backs off, radio screeching in hand, leaving the man behind us fumbling for mumbles & coughs beside his lonely wife — masked man backing off saying nothing but 'Ha ha' 'Ha ha' 'Ha ha' at the mid-point of his razored voice. 'Ha ha'. The proverb for today is Ha ha. And he just keep on going hide & stumble away with the power in those legs & the twist of that dial: listenin in to those secrets, there's someone in there talking confusion & M.M. the lone listener quits the stage, turned his back on this world in the saddest story of land & rain.

Platform defuses. Silence: like a click turned down off of timebomb. People start getting easier again. The driver turns up & lets us all on. Voices raised to a low hushed rumble. We're disappointed, having missed that Jenny girl & wasted busfare, wasted time. Money & time. We've wasted them. We get sit down. Uncomfortably stretching & putting our coats up above us on the rack.

The engine starts up & the full coach steams up from inside while the exhaust fumes blister in the outside rendering all invisible

— the old woman still sat on the bench beneath the messages fades slowly then the picture of she die. We move off. Low soporific throb of the engine, voices all around us (conversations inaudible) add to the drone of tyres on the hard road & Lorries as they steam past.

Within a very short time Jo has curled her head against me in sleep — its nice because its warm where she touches me in the cold bus of other dozing passengers. I try to sleep too but somehow, you know, I cant. There's something unfinished in the air. My mind drifts back to M.M. but this time in some ½ sleep state & my thoughts of him get swirled up with snatches of overhear & scraps then of casual dreams. First thought in head is that proverb. Jus what is the proverb for today I couldn hear him but I keep thinking I keep a list of possibilities in my head while bus loads of school kids pass & repass on the Motorway, looking out they wave & make over-clear thumbs up gestures in rehearsal for never-to-come comradeliness with lorry drivers etc, collecting waves from holiday makers plus the occasional two fingers signing 'fuck off'. I had two possibilities at the end:

(a) Dont care was made to care
Dont care was hung
Dont care was put in a pot
And boiled till he was done.

(b) Quo vadis

Yeah. Quo Vadis. I thought that might be the one.

'N' I think back then (on the coach) to what I heard (imagined) him saying earlier. Like this:

'I was here I mean way back, before they took the trolleys away — I walked this place before the Queen came round & laid the stone to earth. She buried it here that afternoon with the mayor looking on & the papers. She buried it all & went away' & that gets me to thinking I mean it gets me thinking about that stone he's talking about — that bloody stone of concrete — I think I know where it is. Im ready for it — that dump he lived in, that dump with echoes of Spain (the tumbledown 'campsite' Jo & I were forced into, great Travelling story) — he used to hang out there & doss down — his the remains of burnt up magazine, his the shit on the window pane — him the one who scared off the gangs of young kids looking for somewhere to fight & bum — he'd wander round that place like a Zoo at 90 mph — weird stuff — years ago now it was, years ago, before they took the trolleys, before they took those lost shat on animals back to the supermarkets & the clean — I can see him those yrs back now, stalking round the place — just a weird kid — he'd hang out at the entrance to the rubble site like it were his garden or his alley or write his name on back of the sub contractors Van. He'd not wear the mask back then — his face youthful tho' his eyes all dark & closed up sly like wounds to stop the world world world getting in — a sort of darkness in his manner — but the real turning point coming in the summer of '74 when one day after some long situation in the gradually rising building work he ends up some miles away at a completed high-rise — that fantasy, that projection of the construct he hangs about in — an he stands & looks up at it — 100s' of feet of stairway, balcony, glass & elevator all RISE UP — even in the daylight there's lights on up there, there's loves on up there — and his ears take in the messages — blown on the wind — a soup of voices at the high rise so the radio from 219 meets the voices from 354 and the screaming kids on the access rank and the man speaking softly to himself & staring off the balcony at the low 100s — all these sounds merging with a flutter of pigeons wings remember them pigeons at bus station — the respect they had for breadless he — their wings clapping in the soup of voices — a 100 tv's and radios embrace high above the yellow marked out no-go areas below the balconies (the dustmen wear yellow safety helmets here too for fear of bein dropped on) — and the endless drone of the elevators, their doors closing ineffectually plastic on the hands of young kids who lark about, who write someone else's name on these doors with marker pen . . . I can see M.M. stood before this great swirling mess of voice & cry — he look up, up — and then his mind take a holiday.

That night he packs his adidas ex-school kit & sports bag (still marked with the name of a girl he never luved nor anything, nor ever got owt from her either) packs it with a couple of pair of jeans, & shirts etc. Also his darts & air pistol also signed photo of Boy Caliero (Boxer It. Heavywt) also he nicks bread from pantry & also nicks 'Mr Satisfied Pork Dripping (8oz tub)' from fridge. All this while mam & dad are showered in the blue lite of the tv, washed in its soundtrack of bitch voices & car men (he hears them even as he closes fridge door silently & hears them still further as he slips out of the house, the world & away.) In the street at midnight, most of its lights off & he a little lonely he makes his way to the place — the building site — builds him a fire in a corner & pisses down a drainpipe. A new life begins as he puts up the Caliero pic with found carpet tack & lays down to sleep on the dusty ground. The voices from the soup at the high rise — all thos manmen & girlmen talking their way to him in the night of his dreams, punctured only by the gun clap of pigeon wings in flight across the velvet sickness of his life.

Masked man (as yet un-masked) sleeps hard on the cold ground that nite. The next day, passing the high rise on the way he buys a guy fawkes mask. First of many. Rhyme in his head all smashed up repeatit:

Dunt care woz mede to care
Dunt care wes hung
Dent care was pit in a pot
& boiled til he cum
Dont care was made to care
Dont care was hung
Dont care waz put in pot
& boile til he wos dun.

He sing that silent while he dogs his lost way through the crowds of crowds.

My poor head reels & reels on the bus. Its so hard to think it all out. Jo's head all nodding next to me, uh, uh, with sleep.

For masked man in my head all years pass, yrs in which they build on the building he dosses in, yrs in which he continues takin orders from the soup at the high rise, discovering also the radio & the figures & figure-ines that inhabit it — those strange lies he follows behind the blackness of his face — & all that time he stayed there he collected stuff from litter bins & bus shelters, skips of crap & shopping bags, junk & treasure, & he kept notes too, & scurrying it all bac home & sunk it in the brickwork, hidy holed it away between the bricks & into the foundations until the whole building (its deserted corridors half built & empty at night) is laced with his secrets & his nightmares — records of his dreams scrawled onto kleenex — conversations with an unmet friend. All that hidden in the builden as it rose.

Yrs later the when in Dec 83 or Oct 84 when the Queen laid the last brick at his highrise he moved out. She 'buried it for him' & he moved on. She signed & sealed some strange bargains, deals & pacts with the layin down of that final stone & he grinned in the background at the ceremony & he packed his no bags & told his no friends he was moving & he moved on off. He'd met some pretty royal people in his life.

And all that's there left now is the smell of ashes in those modern rooms & his figure (occasional) real or ghostly that stalks the crisis of that sickening high rise. Thats him under pools of corridor light. That's him (with radio) under dripping water pipe. Him jammed the elevator & crapped in the bath. Him crying alone in the stairwell at midnight. Make way sunshine cos the dark ghosts are comin up — there's got to be room.

The coach by now is thunder on the rd. Jo wakes up with a start & there are raised voices from behind us. A woman cryin.

I have one final image of him before we arrive. Sat in caf this time for some reason, talking over the noise of pinball to the old woman from the bus station & she's a sayin 'If I was a kitchen what kind of a kitchen would I be?' — He's sittin down with her over cups of t going cold and they're playing that game & he says with face still masked up 'If you were a kitchen you'd be covered in blood.'

'You're daft. You're plain daft,' she says, 'You cant say that.'

'I can,' says he, 'I jus did. If you wer a kitchen yourd be covered in blood.'

Then he turns his face away from her & looks out the winder & the pouring rain. Ha ha speaks he inside his head. She ignores that. A long & still shot of that brutal face all green & orange plastic spit its teeth out. Perhaps the slightest shot of movement hinted in those spaces for eyes — steam rising from the grim cup beside his blak gloved hand. Then that's it.

Behind us now the woman crying has become a bit of a row & as she's getting off in Sheffield she's a pawing animal at the coat of this 'ard looking bloke and he's looking ahead like nobodys business & she's sayin 'I'm sorry Im sorry Im sorry' like a lonely story of land & rain. All the way home I think of her & that masked man — all houses on City Rd all tucked in safen sound from him, that mad mad brother & when sunset comes I weep a little & spit for both of them. Lord release us, give us room.

BORNEO

Patrick Gale

Bee took a sandwich, doing her best to fill the gap left behind, and opened the French windows onto the garden. She stood on the steps for a moment then saw that the 'whirligig' clothes line was still out, laden with knickers and bras. Stuffing the sandwich into her mouth, she strode out to remove the wretched thing from eighty disapproving eyes.

Tony had died on a draughty Sunday in late Autumn. They had had some friends to lunch after Eucharist, then the two of them had gone up on the downs to walk off the blackberry and apple crumble. The wind had been so strong that they played games, leaning into it, yelling to make themselves heard. Tony's deputy, Mike, was playing at Evensong so there had been no rush. When they came home, he had sat down to watch the new Trollope serial while she made a pot of tea. She had walked in with the tray to find him lying on the floor, his face twisted, dribbling at the pain. His hands had pressed at his temples as if his head were trying to burst. When the nurse had let her in to kiss her husband good-bye, there had been bruises from the pressure of his own fingertips.

'Coo-eee.'

Bee spun around with a handful of knickers. Mrs de Vere was standing there in a tea cosy hat and second-hand coat. Sturdy, black NHS specs glinted in the sun.

'Mrs de Vere. How lovely.'

Mrs de Vere was not meant to be here. Thursday mornings were usually the time for Bee's Afghanistan Bandage Parties. She would pour out coffee to a collection of the more lonely or immobile women of the area (picking them up by car, where necessary) while they cut up old sheets into bandages for her to send to refugee camps. In fact, Bee hadn't got around to sending any bandages for months, and was stockpiling the things in a fertiliser bag in the basement. She thought she had put off all her regulars. Evidently this one had slipped through the diplomatic net. A pronounced outcast, on account of her thick Dutch accent, disgusting mothbally smell and jealous obsession with the Bishop (whom she was rumoured to have followed from post to post since his ordination), Mrs de Vere was not coffee morning material.

'I was not going to come this morning, on account of my arthritis you see, but I heard that you were having a coffee morning next week so I thought today I make a special effort for the little Afghans, yes?' she burbled.

'Of course. How kind. Actually, I'm giving a coffee morning today, as well,' said Bee, hoping that her breathing through her mouth wasn't too evident, 'So I thought I could find you a chair near the fire and give you a sheet and let you get on with it. There'll be all your friends here. Let's go in, shall we, and find you a cup of coffee. You like it made with milk, don't you?'

Dinah still had to appear with the rest of the cups and saucers. Bee prayed that the guests wouldn't arrive in a rush. She ensconced her unexpected visitor in the gloomier corner by the dining room fire and found her a pair of scissors and an old sheet. Mrs de Vere would insist on humming Lutheran hymns as she worked. Perhaps the spitting of the logs would cover it.

Everyone had been marvellous, of course. They had all heard within hours, without her breathing a word, and for the next month she was surrounded by a cushioned wall of comfort. Bee had seen this in operation on others, been a press-ganged accessory to it herself. She had imagined she would react angrily, stifled by the pressing affection. Her submission, in the event, surprised her. The house had reeked of flowers. Every hour brought another fistful of cards and letters. She was honoured with gifts, as one miraculous; packets of home-made fudge, the solace of chocolate cakes, deep-frozen cassoulets for one, books of poetry with the relevant pages kindly earmarked. There were a small bunch of friends who had sent or brought something every day; a token of love. Once she started to venture out, she could subside into tears in the most unsuitable places, like the public library, secure in the knowledge that someone in the vicinity who 'knew' would rush over with hugs and murmurings. She had never realised before, how many of them had suffered. Tony's hideous death brought such a quantity of pain and doubt to the surface that the community had seemed irrevocably altered. Her affection for it was not increased, but she approached it with new-found respect. That they had all felt the agony of bereavement at first-hand was only natural, far more interesting was the chemistry in death that caused so many of them to lay bare the poverty of their faith. Not a batch of consolations but contained one astonishing recognition of the insane cruelty of existence, of the seeming impossibility of any but a psychopathic deity. The strongest of the latter were written on Diocesan notepaper. Bee was an atheist. It was her best kept secret. Only Reuben knew. She had meant to confess to Tony, but his cheerful faith had disarmed her, and then he had died. The spate of avowals in the wake of his death had implicated her in the community. This was the first cord that bound her in. The second had been their guilt.

The house in the cathedral close was a traditional perk of the post of Organist. Mike took over Tony's job. He had five children as well as a wife. Gently, shamefacedly, Bee was evicted. She had finished her teacher's training after meeting Tony, but had done no work since their marriage. The task of teaching the Baby Form at the choir school had recently fallen vacant and it came with a half-share in a pretty, Regency house just outside the Close gates. It was widely known that Bee got on well with children, probably because she was unable to have any of her own, poor thing, so the Headmaster's wife was approached to approach the Headmaster, who subsequently approached Bee who, to everyone's relief, accepted his kind offer. As the sole woman on the teaching staff, Baby Mistress shared number eight, Chaplain's Walk with the assistant matron. Jennifer was a cheery, horsey type, who lived happily alongside Bee for two years before following the custom of her post, getting herself impregnated by Stephen Simkins (P.E.) after being seen swimming with him in the moonlight and the buff. They were still on their honeymoon, and Bee had the house to herself until the replacement arrived.

She handed Mrs de Vere her coffee, then retraced the smell of hot lemon and spices to the kitchen. Her twenty-three-year-old brother, Reuben, was using a fish slice to slide some newly-baked biscuits onto a wire tray. The frown of concentration and faint baker's flush only enhanced his vulpine charm.

'That's the last batch,' he said. 'How many d'you think'll come?'

'Oh, Christ. It could be forty. There are fifty local members. Twenty of them are in homes or bed-ridden, but the others all promised to bring friends. Oh, Christ.'

'Have a gulp of my gin.'

'Rube, it's only ten-thirty!'

'So? Have a gulp of my gin.'

'Thanks.'

She took the flour-dusty glass, perched on the kitchen stool and gulped. He had descended on her five days ago, tanned, penniless, and suggesting, by his echoing want of future tense, that the stay was indefinite. The tan was Indian. He had been out there for nearly a year, making a small, shady fortune as a jewel dealer.

'I still don't understand why,' he said, arranging cup cakes in rings of alternating colours on a vast, borrowed plate.

'Because it's usually run by Miranda Cotterel, but she fell off her bike and did in her hip.'

He had woken one morning to find himself relieved of every worldly possession, save the sleeping bag around him and a quantity of Marks and Spencer underwear. His copy of *India on a Dollar a Day* had also been left behind, apparently on a whim of superstitious benevolence. His escape involved a Foreign Office ex of his from school then a certain amount of murkiness in Bangkok. Dear Rube was nothing if not resourceful.

'You're not on the Committee, are you though?'

'No. But Miranda Cotterel has some very persuasive friends who are.'

'An offer you couldn't refuse?'

'Sort of, only they think they do it to give me something to occupy my poor, bereaved soul. Rube, you're a saint. Can I do anything?'

'Don't you dare.'

He had dropped out of school at seventeen to enrol in Life's University as, variously, masseur, waiter, singing telegram and escort; all activities pursued under the generic carapace, Travel Writer.

'Bee, do you even know where Borneo is?'

'No. But then, neither do they.'

'Have you read the Charity's magazine?'

'Lot of smiley black nuns, isn't it? Look, let me take those through. I hate feeling spare.'

'Don't drop them.'

'I'm not incapable.'

She bent forward to kiss his gilded cheek and brushed her twin-set on a plate of sieved icing sugar.

'Dolt!'

He dusted her down and pushed her gently from the room.

The clock on the dining room mantelpiece struck eleven. In the kitchen Rube had two kettles, a preserving pan and a pressure cooker full of steaming water at the ready. The two thirty-cup teapots on loan from the WI had been scrubbed and contained equal heaps of Gold Blend 37. He poured himself another generous gin. Interleaved biscuits and radiating rings of small cakes waited on the sideboard.

'Will you have a biscuit, Mrs de Vere? Those ones are lemon. Very good. Freshly baked.'

Mrs de Vere lowered her busy hands to her lap and gave Bee a stare. Her lenses were thick, full of milky eye.

'I must not be eating biscuits or cake neither. They cause me to choke. I had an unpleasant experience as a child and have been prone to choking ever since. But you must have one, thank you all the same.'

'Oh dear. Yes. I think I shall.'

Bee bit off a piece of biscuit. It was still faintly warm and crumbled delightfully on her tongue, but the door bell rang and she had to swallow the rest in a rush.

'Bee. Anyone here?'

'Dinah.' Dinah Stapleton, friend with cups and saucers. 'Thank God. No. They're all late.'

Dinah was the school secretary. Urbane and discreetly pagan, she survived on an illusory sense that her every pleasure was illicit. She conducted her friendship along conspiratorial lines, making a point of arriving among the first, whenever Bee was entertaining, so as to enjoy a snatched conversation, sotto voce, in the hall. She heaved her basket-on-wheels up the steps, scowling at each clatter of the school crockery within, then stopped dead and pointed at the alien coat hanging on a hook. She mouthed her enquiry,

'Whose is *that*?'

Bee grinned and beckoned her into the kitchen.

'Hello, Dinah.'

'I say. Home is the sailor. Hello, Reuben. Have you been terribly busy? Don't answer that. Bee, who?'

'Mrs de Vere.'

'What? Why?'

'Quite. She's not meant to be here, but she didn't realise that the Bandage Girls were cancelled for this week, and she lives right up on the hill so I couldn't very well turn her away.'

'Well no. Of course not.'

'Bless you for bringing all that.'

'Yes. We must shove it on trays for you. Come on. No rush, though; they'll be at least another ten minutes. Oh yes. I've got something horrid for the Bring and Buy . . .'

'Damn! The stall. I still haven't . . .'

'It's all right,' soothed Reuben, placing a slightly unsteady hand on her shoulder. 'I did it while you were boiling Dame Vermeer's milk.'

'Thanks.'

Dinah was clattering out a third trayload.

'Your stalls are always so well stocked, Bee,' she said, 'I don't know where you manage to find so many unwanted Christmas presents. Don't you get any you want to keep?'

'Not many. What do you mean, ten minutes?'

'They're all at the Deanery.'

'Why the hell? They know they're meant to be here.'

'Didn't anyone tell you?'

'What?'

'You picked an appalling day. *She* invited everyone to a rival do about a week before you did. Boat People.'

'Why didn't she invite me?'

'The crib gaffe.'

'I only gave it a bit of a dust and changed the dead flowers. You'd think she made the thing by hand, she's so prickly about it.'

'She did.'

'It was one of those plastercast kits.'

'Well, she made the manger.'

'Excuse my butting in,' said Reuben, 'but they're here.'

He had seen them walking up the drive. Bee hurried into the hall and opened the door as Mrs Clutterbuck reached for the bell-push.

'Daphne, how lovely.'

'Hello, Bee. You know Mrs Thomas. And this is my cousin Jane.'

'Hello.'

'How d'you do?'

'Come in.'

'Hello, Dinah.'

'You've been terribly busy.'

'Is that the errant brother out there?'

'Look at all the biscuits.'

'Marvellous spread, Bee.'

'Oh. Mrs de Vere. How nice.'

'What are you doing with that sheet?'

'Rag-rugs? Oh I see, it's bandages. Lovely.'

'Milk, no sug. Perfect.'

'Wonderful bikkies, Bee.'

'Reuben's actually. Coming. Hello. Come in. I'm Bridget Martin,' said Bee.

'Hello.'

'Hello.'

Miss Trott. Miss Deakin. Mrs and the Misses Hewlings. Penny Friston. Marge Brill. Reverend and Mrs Pyke. Reverend Yeats. Sister Veronica and Mother Lucy from that strange community at Perton Bagshawe. Rapidly the dining room filled and the temperature rose. The hooks were laden with tweed and scarves and a pile of coats began to form at the foot of the stairs. Bee stopped answering the door and left it propped open with the umbrella stand. She realised that she should have served coffee from a table in the hall for the dining room, and by degrees the drawing room as well, were becoming so crowded that it was difficult to manoeuvre a coffee pot, cream jug and sugar bowl simultaneously. Dinah had manned the Bring and Buy stall and was therefore cut off at the far end of the room. Bee stood helpless outside the dining room door, tray in hand, and made explanatory faces at Miss Wooding and Mrs Lloyd-Mogg who were staring mournfully at their empty cups.

'Could you? Excuse me . . . er . . . could you?' she tried a few times, but went unheeded by the stockade of rounded backs.

Reuben appeared at her elbow.

'You'll have to shout,' he said. 'They won't mind.'

'I can't.'

'Coward.' He faced into the room and called out, 'Ladies. Ladies.' The din in both rooms dissolved at once into mildly indignant question mark noises. A score of puffy faces turned and stared. He was quite unabashed. 'It's rather hard for us to get to you, so if you'd like some more coffee — and there is plenty — would you like to step out into the hall?'

They stepped out with a vengeance. Reuben set up a pouring-station at the hall table, as a queue formed, thrusting the second jug onto Bee. She toured the drawing room, seeing to the less mobile. These sat on sofas and chairs, sticks at their sides, offending wrists or legs laid ostentatious before them. Miss Coley. Barbie Sears. Miss Rossington and Miss Pidsley. They showed no sign of enjoying themselves or guilt at being waited on. The room was just large enough for each to stare without encountering the eyes of the others. Bee exchanged a few words with each in turn, asking after their health and less healthy friends, checking that each had secured a copy of the magazine, watchful for any anxiety about where they could 'powder their noses'. Then she crossed the hall, with muttered thanks to Reuben en route, and endeavoured to teeter through the suffocating room to Dinah. The latter was counting a wad of notes in a shortbread tin.

'Dinah, are you all right?'

'Fine.'

'You've taken loads.'

'Always the same. You do a roaring trade in the first ten minutes. Everyone brings a thing, buys a thing, dumps it, and there an end.'

'Yes.' Bee recognised a jar of rhubarb chutney she had made two years ago, which had evidently been doing the benevolent rounds ever since. All her original horrors had been sold, and replaced with not dissimilar fare. There were a dry-looking sponge with thin pink icing, two tins of lychees, and some elderly paperbacks. There were also some quite passable lavender bags which she would pocket, if no one else did. 'How's Mrs de Vere?' she went on. 'I couldn't reach her.'

'Oh, she's okay. Ripping and rolling away. There was a lull after Reuben summoned them into the hall, and I managed to get over and have a chat. Someone had given her a collection of those heavenly biscuits, and she was quite cheerful for once.'

'But she's not allowed biscuits; she said so!'

'Well, she was munching away. Said how good they were. Hang on. The cake, Mrs Frist? Oh, I dunno. What do you think for the cake, Bee? I haven't had time to price it.'

'How about fifty pee?'

'Fifty pee it is.'

'But is it fresh?' asked Mrs Friston, giving the article a sharp poke.

'Oh I should think so, wouldn't you?' Dinah used her school dinners tone, and took the customer's uncertainly proffered coin. 'Thanks. There we are. Have a good tea.' She dropped the takings into the tin with a clatter. 'Her Nibs won't be pleased.'

'Why not? They all went to her first.'

'But that's just it. You always go first to the thing you're going to leave. I think the dear trouts are here to stay.'

'Now now. We'll be among them before long.'

'Don't,' said Dinah, who was several years her senior. She looked across the bobbing tussocks of grey hairs and blue much as she would survey the field at the boys' football matches. She addressed Bee in an undertone without turning. 'Is he coming, then?'

'Dick Greville? Yes, but he'll be late.'

'Not the Precentor, you ass; you know, *Him*. Is he?'

'Teddy?'

Bee smiled involuntarily as she spoke the name and Dinah laughed aloud.

'Well, is he?'

Bee felt herself redden.

'He said he'd try. Now I must go and help Reuben.'

Teddy Gardiner had kissed her all over her sofa. Over six foot, with dark leonine hair and eyes of unexpected blue, he had arrived on the teaching staff the year before she did. He was a lay clerk in the Cathedral, singing bass, taught English and coached the first fifteen. His body might have devastated were it not for the sense that it was the unconscious creation of wholesome pleasure, not an effortless endowment of birth. She had noticed him at once, but had stilled her interest with the reflection that, while no great beauty, Tony was blessedly indolent. Dinah had taken an immediate shine to him, but had passed unnoticed and so recovered. Just three weeks into Bee's widowhood he had come, grave of face, to express his sympathy. He had said how sorry he was to hear, she had said not at all, then they had sat side by side on the sofa talking about the Dean's latest sermon and the tummy bug epidemic. The talk had faltered and, after a finger itching silence, they had slid into a wild embrace. Things would certainly have progressed had he not kicked over the sherry bottle. Jennifer had come home in the middle of the mopping-up, and he had fled in confusion to supervise the boys' prep. Over the twenty-four months that ensued, his sporadic courtship had not gone unremarked.

Bee made her way back to the kitchen, pausing only long enough to be told that the rival do at the Deanery had been the usual dour affair and that most of, if not all, the guests had come on to hers. She found Rube sitting on the draining board swinging his legs. He was not alone. He was nose to nose with the young Precentor.

'Hello, Dick.'

'Bee. How splendid.'

Did she fancy that guilty start?

'I had no idea you two knew each other,' she said. Dick Greville, who sang like an angel, was teaching the choristers plainsong technique, and was rumoured to be a favourite at Clarence House, coughed and said, 'Well . . . er . . . Yes.'

'Mrs Hewlings just introduced us,' said Reuben sharply. 'But actually we'd met once before at the Brills'. How is everything?'

'Oh, fine. Fine. Nothing left to do now but chat. Reuben's been a wonder, Dick. He took over all the baking for me.'

'Oh, really? How splendid.'

'Yes, well I was just saying I'd show our Precentor the old wasps' nest in the summer house.'

So saying, Rube opened the kitchen door and stepped out into the back yard. Dick, who had a reputation for purity, hovered on the door mat, wrinkling his brow.

'Are you . . . er?' he asked Bee.

'No thanks. I'd better take round the jug again.' She beamed.

'Oh. Right. 'Bye.'

He shut the door behind him. Bee leant on the kitchen stool and heard Reuben's laugh around the corner. Then she watched the two of them cross the lawn and, after a hasty look round, vanish into the gloom of the summer house. She had found a dried-out wasps' nest in there, glued to the rafters. Reuben had never seemed particularly interested.

She made a fresh jug of coffee and set out to re-fill cups. Everyone said how much they were enjoying themselves. No one had left, although a few had deserted the main body to go upstairs on an 'explore'. Sister Veronica's stout-booted form was trotting across the half-way landing as Bee crossed the hall. She saw Bee in a mirror and stopped, turning with a twitter, a smile and a sparrow flap of her hand. A deeper voice barked from the landing, 'Come on, Knickers, you'll get left behind,' at which Veronica hesitated minutely before scampering round the corner, out of sight. Bee saw Dinah surreptitiously collecting cups and saucers from behind drinkers' backs. Her friend caught her eye and gave her a wink. She turned into the drawing room.

'More coffee, girls?' she called, feeling suddenly tired.

'Rather. White and two sugs. Isn't that naughty of me?'

'Oh but no, I think there comes a time when . . .'

'Black, please. Yes, that's lovely.'

'Whichever's easiest . . . Oh well, darkish brown then, please.'

She met the chorus with bland smiles. She reached Miss Rossington, whose leg was stretched out on a pile of cushions and a footstool and found that she was fast asleep. Slowly she lifted the cup and saucer from off the woman's lap and slid them onto her tray. She turned and saw Teddy. Everyone else saw her seeing Teddy, too, and carried on chatting with eyes and minds in suspension.

'Hello,' he said, 'I'm late, aren't I?'

'Yes, but it's sweet of you to come at all.'

'Oh, nonsense. I mean . . . Borneo and things are . . . well. Let me help you with that. Are you going to the kitchen with it?'

'Yes.'

He took the tray in his great hands and swung out the way she had come. She watched his shoulder blades beneath the Harris tweed and wished again that he wasn't quite so sporty. In the kitchen she took the tray from him and opened the basement door.

'In there. Quickly.'

He obeyed. She glanced into the hall to see that she was unobserved then darted in behind him, closing the door. She shot the bolt and turned on the steps.

His thick arms grabbed her in the dark and pushed her back against the floor polisher and some pampas grass she was drying for the harvest festival. She sought his mouth and pulled his rugger thighs against her. He smelt faintly of Old Spice. She ran her fingers into his tough hair and pulled his head back so that she could take a series of rapid bites around his adam's apple. With a moan he broke free and thrust himself hard against her, making the shoe-cleaning things rattle in their box.

'Now,' he said.

'No.'

'Yes.'

'I say *no*.'

'Mrs Martin? Mrs Martin, are you there?'

'Blast! Her Nibs. Get down there and count to a hundred and fifty before you come out.'

He lurched down the stairs, kicking over a fertiliser bag as he went. Bee flicked on the light, smoothed out her skirt and twin-set, and slid back the bolt without a sound.

The Dean's wife was standing on the kitchen doormat. She was a tall, ugly woman and strained her goldfish eyes to see over Bee's emerging shoulder. Bee shut the door behind her.

'Mrs Crewe. I'm so glad you could make it.'

'Well, I'm not really making it, you know,' she snapped. 'I'm looking for Mr Gardiner. I gather he's here.'

'Yes. He is. Why do you need him?'

Bee set out firmly for the hall again, forcing Mrs Crewe to follow her. She glanced out of the window as they went, noting that the summer house door was still shut.

'I gave a coffee morning today as well, as you probably heard, and he promised he'd come and help move my trestle tables when it was all over. He wasn't going to come until nearer twelve-thirty, but it finished a little earlier than planned and the Dean wants the room free for his heraldry class tonight. Mrs Friston said Mr Gardiner was here, so I wonder . . .'

'Yes he is, as I say. I'm not too sure where. He followed me out to the kitchen then said something about going round the garden to take a look at my leaning wall for me.'

'Oh really? Well, perhaps I can find him there.'

'Mrs Crewe?'

Teddy walked in through the open front door, his hands thrust deep in his pockets. Bee flashed her praise.

'Ah, Teddy, there you are.' Her Nibs threw a glance at her hostess. 'I'm afraid I'm going to kidnap you a little early.'

Without a word of thanks she stalked him from the house. Once again Bee faced a ring of enquiring faces.

'Has anyone seen the Precentor?'

'I thought I saw him earlier on.'

'I wanted to ask him about that dreadful Series Two.'

'Oh yes. King James is so much more . . . well . . . it feels more *right* somehow, doesn't it?'

'Of course, poor Mrs Crewe does have an awful lot on her plate.'

'Fifty-two, isn't she now? I must say, it's lasting rather a long time.'

'Bee, quick,' Dinah's face was colourless, 'in the dining room. It's Mrs de Vere!'

'Mrs de *Vere?* Is she here?'

'Well, perhaps she's just joined. There was something about new members.'

'I thought perhaps the Committee . . . ?'

Ignoring the chatter around her, Bee ran into the dining room. The grey-haired sea parted before her. In her chair by the fire, Mrs de Vere was writhing. One hand flailed before her, where it had dropped a coffee cup, the other plucked at her throat. Her vein-strung legs, bandaged at the ankles, twisted and kicked in their sensible brown walking shoes, and her old wool skirt was riding up over a greyish petticoat.

'God, she's choking!' Bee exclaimed, rushing forward. 'Dinah, could you ring for an ambulance?'

With little or no idea what to do, Bee reached the old woman and unbuttoned the top of her blouse. The lapels of her cardigan were studded with crude costume jewellery. A gold chain hung round her neck, tinkling with good luck charms.

'Mrs de Vere! Mrs de Vere!' she shouted, and banged her

furiously on the back.

'Yes, ambulance, and quickly please. We have an old woman choking on a biscuit here.' Dinah's voice rang out in the stunned near-silence of the hall. 'What? Oh yes. Number eight, Chaplain's Walk. But it's one way, so you'll have to approach it from Bridge Street, at the other end.'

Halfway onto the floor now, Mrs de Vere was turning grey/blue. Her glasses had fallen off and her milky eyes were wide with pain and terror. Her breath came in deep agonised sucks that made her teeth whistle. The other guests kept outside a neat four-foot radius. Some stared blankly, others touched their mouths with listless fingers or picked unthinkingly at their clothes. Reverend Pyke was among them. His wife turned on him.

'Jack, darling. What did you do to Kathy Roach that time? Quickly. Try to remember.'

'Well, I . . . I punched her. You always have to punch them hard on the solar plexus.'

'Well, do it.'

Breathless from belabouring the gasping woman's back, Bee looked up in despair.

'Oh yes. Please. Try anything you know. She's going to pass out any second.' He dithered, finding a place to set down his cup and saucer and she felt her anger rise.

'Well come on, then; she's dying!'

He darted forward, rolling up a shirt sleeve.

'Hold her back so I can get at her,' he said. Getting behind the armchair, Bee took Mrs de Vere under the arms and hauled her upright. 'Steady. Steady.' His voice was quavering. Bee noticed how black the hair was on his fist. 'Now!'

With a grunt of effort, he punched hard at the top of the ribs. Mrs de Vere's hooting cry was hidden by the gasp from the onlookers. Her sucking whistles continued, only fainter.

'Upside down,' called Dinah. 'We'll have to get her upside down as if it was a fish bone or something.'

'Yes. That's right.'

'Upside down.'

There was a suggestion of hilarity in the rejoinders. Swing the old trout upside down.

'I'll take her legs,' announced Reverend Pyke.

He took her by the ankles and walked round, almost ponderously it seemed to Bee. With her feet over the back of the chair, the choking woman's skirt flopped down onto her waist.

'Now, jiggle her up and down a bit,' called Miss Coley, who, chronic disabilities notwithstanding, had found her way onto a dining room chair at the back of the crowd.

'You'll have to be quite fierce, though, Jack, if we're to shake it loose.'

Urged on by the well-wishers, Jack Pyke jiggled her up and down quite fiercely. Her tongue lolled outside her bloodless lips and her straggly hair began to swing against the carpet. Somebody laughed.

Bee could stand it no longer. She bent down and cradled the woman's jerking shoulders in her arm.

'Stop. Stop. For God's sake, stop! I think she's dead.'

But Reverend Pyke appeared not to have heard. Sweat streaming down his scarlet face, indignant from the fire, he continued to jolt his patient.

'Just a few more. I think we're nearly there,' he gasped.

'No, Jack,' his wife called. 'Stop. Stop.'

She ran forward and laid a hand on his arm. He looked at her, then down to where Bee, near tears, was trying to lift Mrs de Vere back to dignity. He let go of the ankles and followed his wife from the room. With Dinah's help, Bee turned the old woman round so that her feet were on the ground once more. The crinkled head dangled to one side. Dinah listened to her heart.

'She's dead,' she said.

A sigh – half apology, half disgust – ran through the crowd. Behind Bee's back they began to find their coats, telling each other that perhaps the most useful thing they could do was to get out of the way and let the ambulance men deal with it.

'Where's the Precentor?' asked Mrs Brill. 'I did so want to ask him . . .'

'Perhaps tomorrow,' hushed her daughter.

The ambulance men duly arrived. As the two of them rolled Mrs de Vere onto a stretcher and covered her in a royal blue blanket, a nurse who was with them assured Bee that there was nothing more she could have done.

'Looks as though she had a good run for her money, though, doesn't it? At least she went out enjoying herself,' she said. 'Better than for it to happen alone.'

'Yes,' agreed Dinah. 'There's always something worse. Look, Bee, I'll ride up to the Hospital in the ambulance to see if they need any details or anything like that. She won't have any next of kin that we know of. I'll get back as soon as I can.'

'Bless you,' said Bee. 'I'll cope.'

She stood in the porch and watched the forlorn little procession wend its way down the drive. Dinah was chatting to the nurse in the stretcher's wake. The coats had all gone. Bee walked with a tray around the drawing room, picking up cups and saucers, then did the same in the dining room. She plumped out a few cushions, re-arranged the armchairs and walked over to the Bring and Buy stall. The lavender bags were still there. She slipped them into her pocket, then took a half-eaten biscuit out of the shortbread tin and counted the money. They had taken twenty-five pounds. Without the float, that was nineteen. The remaining issues of the quarterly magazine had been knocked onto the carpet in the excitement. She gathered them up, threw them on top of the glowing logs, watched them flare up, then carried the dirty cups and saucers through to the kitchen.

There was still no trace of Reuben or the Precentor. She assumed that they had discovered a shared interest in Kashmir or something, and had gone for a walk. She stood at the sink, squirted some washing-up liquid into the bowl and turned on the hot tap. As the foam rose, she picked up the rubber gloves and blew into them to turn the fingers the right way out. As she pulled them on, someone pressed up behind her. She jumped, then realised who it was.

'She let you go early,' she said, leaning her head back onto his shoulder as his hands ensnared her waist.

'I heard what had happened, and thought you might need a hand.'

'Oh Teddy, Teddy,' she murmured as he licked one of her ears, somewhat clumsily. 'I want you to put me in your little red car and drive me fast anywhere else for several hours.'

'Actually, the big end's gone,' he apologised. 'I've only got the bicycle at the moment.'

Over the browning leaves of the geranium on the windowsill, she watched the summer house door open. Reuben emerged with a delicate yawn.

'There's a drying-up cloth on the back of the door,' she said.

DOWN THE LIGHT-WELL

R. M. Hale

Slowly, he pivoted on his buttocks and swung his yellowing legs through the crumpled pile of grey sheets and stained blankets. He pressed the balls of his feet warily to the smooth lino and felt the blood buzz down his arteries and through his blue/black veins. He looked at them dispassionately – a line of small slugs inching their way up his withered limbs. What a horrible dream, he thought. God, what a horrible dream! The greenness of it stuck to the inside of his eyelids, as if he had looked full at the sun and screwed his eyes shut straight after. The dream had been like drowning in the slimey light of a cathode ray tube, pinioned by the phosphorescent blip darting from the heart of the instrument. And there was nothing inside the tube; he knew, he had dropped one, and the glass had all smashed inwards. Get caught in a vacuum, and your breath would all be sucked outwards, wouldn't it? Leave your lungs squashed flat together, like the bread in a damp sandwich.

The dream scared him most, because it showed that memories he had hoped were long dead were soaking back through to the surface of his mind. He knew the facts of his past well enough – what was what, where he'd been and even, in a life full of swift and necessary changes of name and character, mostly who he had been. Slipping from person to person had always been easier because the sensations of his life gone by had always seemed suspended far away, hardly worth troubling over. But, in this dream, he had been back in that submarine, and not just ironed-in by the hull and the walls of green water beyond, but glassed into the radar. The 'Green Eye' they had called it. At the back of his throat was the taste of a biting memory . . . that thin green wisp of chlorine gas, generated when a battery cracked and its acid seeped into the saltwater bilges.

His long progress of temporary lives had sprung from a sudden impulse to escape that creaking tomb. He'd hoped that the images of the place had evaporated into the fresher air he had found outside; it was frightening, so many years later, to find that they hadn't. He knew the cause of it — that bloody ham; a grumble deep in his bowels confirmed it. He slapped across the bare lino, unlatched the front door, and peered cautiously down the passage. He didn't want to meet anyone. As it was clear, he pattered past the banisters and into the heads. And that was a word he would hope to have forgotten.

The ham had been saved up for months, hidden away in the top cupboard. Stupidly he had left it on the table the day before, meaning to open it for lunch. As he hadn't felt so well, it had sat in the sun through the long afternoon. In the evening he had stirred himself to open it. But, instead of the smooth oval joint wrapped in cool translucent jelly, a livid slab of pressed pink flesh slopped from the tin and skidded across the cracked plate on its slick of yellow oil. He chopped it to a tombstone shape, shaved off some thin slices, then squared it up. But barely ate any of it. Tasted like spam.

Anyway, that's got rid of that, he thought as the cistern clunked.

In the kitchen the fat had congealed over the meat. He didn't hesitate in lobbing it through the window, from where it hit the dustbins four storeys below, booming like a distant depth charge. His windows faced west, and he saw from the stark shadow thrown forward by the corner of the block that it was going to be another bleak, hot day. He put the kettle on the hob, but only a thin layer of black dust remained at the bottom of the tea packet. He would have to go out. He was distressed to find that, but for his trousers, he was still dressed from the night before, so he tugged off the dog-collar for inspection. Dirt rippled around the off-white celluloid, so he stuck it under the tap and listlessly scoured it away with his thumb and finger. So last night he must have taken off his shoes and trousers, wrapped himself in the bedclothes and simply passed out, undersea. After the ham, he remembered only the drab magnolia emulsion on the wall flushing with the sunset, and the shock of seeing his silhouette — a hunched old man with a long thin throat. He'd sat on the edge of the low bed for hours without moving, just staring at the wall. He had not been out into the heat for three days now, and couldn't recall when he had last spoken to anyone.

He had been a vicar for many months now, ever since the moment an impulse had taken him into a theatrical costumiers, where he had purchased (not stolen) the dog-collar and the thin grey flannel bib. It marked his retirement from all the mask-shifting his long-ago desertion had caused to become the pattern of his life. A reverend was a respectable role; surely he deserved some quiet respect now. Spending the twilight of his years in a country parsonage, surrounded by orchards and cottages; that would be nice . . . Still, at least the collar had secured the room for him, and the little kitchen. Where would he be otherwise? And he had his chapel; he had even preached a sermon! He couldn't think why, but this time he didn't want to cheat on the part he was playing. Not for the God stuff; that was as nothing. Nor because of the collar – he'd come across padres, bishops, monks and the like all over, and knew there were as many gents and bastards among them as near any other group. He just knew that he would not cheat on himself this time. That was why the meeting was frightening him . . . and hadn't that been in the horrible dream too?

By chance, he had found a letter stuck beneath the door of the chapel. It was a circular inviting all the brothers/sisters in Christ of the senders to join with them in a discussion group and prayer meeting devoted to the relationship of faith to the ever-changing nature of modern society. 'We are the "Interface Community Troupe",' it told him. The print had been difficult to read; there was a list of dates and venues but he couldn't make them out. One of them was bound to be the chapel, otherwise why would they have troubled to deliver there? As it was his chapel, he would have to go. Weeks later, another note appeared, this time a handbill specifying no days and no locations, just 'in your area!' and 'soon!!' Surely his new brothers/sisters would expect him to contribute not just his presence, but a sermon too. The given theme was 'Hi-Tech Heaven'. He had even met a woman posting a notice in a shop. It spelled out the words 'Interface' and 'Hi-Tech Heaven' in stubby felt-tip capitals and was accompanied by clumsy caricatures of children staring at an oblong screen. Above them was a bulky cloud emitting thick streaks of red and blue, signifying, he supposed, celestial light and so divine approval. The woman had cheerfully pointed to a moon-faced child and said:

'We must learn from the kids; you'll be joining us, I know, Brother.'

He'd have to go, he knew he'd have to go, and his guts knew it too; they nagged him daily — that must be the dread on waking. And now during sleep too. The idea of participating in anything scared him — look at the result of his sermon. Only an anonymous crowd was a friendly one, that much he had learnt from his years alone.

'Trouble is,' he said aloud to the kitchen, 'what do I know of this computer stuff?'

Even the sound of his own voice, the words slurred by the fur on his tongue, sounded unfamiliar and unsettling. The date must be due, he would have to move. Picking up his clergyman's linen jacket, with its dark sweat stains in crescents beneath the armpits, he wandered over to the bed in search of socks and trousers. He must try to get out early, stay out of the sun.

* * *

No one seemed to live in the street now; most of the houses were crumbling. It all looked set for the bulldozer. The chapel was inconspicuous, sheltered at the side by the railway embankment. Once part of a large school, most of which had been demolished, there remained the chapel itself, a long narrow room used until recently as a playgroup centre, and, above them both, a lop-sided hall with a stage that faced away from the floor area. The roof was still quite sound. It would all come down soon but, till it did, he had adopted it for his own. He even had a set of keys, though he had yet to find the locks they were meant for. They made a good appearance when he reached the door — not that he had ever been questioned. He came at mid-morning; its other users seemed to come at night.

He entered cautiously. If anyone were waiting, he would kneel at the altar rail and mutter to himself for a bit. It was just going through the motions but at first it had seemed quite purposeful. The chapel was empty, and a swift inspection showed that there were no additions to the scrawlings on the walls; no sherry or cider empties in the pews, and no would-be voodoo burnt-offerings on the altar. Nothing had been stolen, because there was nothing left to steal. Only the cupboard in the vestry was locked; it held a tattered collection of psalters, mildewed prayerbooks and missionary leaflets. He had once had it open, but now it was jammed shut; he didn't want to see the leaflets again, with their wall-eyed old women clutching fly-blown infants in their fleshless arms. They would probably all be dust by now. Another pane of the arched window was out. You could trace his slowing efforts through the gaps in the stained glass, where the sombre Victorian colours were replaced first by strips of coloured cellophane, then hardboard and, lastly, scraps of cardboard. Looking at it now, he marvelled that he reached up so high on those rickety steps, since stolen. A brilliant channel of sunlight flowed through the fresh gap. The dust his shoes kicked up spiralled heavenward. Jacob's Ladder, he thought. The only bit of Bible that's stuck in my mind from the Old bit. He wouldn't dam it up this time. Jacob – had a stone for a pillow, didn't he? Must've hurt!

The hall upstairs was empty too. It still retained the debris and decorations of last year's Christmas party, run by the Rev Underfoot. He felt the crackle of a newer tinsel – scraps of dull, charred aluminium foil stained with a dark tar, lying in a litter of dead matches and tubes of spittle-stained rolled cardboard. He hadn't understood; the Rev had explained. One day there would be something dead slumped on the heap of discarded hassocks lying in the wings of the narrow stage, like a wall of sandbags. Not this morning though. The Rev knew his way about, both around the city and up and down the Testaments. If he didn't know a quotation, he invented one. Nebuchadnezzar 3 was a favourite. There was a tacit recognition the moment he found the Rev sizing up the hall – each knew that the other had assumed the cloth, rather than had it conferred.

'Leonard, my friend, my case is as simple as it is legitimate. I was pre-ordained to the ministry. My mother felt it in her water!' he had once said, his shrewd dark face beaming confidence. His belief was thoroughgoing, but his tolerance of the established churches less so and tended to overwhelm more reticent clerics and set the city's racist fringe seething. Since that February evening, Leonard, as he called himself to the Rev (who was known by the title, and never gave a name), had even addressed his cheerful congregation in a room above a pub. 'Wherever two or three people are gathered together . . .' someone had said. He hadn't said much — mostly babble off the top of his head, really. But it seemed to go down well enough. The trouble had come later.

A train rumbled along the embankment outside, shivering the floorboards and jolting him to a decision. He'd go and see the Rev. They'd have a half of Guinness and the Rev would tell him all about this 'Hi-Tech' business.

* * *

They sat together in the conspiratorial dark of the public bar; he sipped at his stout in some discomfort. The haze of smoke itched his eyes and the drink wasn't going down well. Worse, the Rev seemed to be brooding. The small glass was all but hidden by his huge fist. You'd expect him to down it at a draught, but he didn't drink. He slipped a coin into the apparatus contained within the table at which they sat. Luminous green planets effervesced across the screen in the centre, then dissolved into a galactic night, soon invaded by ranks of moving ciphers which squirted tracer in the approximate direction of the Rev's groin; but he squirted back and they disintegrated into a mere fizz of particles, to the sound of a hollow boom from somewhere beneath the table.

'Your play, Leonard!'

He shook his head.

'What are they teaching our kids, these "Hi-Tech" Interfacers of yours, Leonard? Heaven as a data processing complex — humidity controlled, air conditioned? User-friendly terminals for angels, God behind a fat, green VDU, giving a poor dead soul a visual read-out of his sins on this Earth? Press return, await judgement. "Hi-Tech Heaven" — just a game of squiggly red devils being zapped by neon white angels. 50 points a devil; 500 bonus for a pot shot at Satan.'

He took a long pull at his glass, swallowing down the lot, but for a thin rind of ivory froth above his broad, dark lip.

'And what would our print-out read like to them? But they'll never know; you and I, Leonard — we will never be the integers in anyone's social matrix. We have lived with heart; I see the Lord in you, Leonard. He's like a little Frank Bruno, with your heart as a punchbag, pounding the blood round your body, the bruising that keeps you human. Your worthies will never understand us. Yes, they recognise the issues, yes they try, righteously try. But they don't feel it in their hearts and bones. There's a repulsive virginity in them . . . can you understand racists until you've found their animal shit in crisp bags on your altar . . . the dole, if you've always had wealth?'

He had never before heard his friend speak in such a fashion and it distressed him beyond expression, though most of what he said baffled him; but being thumped inside his chest, he felt that.

'You preached against racism in words we understood, Leonard. I'll remember you in my heart for that.'

What was happening? It proved that the Rev was returning to Southern Africa. 'Free Nelson Mandela,' said a voice from the juke-box.

'Free Nelson Mandela!' said the Rev.

He hesitated, then said, 'Then I'll buy you another.'

He laughed. 'You know, I've never much liked this sour black stuff!'

* * *

He started his technical research along the stack of shelved trash in low spirits. He paused over a magazine featuring a menopausal starlet, rigid in a pose of impossible muscular dexterity, an airbrushed grin glaring with the enthusiasm needed to sustain a three-page feature, the full gloss cover and the banner headline offering fitness and fun at fifty for any who dared purchase. God, how old was he now? He leafed through; spiritual relaxation, the garish matron informed him, was the source of her lustre, abetted by diet and the now-revealed exercises of her own invention. He was struck by the thought that here was a framework he could use, should he ever preach again. Diet — bread/wine; age/youth; comfort/relaxation . . . 'age, youth — like your man said, Leonard; simply dreaming on both,' his friend had said as they were parting at the pub. He hadn't really worked out any of what he'd been saying. Didn't feel quite up to it today. 'When you reach the burn . . .' began the magazine woman's piece, but he couldn't read on.

Wonder what Christ's diet was like then. Were bread and fish sufficiently high in fibre? He'd always wanted to try barley bread, it sounded delicious. There was a picture of the Feeding of the Five Thousand on the wall of the chapel playroom, where the bread had a beautiful golden crust. Nicer than honey and locusts. Honey with the comb left in it; he'd always wanted to try that too. No wonder Jesus was so thin. He thought of the familiar images . . . amid a flock of woolly lambs and brown-eyed donkeys, with a Sunday school glow. Or more grown up — hanging from the cross, the cadaverous hollow beneath his ribs. Or dead — that scorched sheet he'd seen on a poster in the library. He couldn't make sense of it today. He surveyed the rack and got mixed up. Jesus, not in dusty sandals and a tattered tunic, but a hunk of manflesh, posing in trainers and his sponsor's strip. The images were horrible. He turned away.

He felt a grumble in the bowels. Another time and this would have sent a tremor of relief shooting up his spine, but with a long afternoon's researches ahead of him he had neither the time nor the spare energy for the long detour. The hot weather was a curse on his digestion; first a misery of retentive aches, and now that bloody ham. Usually he found that only a long session in the public library (archaeology section) could loosen him. No chemical laxative matched the purgative power of the Dewey Decimal System, and in no publicly accessible convenience did he feel quite as secure as in the gents at the Municipal. Just scanning a bookshelf now seemed to be bringing on a sympathetic response in the wrong place and at an unwanted time. He struggled to bury it by trying to take his usual observer's interest in those about him.

Each section of magazines, he noted, attracted a distinctive cluster of browsers. To his left, three girls with shaven temples and peroxide braids squatted on the floor and argued playfully over the crossword of a flamboyantly coloured music paper, which they had spread loosely across the floor.

'Got a pen, vicar?' asked a shrill northern voice somewhere below him. There was a yank on his trouser leg to make the point. He looked down to see a sharp young face gawping up at him amiably.

'Surely, my child.'

They looked an agreeable trio, so he dutifully played up to their expectations. He handed down a red plastic ballpoint, with 'Africa Poverty Action' embossed in gold on the side. It didn't work; nor did the four thousand others he had discovered in the vestry – and he had tried most of them. He moved before the shortcoming could be discovered. From a protective screen of 'Romantic Fiction' he heard a screech. Perhaps they had a clue.

'"Punk peak pleasure" – two words.'

'"Nipple Erectus!"' shrieked a reply.

' "Tender Rosebuds" '? said the lead title opposite him.

'"Orgasm Addict",' trilled the girls in chorus.

They tried to write the solution into the appropriate boxes, but succeeded only in scratching the page to tatters. With cheerful resignation, they tossed the pen in its owner's direction, upturned an RF display case and ambled out, through the double-doors and into the oven of the outside.

He dithered for some minutes more, before searching out the racks he had really come for. A docile gang of young professional salespeople were ranked about the new technology brochures, grouped almost in the respectable order of a primary school photograph. As he had no idea of what to look for, any excuse to delay confronting this silicon desert was welcome, so he inspected the enthusiasts for a few moments before finally peering past into the shelves themselves. It was a confusion and a disappointment. The magazines were virtually indistinguishable. There was a dull spread of typewriter keyboards shown at various angles; some had sort of cash-till bits attached to them, and most had little tellies stuck on top. They were tarted up with splashes of colour, mostly in the form of prisms and spectrums on the telly screens, or as rainbows sprouting out from just about anywhere. There were bludgeoning slogans composed of jargon and exclamation marks or simply jumbled letters and numbers. It was a code he could not understand.

Suddenly it all blurred. He felt a hot blackness across his eyes, his knees sagged and his armpits prickled in warning. His thoughts stilled a moment and deep inside his chest he felt a gentle nudging. He feared that to heave the air in might hurt too much, so motionlessly he concentrated on a word, any word. The first to come into focus was 'interface'.

'. . . interface, interface . . .'

The air fluttered into his flat lungs and he began to revive. Just as he was about to move towards the whirling fan suspended from the wall, there was a stab in his side just below the ribs. It came from the four jabbing fingers of a gaunt youth, who stared fixedly at him whilst waving the fingers like a film-actor's Luger. The Rev called him Filthy Morrison on account of his brutal methods of expressing his racial intolerance. Since preaching to the Rev's congregation upstairs at the Red Lion, he'd been marked out by the fanatic. He broke the chapel windows and daubed most of the slogans. This time he felt too stretched to be scared. Instead he found himself inspecting his assailant.

Funny, he thought, how even with a summer hot enough to scorch through concrete, there was not the slightest shade of a tan on the racist's sallow face. Only a few ginger bristles, like dead insects' legs, punctuated it; together with a scatter-blast of blackheads.

'More tea, vicar? Huh, huh.'

When he was sure that every customer was aware of his presence, Morrison continued his performance.

'Nosing around for the nubiles are we then, vicar? Huh, huh.' He seized a fistful of magazines from the top shelf (male interest/leisure), waved them to his reluctant audience, found a centrefold and thrust it into his face. He could smell the oil-based ink; he shut his eyes.

'You a tit man, vicar?'

But the vicar had turned his head away. Morrison wiped the glossy sheet across his face, as a dim awareness that he was starting to look stupid crept into his skull. The vicar had staggered against a shelf and was gasping slightly. He wished those girls had stayed. 'Fucking bully!' they might have said. His shut eyes were hot and round, and a fierce electric pulse seemed to shoot from temple to temple.

'Oh no, I'm so sorry, vicar,' continued Morrison with frenzied sarcasm, 'we don't stock the sort of magazine you're after. We're all sold out of choirboys showing their fucking bums.' He appealed to the shop: 'Got a little brother. In 'is choir. He'll tell you all about this . . . this . . .' But he was unable to find a word. Each member of his embarrassed audience was engrossed in the book, paper, record sleeve closest to hand.

'You lump of shit, queer, nigger-shit lover. We'll have you . . .'

The doors were held open for him as he escaped the assault, only realizing as he reached the pavement that his left hand still clutched a magazine, its pages already warped by the sweat of his palm. He stuffed it in his bag; he wasn't going back in there. He followed the broken geometry of the precinct until he reached the open street; then he doggedly wandered to a small, dusty square and an undisturbed bench. Everything seemed covered in this dust, fine as cement – shoes, cracked lips; in his eyes.

* * *

The unwatered lawn was tawny brown; idiot blackbirds gawped across at him with wet eyes, their wings splayed brokenly over the grass. The random albino splashes across their greasy feathers looked as though they had been flicked at with a wet paint brush and been too listless to move. Must all come from the same nest, he thought; keeps it in the family. The Rev once described God as that selfish genie, helter-skeltering up and down your DNA; if he did believe in him, he didn't seem to hold a very high opinion of the Lord. He wondered about that in-breed Morrison, and supposed he would be on the dirty end of more trouble. Perhaps it would mean more than broken windows – perhaps those crisp bags full of excrement lying on the altar, hosting a colony of blowflies. He might get hit in the street, if he were out late.

He thought about Morrison's brother. How would he have coped with him, were he a long-term vicar? A clever Morrison would play it two ways; trap you with invented confessions, and half an hour later would be trumpeting that the vicar had 'had a go at him' before he went off queer-bashing. That sort of brat could really tie him up on this Hi-Tech business. He looked at the magazine he had removed from the shop. Habit. Couldn't understand it. He put it back inside the plastic carrier and slotted it through a gap in the bench-boards. His fear of the meeting was all worn out. He felt staked out by the heat, and his mind couldn't move that far ahead. He looked at an old dosser on the opposite side of the square. He seemed to be struggling feebly in his sleep. He's halfway on the swim to the crematorium, he thought; glad I've not ended up like him. Fought the Germans, don't doubt. The whining noise inside his head was intensifying and he had to shut his eyes to try and damp it.

He remembered a German pastor talking in swift guttural phrases at some meeting before the war. It was translated in an undertone by an intense curate with curling fingers and hanks of greasy hair, the colour of dirty plaster. You could pick out the odd word before the translation, words like 'Gestapo', which became 'special policeman'. Despite the curate's politeness of phrase, a cold hand fingered the innards of all present. They all walked out into the summer – Eastbourne before the war. Hot as now, but then he could absorb the sun; not slowly desiccate, but walk on the shingle, catch the breeze off the sea. He'd never been though . . . filmdream perhaps. Nice girls in hats, whitewashed walls, slipslap of wet feet on promenade flagstones, thick white gloss on the railings . . .

* * *

He came to with a start. The sun had shifted and his left side had lost its feeling. Hurriedly, he lumbered off.

He wandered into the afternoon along unfamiliar streets, banking on a vague feeling that his sense of direction would return and guide him right. His walk was a shuffle and he had to stare at the paving stones to keep the beating sun from his flaming forehead. With his eyes on the cracks, he saw none of the panic outside the flats to his left. He heard some confused sounds, but they didn't carry clearly on the dry air until they focused into a single voice screeching, 'Vicar! Vicar!'

'God, that's me!'

'Vicar, it's the old man!'

He turned dizzily and found himself walking towards a group of grey-haired old women. Younger than me, he wondered. They clustered round him and propelled him into the narrow hallway, talking all the while. They thought an old man was dead in a bath, but they weren't sure. They hadn't really looked, would he look, he was a vicar after all . . . yes, after all, he was. They had decided his role as naturally as they had decided who would telephone the police station, the doctor, the ambulance. His job was simple. He had just to go in there, and see.

The hallway was cool and too dark for sight after the glare of the street, but the animate support of the women around him meant that he had no need of it. They made their way up flight after flight of steep, uneven stairs until they reached an empty landing. He stepped on to it. The others drained away, leaving him alone and staring at the crack of a partially opened door. They had opened the door, but no one had been in. They knew he'd drawn the water because his neighbour always listened for the plumbing. It gave her something to do. She hadn't heard it filter out. They knew; they'd been expecting.

He didn't want to move the door, and his hesitancy made the loose boards squeal. Aggrieved mutterings drifted up the stairwell. He lurched through and closed it firmly behind him.

The bath had been overfilled with cold water, leaving a wide puddle across the threshold. The man floated gently on the surface. It was a relief to have the dread of the stranger's rooms replaced with a sight he understood. Reminded him of a pickled egg in a jar full of spirit vinegar, rather than the victims he had known from wartime, with their lungs dissolved by diesel or retched-up after inhaling chlorine. He must have run the bath in an effort to escape the heat. Already the toes were deeply rippled. Soon, perhaps, the whole body would be ridged like a walnut or a scrotum. Better get him out then.

The man seemed to belong there; the grey of the worn enamel matched the pallor of the corpse. He removed his jacket and rolled his sleeves up to the elbow, before plunging his arms into the dark water. He touched the bottom; then he fingertipped the man, and pulled his hands up instantly. The water stirred and the old hair swished. If hair still grows after the body dies, does it mean a bit of him is still alive? But then the water calmed and the hair rested lankly down the edge of the bath. Taking a deep breath, he slid his arms back beneath the legs and spine. He strained them upwards and felt the dead hand rest on his wrist. He realised that, in the dim light that stole in from the next room's windows, he could not tell the difference between the limbs of the cadaver and his own near fleshless sticks. He strained again. The corpse did not shift, but the bones and veins now stood out clearly through the taut skin on the underside of his arm, like the skinny wing of a cold chicken. His sleeves came loose and the cuffs flopped into the water. Enough had leaked down the overflow for there to be a gap of several inches between the surface and the rim; he couldn't heave the corpse unaided. Still, he wanted to leave before the police arrived.

He couldn't understand how the old man had managed to turn off the tap, the thread was so stiff. The flanges dug deeply into his palm, but finally it shifted and the water sluiced over a bony foot. He would love to have had a long drink, and let the fresh stream splash over his face. Just what this bloke thought, he realised with a chill.

After slopping him over the side, he wrapped him in towels and fresh linen, since the puny nakedness seemed a horrible indignity without the support of the water to buoy it into movement. He was staring at the hollow spiral, shaped as the water escaped through the plughole, when he heard the noise of boots and imperatives on the stairs. He knew he should leave, but the whirling fluid and rhythmic gurgle hypnotised him. As the last drop ran out, there was a bash on the door. He struggled past the body and had the necessary moment needed to slip behind as it opened. Two policemen blundered in. He darted past on the blind side, on to the landing and straight down the stairs. He sped downwards out of control, with his weight slumped forward across the banisters and his feet dragging and tripping at every step. His rib-cage bashed against the rail and sent pain shooting through his chest. He must not be seen and he must not fall; his bones were as brittle as sticks of chalk. He saw daylight gaping and dived through the door, down the steps and face-first onto the pavement. A reflex jack-knifed him to his feet. He was away and unnoticed, with torn trousers, skinned knees and grazed, stinging palms.

* * *

He couldn't feel his feet anymore; instead of toes he seemed to have bandaged stumps, wedged into his shoes; he only stayed upright through some freak coincidence of balance. The bone-ache was worst in his hips. The pelvis, cradling his vitals, felt fragile as dried meringue, ready to crumble on impact. Yet, somehow, his long bones still staggered him forward, now quite aimlessly. Walking with the late afternoon sun on his back and staring at his shadow as a pool of relief from the pavement glare, he had strayed far from the few streets he knew well. The light had bleached away his image of the city, as a sign fades in a window. Then he had just followed the cracks in the pavement, through a dirty smoke-stained sunset, reflecting the street-slick of the city roads — skid-marks, melting tarmac, spilled oil — which still gleamed as a black sheen in the artificial sodium twilight, after the sun had gone.

He didn't understand these plastic capsules of sickly amber light and his fear of them began to absorb him, for in his mind he now carried images, clear as on a cinema screen, from far back. And he could hear a 'pop' as a gas streetlight ignited, see the bright whiteness creep up the frail asbestos mantle, capped by a slight blue flame — till, in an instant, it caught and the incandescence was benevolently dazzling. Then he thought of a fat, naked bulb, casting a wide arc about the room as the breeze from an open window took it, and it could swing lazily at the end of a fly-stained flex . . . and how the filament cooled to a fierce red, then a gentler orange, when the switch was thrown and the thick metal hair ceased to eat the pulsing electricity. He stopped and watched as the fragments of a shattered windscreen were momentarily transformed into a heap of gemstones as they refracted the lights from passing cars.

Then, amid the fog of dull orange streetglow, he glimpsed a near vertical sheet of plain white, washing up the face of a building and to the tops of surrounding trees, projecting upwards a vivid deep sea splash of green and shadow. As he approached, he scorned the façade of the church, and left his bootprints over the clumsy lettering and innocent cartoons of an out-dated placard, heralding the arrival of the long-defunct 'Interface Community Troupe'. He was drawn by the ultramarine foliage and the deep glass flood-lighting tanks below.

He stared at the beam full on. God stuff; he'd had it with God stuff. The light burned away at his memory — like Very lights, tracer, starshells, magnesium flares. Or like looking down the barrel of a cinema projector. The beam resolved into a memory of a childhood summer. Bright copper pennies gleaming through the clear spring-water of a wishing-well. They seemed so near the surface. He plunged his hand in, but could not reach them. He leaned over further, stretching on tip-toe, fascinated by the ripple patterns playing across his smooth skin. The water was icy and numbed his arm, which seemed to hang from his elbow at a funny angle beneath the surface. He wanted to lay a coin flat on his tongue.

He was stirred to movement by a series of low thumps and thin squeals; he was too starstruck to judge their origin, and stumbled from the path till he found his face pressed thick into the deep folds of a yew tree. The stink of it revived him a little, and he groped his way to the shelter of some weathered limestone slabs. Yards in front of him, a young couple tangled in a gutter-love ritual of suburban voodoo. As they sprawled over a tomb, their torn black garments strewn about them, a song of naïve hell-worship blared out from a makeshift altar. It had thin black candles stuck in empty spirits bottles, the cassette recorder, all within shakily chalked pentagrams, on the concrete roof of the cistern hut.

'Necro! Necro!' choked the adolescent singer.

Only the flickering candles registered on his mind, like the blurred image on the screen of a pin-hole camera.

The boy sprang upright and stared straight at him, gawping in silent terror. The girl put her arms round his thin white back, with its crust of blisters, and hauled him down to her. But he began to gibber when he saw the bony claw twitch in gesture. The old man, for whom the blurs of light and smudges of dark were slowly swimming into a picture, was trying to sign – 'Don't mind me; carry on, carry on.'

'Leg it, leg it!' screeched the boy as he disappeared. The girl drew her knees up to her breasts, sat a moment as both figures disappeared, then slowly gathered up her clothes.

'Necro!' she said with contempt, delicately snuffing the candles with her wetted fingertips.

* * *

He could not move. He was mesmerized by the circle of ghost-selves radiating outwards in a procession from the hunched bundle, misshapen by the lattice of the fence, which strode forward the length of the road, spindled beyond vision and returned as a dwarf at his heels with the next passing car. Their halogen beams were a burning glass, erasing him shadow by shadow. Slowly he keeled over. The fence gave, and the deep shadows took him.

* * *

GHOST WRITING

D. A. Herling

With respect at least to his closing scene, our author is perfectly assured. It holds two characters, probably a man and a woman, and the reigning sentiment, the melancholic yellow light which he thinks he finds in the old, Judaeo–Hispanic song responsible for his fantasy undoubtedly proceeds – if anything can proceed – from an impasse. The melody, its uncompromisingly resigned harmonies, almost acidly delicate guitar accompaniment and the brazen weariness of the high tenor voice imploring its beloved to come that day and sit at the shore beneath the flowering tree – the melody has offered to our author its spirit, withholding from him only the knowledge of what to do with it. Sensibly, he realises that his exquisite image perhaps of frustration, perhaps despair (all these he finds in the music), perhaps even hard, sullen anger, can only end a story, the camera gently sliding back from that fine deadlock on the sands to show the towers of Cadiz, or maybe Barcelona or Malaga. At home in this miniature of notes, our author, temporarily disappointed of the surrounding story, yields to the charms of his dreadfully limited creation.

Not to be seduced by detail, but himself to seduce it! Possessing some skill as a writer, and great experience in the art of observing the blank page before him, our author considers that his involvement with his characters, their backgrounds, age and civilisation, is of prime importance; the more he thinks about the germ of his story which he has so definitely and in such isolation conceived, the better his chances of arriving at a mode of speech, an ambience, a plot. The nearer he can get to becoming the lettered voyeur in the tamarisks, overhearing and overseeing the conversation between the two at the sea-shore, the more obstacles are removed between him and his story. He sees them so clearly, feels what the song tells him to feel so innocently, and yet so knowingly, that he surely by dint of imagination could almost become them. Need he, he muses, preserve even the remove of observing that evening impasse beneath the tree on the shore? Might he not write the story of the lovers from his own experience, made — he believes he *can* make it — identical to theirs? With the experience at least of the man, the singer, imploring the woman to join him in that piercing, soothing light?

But yes, of course the man and the woman never do meet, according to the song. It is entreaty, not description. As sharply as if he had been slapped across the face, our author feels that he has presumed too far. Over-eager, he has already betrayed the song's longing, its plaintive realisation of the impossibility of satisfaction. Stupidly well-wishing, simplifying, over-writing, already he has nearly ruined its tensions, been deaf to the guilt in the man's voice, not looked for the hundred reasons why the two cannot, will never, meet at the shore. As if following a tetchy guide, he returns chastened to his proper place; guilty, a step behind.

The song is far too fragile to be seized with both hands. It must be wooed, followed respectfully.

Like any green lover, our author reels from his first disappointment. It must be admitted that he really is in doubt whether to continue; he feels the stigma of his oafish presumption so keenly. His imagination, which he had thought to exert clinically, with the control of a master, now springs into irrepressible life, abandoning the severe sublime to miscreate scores of chimaeras, horrible scenes of embarrassment. As if it were enough to imagine, and then to assert oneself over the beloved, taking it for one's own image.

Our author's devotion to his scene is no passing infatuation, though. He retreats, resolving to observe, to bide his time before attempting to control.

'Nights I have spent sleepless.' The Old Spanish mimics the sighing and the wakeful yawning, the hours of breathless night spent becoming more and more blind to consequence and the irreality of hope. Our author, now following his vision and his ambition with decorum, has yet to arrive at this state. But, having

conceived of it, he is only moments away from living it hims
And now, indeed, he feels ages of wanting enter between him an
the object of his desire, as the scene he yearns to encompass as the final jewel of his narrative separates itself more definitely from any matrix in which he may attempt to set it. He sees now the crazing in the varnish of the guitar, the yellowing at the edges of the print, as the antiquity his vision assumes makes it still more precious to him, more fragile and more heraldic. Just so, in the later verses of the song, the voice, assured of the melody it has established, bites the words, spits out the archaic 'agora', meaning 'now', as if aware that the pronunciation would change, had changed, was changing at the very moment the word was sung.

Another slap in the face, another flounce away. Our author is miserably brought back to his study as his vision, outraged, flees his tyrannical government. This time his mistake is quite unjustifiable. To dictate the nature of what he imagines from his own difficulty in imagining it. Palpably brutalised, the song, its singer and its setting dart forward out of the clutches of his modern embrace to reassert their utter timelessness. He, wretchedly conscious now of his shameful application of linguistics, labours mightily to re-imagine the purity of his original imagining, contaminated by time as well as presumption.

Strangely, though, he feels after this infinitely delicate operation that he has moved closer to a communion with the envisaged scene of the impossible parley on the promenade of the southern city whose name he cannot know and is fastidious now in not trying to fix. Clearly he must approach it not with stealth, but with a genuine wish to accord it as much freedom from him as it may care to preserve, trusting it all the time not to escape entirely. That, it seems to him, is in keeping with the nature of the man's entreaty to the woman, citing no oaths but rather comprehending a certain bond, established perhaps by simple acquaintance, with all the moments of closeness, distance, sympathy and estrangement that simple acquaintance can well include. Maybe the song, the nightingales of the title, the flowering tree, the hiss of the calm Mediterranean and the recollection of lonely, passionate agony is an attempt to alter the nature of a relationship, a desperately clumsy attempt, strangled by the too much formality which protects against the ravages of the twilight.

Our author is fairly happy with this, feeling for the first time a distinct correspondence between his own predicament and that which he is seeking to subsume. He is, after all, engaged in the attempt to alter a relationship from mere latency to the full passion of authorship. He too feels trammelled by the formalities (he sees them as such) which beset his sincere efforts to define and live with an imagined scene sufficiently closely as to be able to write around it, secure of its being utterly his. He is, as it were, at the point in the relationship where one thinks, 'Well, we're actually very similar.' But here, with that self-destructive tendency which so cleanly edits so many thousands of words, he starts to wonder what kind of a basis similarity is for any sort of living together. Having very briefly ridden on a tiny wave of satisfaction, he is now at pains to rehabilitate — whether justly or unjustly let the reader judge — all that dissatisfaction which his vision is about.

He has lost the ability, for the moment, to describe his image, so eagerly has he followed it. He sees now, not the deliciously resonant stock of archetypal nouns and adjectives which, like a lover's endearments, he had set aside for the purposes of adornment, or in fact, for the creation of his image in writing, but, shockingly, himself. With a fleeting relief, he realises that this mirroring might be the force which leads the man to sing the song to the absent, unhearing, unexpected woman; that there are only the two of them, Jews in that city of Moorish Spain, a ghetto of two. His relief is short-lived, however; every realisation, every thought strengthens the bond, and his all-important will now seems subordinate to the working of events in his mind. His vision no longer avoids, coyly, his considered husbandry; it stands, arms akimbo, eyes blazing, crying, 'Yes, it is you that you see in me, not your imagination any longer, but you, your every notion part of me.' Our author feels as if, tipsy, he had pointed at a star; unthinkingly linked himself to it for as long as it should exist, and that he is being drawn towards it out of the air into claustrophobic space in which his existence is entirely his own affair, he only accountable for his temerity in being there, horribly his own master in the self-willed slavery of authorial contract. He faces the terror of himself being written, and himself to blame, finding in that final discovery still further discoveries that he approaches even more nearly the deadlock of the singer, who can only wish himself physically outside the City, to entreat a woman to follow who his song says cannot.

His posited novel having metamorphosed to autobiography under his very eyes, our author reasonably enough feels shaken. Sitting in a small, not romantically cold or uncomfortable, but ignominiously rented room, which he had hoped as he now sees to pass off as a more glamorous setting (he spares himself no humiliation), he has not only met, but devoured that vision which was intended to end his narrative, and he finds himself no closer to any sort of beginning. When, however, he tries to recall the steps by which he has just come to understand the vanity of writing, he is quite unable to do so. And yet his vision remains, seeming more relevant than ever, faintly alluring despite the intellectual disillusionment with which he now thinks of it. It is still frustration somehow made beautiful, and character somehow made to co-exist peacefully with the far more solid, and therefore satisfactory backdrop of the sun-baked city, luminous in the sea twilight. Our author hypothesises that, to live together, partners must either share no vanity, or the most powerful of vanities; he rightly deduces that his vision and he fall into the second of these categories.

What he now embarks upon is a kind of married life, in which mutual respect exists, and is in addition a firm foundation, but is of the rueful sort. Whilst our author is very, very far from admitting his limitations, he sees them second-hand, reflected in the image to which he is securely tied. He acknowledges that everything which most attracted him at first, the foibles and the appealing idiosyncrasies of the picture he made from the song, now causes him the greatest annoyance upon repeated reconsideration, and that the aspects of his partner which he had initially considered too banal to occupy much of his thought are now the traits which retain most power to charm. Our author is not, of course, so blind as to fail to see in those formerly winning marks the corresponding needs within himself, but by virtue of being now completely at home with his partner he sees the needs more strongly than the favours which were to appease them. Rather than envisage like a fond film director the sequence which gives way to the credits, he now regards his image as the very bulk and body of the entire narrative which, valiantly, he still fully intends to write. It has become indispensable to his work, forming the central part of it, increasing its hold over him every time that, familiar, it appears in his mind.

Our author steeps himself in it, cudgelling his brain to make it spill, not the best storylines, but any at all; the scantiest, the most tenuous perceptions are welcomed eagerly and rewarded with his full attention. He is not alone in this; it must be said that this is the treatment which the middle part of any author's work receives. Our author debates the age of the singer, whether the city behind him has a domed church or mosque, or whether it is towered and crenellated; he argues the case for cliffs or a shingle beach, a yellow or a malarially green tinge to the sunset which enfolds the meeting the song longs for.

Obscurely, at the back of his mind, there lurks the unpleasant intelligence that it is a vision of self-dramatisation which obsesses him; but if it must be self-dramatisation, let it at least be glorious, the guitar exchanged for the high trumpets of the bullring, the thin skirl of the muezzin in the background swapped for Bach's B minor Mass as incidental music. If he must live with this vision of his own yearning after authorship, let it at least be well decked out, pleasant by day if disturbingly his at night.

Despite all our author's efforts to make it into a blockbuster, it remains sullenly itself, himself, a guilty record of the traumas of self-expression which he seeks to make it dispel. Whatever he does with it, it is still a man singing to a woman, already an outsider to the thronged city which gazes over him to the sea horizon, the field of action caught and pinned between the City and the empty, yellow sky. Whatever he does, the woman will not, cannot, come and sit beside him underneath the tree at the water's edge, the world's end, to talk. No more can he retreat into the city; he has cast that away to its own destruction or what it will. And if the key changes, if cadences ring out and are forgotten, the same harmonies persist, lower each time, with each change more rigid, the world shattering again with each change.

With a lucidity which he himself finds alarming, our author is conscious that he has come face to face with despair, the most unliterary of emotions.

The bench had been the outcome of a rabbinical dispute, a fact which, together with the religious genesis of a number of the synagogue's other good works, the community rather vaunted as evidence of piety, while more worldly outsiders from Gerona and Cordoba instead saw only the ridiculous, provincial wrangling of small-town rabbis. Something to do with a Talmudic dispute . . . someone used as an exemplar a carpenter, lost, finally raised such a stink over it that to save his own skin he thought he'd better do something public-spirited and appropriate. In those days the Jews were still allowed to use an area of marshland between the bay and the tanners' quarter as a cemetery; they put the bench there, on a rise in the ground beneath some acacias. Of course no one ever sat on it. It wasn't very well made, and anyway the marshes were held to be malarial; fine during the day, but once the mosquitoes got under way in the evening, 'the nightingales' as they called them, distinctly dangerous. And who wants to go and sit in a cemetery at dusk, anyway? As if the malaria wasn't enough, actually to go and sit among the dead. And plenty of them down there still bore grudges, were the sort that during their lives weren't averse to underhand dealing. Dead, my God! what wouldn't some of those people do then?

Isidro had heard it so many times. 'What do you want to go and sit about that place for? You're crazy! Why don't you go and talk to Rabbi Meir instead; he likes to have some company after he's eaten. Isidro, you know, we thought once perhaps you'd be a cantor. But don't you like music any more? Sure you do. You want to go and waste your time and endanger your life as well. And what good is she going to do you now, the Coen girl? What good? She scorned us here, Isidro, she scorned us, and it's not the place of a son to leave his family, stamp with his foot on all his family's just hopes, for a woman who did us no honour when she was alive, God rest her soul. Give it up; give *her* up. Do something you know how to do — learn to do something then. But at least don't waste valuable time on a fool's errand. Maybe waste your life on it. Is it making you happy, going there again and again? No, it's quite clear.'

But to counsel one who has despaired to despair once more requires a subtlety of persuasion which even the righteous voices of the community were unable to attain. Certain emotions rest happily in the grave, industriously tunnel their way to the published, patriarchal bliss of Zion, there to exchange the myrtle bough for laurel, and high company. Despair is not such an emotion. Misery, yes; fury, undoubtedly. But, for despair, both the grave and the waste-paper basket are infirm vessels. Children, beginnings of all sorts may find beds of their length, and enterprise's old age, though its parting cause more conscious grief, lies tranquil. Images of self, courtable, nubile, even briefly cohabitable, rise and possess, lie still anew, new buried, and again rise up, desperately whole, despairingly halved, remembered, unquiet; forgotten, destroyers.

He sits there, remembering how she had wanted no 'chazzanim', no paid young men to mourn her, in recognition that any attempt at a formal end would be a vanity itself. And he resents that unwillingness of hers to spare him that special haunting; as if the ghost of her life were not sufficient, to be plagued by the ghost of her death as well.

Isidro's affair with the girl had been a torrid one, more by virtue of what was not done, than any specific way in which they violated the moral code of the community, ironically undefined in a society obsessed by definition of laws. Lea Coen came to the city from Granada, already weakened nervously and phsyically by the rancour of the opposition she had provoked there. It was not her atheism, but her approach to the community and its values — or rather, it was not that, but her atheism. Naturally, it was finally her travelling around like some self-styled scholar, without even the token propriety of a husband, which fuelled the feeling against her. A man, if he could have got into such a predicament, would straightaway have been a pariah, beyond social, or any other kind of, redemption. But it was a problem that did not exist for a man.

Lea found herself rapidly becoming the preoccupation of a number of young men, among them Isidro. More rebellious by force of circumstance than by principles, it soon became obvious to her that the partial sacrifice of her own independence would be more than recompensed by the respite which choosing one of her suitors would bring. It was the tone, not the fact of moral stricture which had in the end forced the break between her family and herself; the mistrust before, not after transgression. Isidro's community, still more rigid than Granada, provided for her the opportunity to define further, and against the stiffest odds, her own hatred of compromise.

And yet it was not compromise at all which she hated, but having to behave as if she were wrong when she had not yet done anything, right or wrong. With herself, her own desires, pleasures and satisfactions, she would compromise endlessly. Lea, weighing her reasons for leaving Granada, judged according to the standards of the most rigorous Talmudic debate, that it was a right decision, both intellectually and practically praiseworthy. Her mistake, her only mistake, was then to go ahead and act on it. Far from being the woman of easy virtue which her action stamped her, travelling the sierras oblivious of the most basic decencies of womanhood and the Sabbath, she subjected the smallest details of her life to her own unflinchingly honest moral scrutiny. When, that is, she considered it necessary. Her adopting Isidro in the capacity of mate – the community could find no more acceptable word to define the couple's status – she quite overlooked as an irrelevancy. To her, it was a simple descent to doing what everybody else did with universal blessings. Why then the further ostracisation? She chose him from among the handful of possibles because he was musical, a singer; at least he might be expected to talk less than some of the others.

He did not seem to mind that she could bring with her no dowry, and not even the boon of a strong constitution. But that seemed completely reasonable. After all, he claimed often enough to be in love with her; wasn't that what love was? He suffered fits of melancholy, certainly, often when their spoken conversation had reached the point that the next likely topic would be their future; but then so did she, at the same times, and so all appeared well and good. That they should be the same was infinitely more important to Lea, for the first time in her life, than that they should be right, or even that they should have a future. The future was for her a matter of severe intellectual debate, and in her experience boded pain and little else; it was nothing remarkable then if she chose rather to withdraw into proximity to someone who, if not precisely the same as her, was at least skilled in concealing the major differences.

He, on the other hand, seemed much concerned about the future, a trait in him which she regarded as rather feminine, given their circumstances, but at the same time naturally, and therefore delightfully, assertive. It thrilled her to see in him the outward signs of his deep thought, the melancholically furrowed brow and the silent shifting of position, as he assumed all those burdens which, in the preceding part of her life, it had been hers to carry. When they met in the evenings to stroll around the broadest streets of the city, enjoying the cool of the day and the stares of the old men, against which Lea now felt strangely insulated, she would sometimes look up at him unnoticed, see the hard concentration on his face, and look ahead of her again and smile. For she knew responsibility, knew it perhaps better than she had known anything or anybody else in her decision-fraught life. To see him like that, mentally following paths she had already trodden, writing in volumes she knew by heart as their authoress, was to her a very great fulfilment.

He did not speak to her of what he thought at such times, as they walked from the alcazar to the harbour, and back up the hill to the quarter of the nobility. That part of the city was in theory forbidden to them, and they giggled too much for talk when some old retainer, with a face like Cordoba goat-skin, scowled at them from a massive doorway and spat as he remembered that Rabbi Benjamin was his master's favourite doctor. But she liked Isidro's silences. It was not that the two of them had no need of talk, but that perhaps Lea was frightened of it. Any representation of herself, even the pronoun 'you' (Isidro invariably used the polite, third-person form), was to Lea a misrepresentation. For either of them to make any statement about her, as the rabbis found when talking about God, entailed some falsehood, some shrugging off of issues; not so much an undervaluing — for the rest of the sentence could balance that, and Lea liked to think she had no fear of being undervalued — but a concession to glibness, to the bland acceptance of faults and virtues which could not blandly be accepted. Thus, while her character was made up of constant inner dialectic, the cut and thrust not of the schizophrenic but of the pathological lawyer, she had cultivated, as a second best, an almost boundless sympathy for silence.

How she loved to see the same in Isidro! When she looked across at him, sometimes their eyes met, hers almost glowing, transforming her sallow face. They glowed still more when she noticed how he looked at her, silence closing his expression further before he turned back to the street ahead of them.

Lea was not mistaken in her surmise that he was thinking about the future. She deceived herself (as it is the unkind fate of such people to be deceived by detail) only in her analysis of his reasons for thinking about it. He was learning to court other visions, to conjure new images, and particularly ones which were of marginal relevance to them. Their future together was such a vision; to look at it with his mind when he saw her face was a way of not seeing the face, the signs in it and imposed upon it which assured him that the future was not their concern. To escape that face was not easy; with every meeting the eyes became more prominent, detached themselves more from the body, became themselves the sum, and not merely the expression, of the character. If she could physically have made herself a part of him, it would have been so, by the agency of the eyes, enveloping him, boring into him, trying to become his eyes, the eyes with which he saw the world. It was that which she had to give him; a look, and a way of looking. Her mouth was much subordinate to her eyes and, as the shape of her face altered during those days, it was dominated more strongly by them.

All this Isidro saw, and he exerted his imagination immediately in order to see something else. As if it were his own illness, and a vision of himself which he saw declining, he was careful that, if nothing else, it should remain with him as a vibrant one. He laid plans, became meticulous in the management of his affairs as if he had some great scheme in hand; became in fact the model family man, although without a family of his own, or any honest illusions of starting one. He considered a hundred professions, asked around a bit about each, and made no further enquiries about any. That was unimportant, irrelevant to the preservation of his vision. As Lea weakened, so she retreated into silence, becoming aware herself of his need to dissimulate, fearing to speak lest the faintness of her voice should betray both of them.

For what mattered was not that she was unable now to walk and her breathing strenuous; that at least was completely unimportant. With respect to the detail of her closing scene, Lea was perfectly assured. It was vital — if anything in her situation could be vital — that she should *become* Isidro. So she, too, silently fell to imagining a fictional future for them. Secure of her end, she allocated her forces to conceiving of the beginnings of a life for them both. If they spoke at all, it was of that. Even when talking became physically difficult for her, she followed every report of Isidro's life rapaciously, and he saw in her eyes every solicited detail being passed through the mill of her intelligence, processed and usurped. They were merging into one consciousness; she saw in his expression her own state, and he saw instead of his continued existence, their continued existence or none. Dreamer and vision, life and death, blurred, frighteningly and yet soothingly indistinct. Her decline he observed as if seeing a series of portraits in motion. The sitter was elsewhere, in him, leading an independent existence. Leading *his* existence, looking through his eyes at the portraits of herself. Sitting at her bedside, he would fall asleep, wake and be surprised to find himself whole and well. She, with a shock not separate from that, saw herself only in his reactions, and did his thinking for him, thought of his friends, his parents, his synagogue, his future with her. She seized his mind, to put in its place her own, and died in his sleep.

'No chazzanim!' — no mourning chorus. That had been her distinct command, made long before her illness was any more than a cloud on the horizon. She and Isidro had discussed her death as a matter of course; from the very first it had been a natural means of drawing them closer. The elders of the synagogue, however, were not standing for any romantic austerity. They felt perhaps a twinge of conscience over the case of the admittedly difficult waif who had expired on their doorstep. Besides, the community had got itself a name for litigious zealotry which preceded any of the attractions it could noise abroad to pull towards it scholars and men of culture. For the synagogue to provide for this most unorthodox young woman a ten-strong chazzanim, as if she had been any unmarried daughter of the community, would be a notable piece of generosity, likely to do good where it was most needed. 'After all, there were a good ten of them running after the girl in the first place, were there not?'

Isidro took his place along with the rest, knowing the misunderstandings which would have arisen had he stayed away. She, in his position, would have refused, but she, and that, he reasoned, were dead. And, when he realised what he had done, he despaired. Maybe he realised before he did it and, being completely her, did what she would have done, and pretended to be him. But he was not a sophist, and he despaired.

No, a poor, a wretched joke, endings. No use trying to make them formal. The twist at the end is all too often not really the end at all, just a twist. Our author is a little distracted. He sees before him an unpleasant scene, unfortunately familiar to many who have driven the country roads of England at night. Sometimes a rabbit runs in front of a car, and stops, transfixed by the headlamps. But is it transfixed? Who, our author considers, warming to his task, is in a position to say that the rabbit is panic-stricken? Does it drum on the road to warn others of danger? No. Who can say that it does not calmly take stock of the situation, reach the sublime conclusion that its life is worth no less than that of the presumably living car, and pits its eyes against the headlamps? That they are strong and dazzling, far stronger than the eyes of a fox or buzzard — why should that alter its will to live? Is it not possible that, far from having no vision of itself, that is *all* it has, the sum of its experience, and that the reality of itself leads it to deny the reality of the certain death rushing to meet it? That, until it is dead, death remains an illusion, worthless beside the true illusion of itself? That, until it is hit, it can deny and deny and deny?

Until it is written on the road, at last in doubt as to its ending.

LOOMIS

Mark Illis

He even fought like a dancer.

It was the time of year when everything seems to be gold, the sunlight on water and reflecting off windows, that's the way I remember it anyway, but he brought the night with him. He was born in New York, spent most of his life there and saw most sides of it, he said; he spent two years in London and went back there sometimes but nights in Paris, he said, were where he lived. I can't grasp any particular thought and hold it.

The rails led in an almost but not quite random path all over Europe in the usual student summer holiday way. Booked seats and hidden-money belts in the first week degenerating into overcrowded carriages, occasional meals, the travellers' cheques stolen in Florence, a growing immunity to architecture and nights spent curled in jolting corridors somewhere perhaps near Athens. The Greek beach stands out. Naked bodies laid out in the heat like sides of meat, my sandy Sony Walkman and the big Charles Dickens, spine bent backwards, reaching its end. I remember one Austrian city mainly for its swimming-pool but the sea on this beach . . . caressing and yielding, not Greek but somehow all-belonging. The wind-surfers, arched in grim effort, skipped over it like fleas on the back of some huge benignly indifferent beast. The low white buildings of the town, dazzling at noon, crept up the side of the hill shoulder to shoulder like anxious sheep. Turn three corners and you are in the Labyrinth, guided by painted hands pointing in the direction of the hotel, granted by some kind Ariadne.

He even fought like a dancer. In his act, in Les Halles for preference but wherever, he'd twist and mime with weird music in the background and draw yards of string with razor-blades attached out of his mouth. He'd mock his audience for their passive television-watching attitude, but he needed them, he needed the response of an audience the way a tennis player needs a good opponent to bring out the best in himself and to give the game a meaning. But I only saw that act once and I'm prone to fit people into the categories I think they ought to go into. I think I saw him as a part of the night and of the streets and in a way I think I was right in spite of my lack of realism.

I met Helen in Budapest. In a city like that when you know you're not just abroad, when you feel displaced into a completely different kind of society, you find yourself drawing nearer to other tourists instead of consciously avoiding them. The herd instinct must be present in all of us to some extent. And after Budapest we stayed together through Vienna then Salzburg and on to Basel. Youth-hostels are unpredictable and a lot depends on the warden but Basel was best because Helen had her own room and the warden didn't give a damn. It was raining when we got there. Someone had said I had to be in Switzerland on August the first for the celebrations of independence. Someone on some train who posed as an expert on Switzerland and said that one really ought to be in a small village where one could get the real atmosphere. Basel was as close as I could come because I had to be in London on the third.

In the afternoon we swam in the Rhine. The Danube in Budapest was a disappointment because it was a mucky green and it smelt. The Rhine flows very fast through Basel, or it did when we were there, and we jumped in from some steps down to the water near the hostel and swam or just floated down-river like slick swift fish as far as the cathedral. Then we got out and walked back, drying in seconds and then jumped in and floated down again, racing or rolling in each other's arms and laughing almost too hard to stay afloat. If we'd stayed there we'd have ended up in Cologne or Holland or swept out to sea.

In the evening I went for a walk on my own, just walking without any particular objective in mind, wishing that the holiday could go on longer. Around me in the darkness, beneath the deep shadows of offices and flats, stalls were rising, I watched their flimsy skeletons being dressed in bright colours by men and women talking eagerly of the next day. A man at the top of a long thin ladder was tying a line of flags to a tree decked with light bulbs like some odd new fruit. The flags draped around his shoulders and wound around the ladder so that he looked like a kind of make-shift decorative pillar.

It happened in a narrow, empty street lined by closed doors. I was standing indecisively in the middle of the road with a growing sense that I was lost when a small man in a huge dirty fur coat appeared, asked me if I was American and went on without pause to offer me grass, coke or heroin. In his thick accent the words sounded almost comical but his expression was ugly and in a bad mood and, not thinking, I swore and pushed him away and walked on, already aware that I'd made a mistake but sure when my shoulder was grabbed and I was spun round to see three, one with a knife, before I doubled over as the pain and the whispered hate hit me together.

From the ground behind the boot I saw a fourth figure, I took it to be one of them, standing head turned in an even narrower, darker side-street, watching. I took the kick in the shoulder and rolled into a filthy puddle, my breath like a sob, my skin trembling, expecting the slice or stab of the knife. Instead I saw him, he had walked unseen between the other two, kick impossibly high, catching the man in the fur coat in the back of the head. The other two were beginning to react as he spun, he fought like a dancer, and hit one with an arm like a piston in the face and turned, oddly still, looking at the third. At that moment the hand of the first slapped the ground in front of my face, splashing me with more of the slime. It hung like muddy dew from the nylon fur. Absurdly I remembered the little pointed flags hanging from the man at the top of the ladder, looking in the thinly illuminated darkness like drops of dew about to fall.

The third man stood equally still, appraising. He stretched the right hand out slowly, the one with the knife, holding it with the tips of his fingers while with the left he slowly opened his jacket. He dropped the knife but it didn't fall. In his left hand was a second knife and the film suddenly jumped from slow motion to unreal speed as he slashed savagely, lips curled back, but his attacker pivoting on the toes of one foot had caught the first knife twisted and now cut the man's face apparently in one movement.

That was the end of the fight. The one with the knives staggered and then ran, hands clutching his face, the blood oozing between his fingers seeming as muddy as the puddle I found I was still lying in. The other two, who I remembered had each been hit only once, were lying still. He bent over them. I wasn't sure if he was looking in their pockets or just checking that they were all right. Then he helped me up, saying in French that the one with the knives would be proud of his scar. I answered in English and thought for a moment I saw disappointment or displeasure in his face. That was how I met Loomis.

After that there is light and darkness, eyes staring with the uninvolved passivity of television-watchers and gradually returning consciousness, stumbling and then straightening. The dingy, closely-packed old streets, a nightmare version of the bright white houses of the Greek Island, had given way to ugly well-lit concrete in a wide boulevard with neon and even trees. Somewhere someone was laughing intermittently and a little hysterically and I thought they were laughing at me. Somewhere else voices were speaking seriously, a little intensely. I felt withdrawn, as if sitting in a room hearing these sounds outside a door, the window.

Sooner or later we were in the coffee bar in the hostel with Helen and then, before I'd said more than a few words to him, Loomis had left. 'Does he think he's the Lone Ranger?' said Helen.

'Maybe he is, he saved my life, you know they were going to kill me, those guys in the gutter, and the guy on the train said one ought to be in Switzerland . . . funny I thought it was supposed to be so clean.'

I was spilling my coffee so I put it down and then I found I was crying into it. 'It'll cool down very fast if you do that.' She came round the table and sat in my lap which was much more comfortable altogether and I didn't cry for very long, she was more comforting than coffee.

'He fought like a dancer. Like someone in a film.'

'I almost wish I was there,' she smiled at me, 'But I wonder why he left like that.'

'I don't think he likes us. Students on holiday, thinking a few weeks on trains in Europe is something special.'

'Well, sod him.'

At any other time I would have agreed. I'd seen Americans

wandering round Florence with eyes that were comparing it with back home and finding it wanting, I'd heard them talking about the McDonald's in Vienna and I'd seen them posing on the beach in Greece, but I was already looking at Loomis with a narrator's interest.

When I slept it was surprisingly well, I only woke once with a vivid split-second image of the three of them in front of me. After that I dreamt of Loomis rifling their pockets as if looting corpses on a battlefield. I had decided not to go to the police, I didn't want to get involved.

We saw him the next day where he'd said he'd be, in a pedestrian precinct surrounded by shops even gaudier than usual for the special day. In the centre of one row was the town-hall, painted in bright colours, and along its balcony were the stone heads of various animals which seemed on the point of biting and tearing the wreaths and tassels decked around them.

We watched hanging over a railing from the first floor of one of the shops; he was like a wild animal himself as he prowled within the closely-packed circle of people. His act although not original was superb, he was light-fingered. I watched for the look or word or movement which would betray his image but nothing came.

Basel is three countries in one and he spoke to us in four languages — English for the tourists — rapidly and unselfconsciously. Helen, who had been scornful the night before, was totally engrossed.

When the act was coming to its end we came down to the precinct to meet him, pushing through the aimlessly dispersing crowd. He was talking to a policeman and for a moment I thought he was telling him about last night, but he was angry, his French marred by an American twang on the vehemently stressed syllables. The policeman seemed unconcerned, protected by the bland, precise nature of the rules on this day as on any other, gazing at Loomis as he might have gazed idly up into the sky.

Loomis caught sight of me.

'Cą va?'

'Bien,' I smiled. 'Got a problem?'

'Got any cash?' he said it without expression and I didn't look at the little plastic bag in which he had just collected the coins of the crowd. I paid the money, about ten pounds, and we went to a bar.

'Pigs and instant fines,' said Loomis 'are a bad mix. I hate Switzerland.'

He barely acknowledged the gift, but I didn't dislike him for it. I didn't try to kid myself that he wasn't interested in money, I was just satisfied that he was different. When the sweat from the act had dried he had a charm that didn't seem forced and a smile without reservations, but it was his air of infinite self-sufficiency that impressed me. He didn't seem perfect, least of all in my own, slightly conservative eyes, but he was different, like a living fiction. Even the bar we were in was appropriate. It was underground, long and dark with a low ceiling with painted pipes running across it, candles on the tables and incongruously at one end a chandelier glittered, small tear-shaped glass beads occasionally tinkling, over an empty dance-floor about the size of a small rug. It was full of locals of course, no tourists, authentic.

Loomis had left his huge ghetto-blaster with the barman, whom he knew, and was looking at the juke-box.

Helen turned to me. 'It's damp in here, isn't it? And there's no air.'

'Atmosphere,' I shrugged.

'I'd rather have air.'

Loomis came back and sat down as the first of his records began to play. He put the bag of silver on the table and it slithered outwards under its weight as far as the plastic would allow it, like a glass of water frozen as it spilled. We spoke over it, as if ignoring somebody else's mess left on our table. I was afraid that he'd be egotistical and the self-consciously continental American but he wasn't very responsive when I asked about him. He seemed glad to have company, and he asked questions about parts of London I'd never been to. I asked him about his fighting but he didn't want to talk about it.

He said that he didn't mind being alone but that he could always find friends when he wanted them. He was right, around Europe I had met many people whom I could move around with for a few hours or a few days and then part from amicably. But for some reason I noticed the casual way he talked about friends. Someone who uses the term so casually can't attach much meaning to it. Like a man who talks about a war in terms of scenarios and kill-ratios.

After a few songs he asked Helen to dance and to my surprise she agreed. The juke-box obliged them with a recent hit as I suppose he had known it would. They danced without touching alone on the tiny floor and although Helen did her best it was as though she was standing still watching him. It was a corny song, nothing like the music he played on the tape for his act, but he moved as if mesmerised by the sound and after it had reached its climax he collapsed theatrically to the floor showing his egotism after all but in a friendly way which suited the mood.

Lying there so strangely sprawled he seemed for a moment to be pausing between one act and another and I felt uncomfortable. Helen paid for the drinks, her bag up on the table seemed a much more solid thing than Loomis's. He seemed to notice that himself as he slipped his bag of coins into a pocket in his jacket, the look and the action reminded me of my dream. We left him performing again, having arranged to meet that evening.

Helen wanted to sleep before going out so we went straight back to the hostel. I had an empty sort of afternoon, I nearly went to wake Helen for a chat, and as I packed my rucksack that night I had the strongest feeling yet that the end of the holiday had come. I sat on my bunk feeling a little lost, not really where I wanted to be, not knowing what I wanted to be doing.

I met Helen in the coffee-bar. 'Do you want to go out tonight?' She was surprised. 'Have you got a better idea?'

'I don't know, I thought we could get a train and go to Greece, but together this time, or Morocco or something.'

'I'm going to Italy. I'm not changing my plans now for anyone. I'll see you in London in a few days.'

'There's not much in Italy you know. Just buildings and paintings and stuff.' I didn't know why she had answered me so seriously.

'Come on,' she said, 'have you got your things?' She put them in a bag, the passports and travellers' cheques, it wasn't safe to leave anything valuable in the hostel.

The road the hostel was on was quiet and the single line of flags along the buildings opposite looked lonely and miserable, but as we neared the river the crowds grew quickly. Loomis was an almost furtive figure beneath a particular tree watching the faces flowing past him. Lights shone with small, limited glows in the branches above him, illuminating a few leaves and individual flags.

He nodded a hello and told us to follow, turning and slipping through the wandering crowds like a shadow or a single dancer on a stage full of extras. We pushed after him as if wading through water, as if we were the messy wake to his slim cruiser, and I began to resent our apparent dependence on him. I reached out and caught his shoulder and he spun surprisingly fast, on his toes for a moment as if ready to run. I spoke quickly, trying not to seem taken aback. 'Where are you taking us?'

'To the best place to see the fireworks. Why?'

'Can't you slow down a bit?'

He gestured to the people moving impatiently around our little group and on down to the river. 'Look around you,' he said, 'make your own minds up.' And he turned and went on.

'Come on,' said Helen, pulling me after him, 'he knows where to go.'

Why should he know where to go to get the best view of the fireworks on Independence Day in Basel? But I followed anyway, he exuded a competence and confidence that made lack of faith look stubborn.

Our faith was rewarded. We found ourselves in the middle of a bridge almost overlooking the barges carrying the fireworks. The Rhine swept through the arches of the bridge spitting noisily, and the first rocket, premature perhaps because it was followed by a silence, spat stars down towards us, each of which was revealed as a point of a larger star which gleamed for a moment, then fell and disappeared, the dark pinpoints instantly swallowed by the darkness like drops of water in a pool, dew dropping into a muddy puddle. Sighs escaped the craning necks and open mouths around us.

It was spectacular, the best fireworks I had seen since Disneyland two years before. I like fireworks. For a few moments they are brighter than neon but unlike neon they are too sudden and too brief to seem like scars on the night. Perhaps some of the people there were thinking about independence, I don't know.

When they ended, in a colourful, noisy finale, Loomis was quickly on the move again, to find seats at a table by the river, he explained, before all the tables were filled. He had seemed unmoved by the fireworks and for a minute he reminded me incongruously of one of those tourists who hurries from sight to sight through a sense of duty rather than inclination. His mind was somewhere else and he wasn't very interested in what was going on, perhaps he needed to be the centre of attention and disliked being part of a crowd.

He found a great place for us to sit. The river rushed past, around the moon the clouds were silver-edged, unravelling, bulbs partly illuminated leaves and flags in the trees and everywhere people bustled shoulder to shoulder, ate elbow to elbow, talked and sang to enthusiastic, ragged bands. Even on a night like this I would have been surprised if he hadn't found a good place for us to sit. It was the scene for something important to happen.

'Couldn't you be making money tonight?' asked Helen.

'Sure, there's a fortune to be made tonight, but not through my act. The Swiss want to see the Swiss tonight. My act's mainly for tourists at the best of times.' He grinned at her.

The grin annoyed me, it didn't fit the image because it was too generous and it therefore spoilt my own image as an imperfect but omniscient narrator. 'So where is the fortune to be made?'

He was sitting next to me, Helen opposite, and he leaned towards me, put an arm around my shoulders and spoke in a loud whisper. 'Pockets. Isn't it obvious?' As he spoke he moved away again and with a slight flourish he laid my wallet on the table in front of me. He was light-fingered. Helen laughed delightedly. 'Slick. Very slick.'

I think I have a threshold beyond which human company becomes a necessary evil. It's nothing to do with boredom and not much to do with irritation, it's just some anti-social gene inside me that makes me want at least to observe but preferably just opt out.

I found myself pining for the Greek beach where the sun dulled your senses and, except for the passing of the Dickens, it was timeless. Where somehow, if you chose to speak to someone, you found the sun had stripped away most of the hesitation as if defrosting your insides, but most of the time you just didn't choose to.

So Helen and Loomis talked and I watched and drank from the big glasses with the froth running down the sides. Looking into the froth, I found, was almost as mesmerising as staring into a fire, stimulating inwardly-turned thoughts. Why should I, an aspiring writer so probably the world's ultimate egotist, be antagonised by egotism in someone else? Probably just because he didn't fit the image I wanted him to fit. I should be grateful that he fitted one particular image well enough to be able to save my life by beating up three opponents. Maybe they wouldn't have killed me, but either way I would always know what it was like to feel close to death. The kind of experience that's good for a writer. Somebody told me that Tolstoy sat with his brother as he died in a small village in rural Russia some years before he wrote of Levin in *Anna Karenina* sitting with his brother as he died in a small village in rural Russia. All experiences, I suppose, must eventually be material for a writer, however personal or painful. Slightly cheered up by the thought I pulled my gaze away from the remains of my beer and noticed that my wallet was still in the middle of the table, as Loomis's little bag of cash had been earlier. I put it back in a different pocket.

'Back again?' said Helen.

'Sorry, I was thinking about English beer.'

'I wish they had gin and tonic.'

'White Russian.'

'It's time to move on,' said Loomis, 'I'll take you where you'll get a whisky sour.'

So we moved on, although nothing important had happened.

The streets away from the river were almost empty and cluttered with debris, as if a party had ended. At one point a line of flags had unfastened itself and was draped around the trunk of a tree displaced, reminding me of the ones I had seen the night before.

The club Loomis took us to was surprisingly bland, he apologised for it as if he owned it, but it had a bar serving more than beer.

Helen bought the drinks, taking money out of her bag from amongst travellers' cheques and passports.

'Is that safe?' Loomis was peering into it, 'I thought tourists wore money-belts.'

'That's mainly the Americans,' I said.

'It's safe as long as I hold on to my bag,' said Helen, 'it's safer than the hostel anyway.'

Loomis looked at me and raised his eyebrows. 'Some people would take it whether you were holding on to it or not.'

'Where do you keep your ghetto-blaster and your money and stuff?' I asked.

'There's usually someone to leave things with,' he shrugged, 'if not there's left luggage at the station.'

'I won't have to worry about muggers with you around, will I? You'll just tap-dance on their faces or something.'

'Friends in every city? You must have a great circle of contacts.'

'I never did learn to tap-dance,' said Loomis, and to me, 'I make friends easily. What do you mean by contacts?'

'You mean you save lives on a regular basis?' I said.

'You don't sound very grateful,' said Helen.

'Why would I be tap-dancing anyway?'

'He said you fought like a dancer.'

'Before you'd seen my act. That's very perceptive, I trained as a dancer for a long time, they're the fittest people in the world. I guess you see things more clearly when the adrenalin's going.'

'When you're terrified, you mean.'

His charm didn't waver at any point. He talked and smiled as if he hadn't noticed any change in my mood, or as if he was overlooking something embarrassing in a friend. It reminded me of the way we had all ignored the pool of money on the table at lunch-time, or of his quiet acceptance of my gift shortly before that. Something made me want to throw a stone into that charm and watch the ripples, I didn't trust it because I thought it was hiding something and with my narrator's egotism I couldn't leave it hidden.

'I'm tired,' said Helen, 'I'm on an early train tomorrow.'

'So am I. What's your next move?' I asked Loomis.

'I don't know. I may have a holiday.'

'What would you do for money?'

'I'd arrange something.'

Outside it had begun to rain and the few figures left in the streets were hunched and hurrying, the fireworks forgotten and the decorations ignored. An occasional car pulled away from the kerb, its lights briefly dazzling, picking out for a moment the individual rain-drops sweeping across its path or the detail in the trunk of a tree. At the bridge Loomis asked us to wait as he moved carefully down the steps towards the water. We walked forward a little, on to the deserted bridge. The river seemed to be faster than ever, the rain puckering its surface in the faint light from the street-lamps above.

'You weren't very nice tonight,' said Helen. 'Were you jealous?'

'No,' I said, surprised. 'No, I wasn't jealous. Should I have been?'

'Maybe we shouldn't meet back in London.'

I looked at her but I couldn't tell if she meant it.

'It's up to you.'

I took out my wallet and opened it. All the money was there.

'What are you doing?'

'Maybe you should check the bag.'

'Why?'

'It worries me.'

'I don't understand.'

'It's an odd feeling to piss in the heavy rain.' He moved quietly as well as quickly. He laughed. 'Did I surprise you?'

At the end of the bridge he said he knew a short cut.

'Where do you have to go anyway?' Again we were following, dependent on him.

'Same kind of direction as you.'

So we followed him and inevitably I began to realise that we were approaching the street in which I had been attacked. There seemed an appropriately circular motion to everything and Loomis was the pivot, like a stage manager or director. It seemed now that the circle had been turned very quickly, just as it seemed now that a six-week holiday had lasted only a few days.

'I don't think this is the best way,' I said.

'It'll do.' He put an arm around Helen. 'Are you cold?'

'No.' She shrugged out of his grip. 'Are you two about to have a big macho scene?'

Loomis looked at me.

'I hope not,' I said.

'Well, I don't want to get involved,' said Helen. 'I'll leave you boys to sort it out.' She looked at us, hesitated and then went back the way we had come. Loomis looked at me impassively and then with a sigh opened his jacket. There was the chink of metal on metal and he took out the bag full of coins and held it out to me.

'This is about what that fine came to,' he said, 'do you want it?'

'No.' Now that Helen had gone most of the tension seemed to have gone too. 'I don't know . . .' I began.

'I've never stolen anything from anyone in my life,' said Loomis. 'My father is at the embassy in Paris. He's rich. Does that satisfy you?' he smiled angrily. I watched the water dribble off the little bag he was now holding by his side.

He seemed to be angry that I now knew he had nothing to hide, as if he enjoyed cultivating an air of mystery. Unless there had been no air of mystery and it was just that I prefer the characters of my imagination to real people. Anyway, I never knew Loomis at all, not even then.

There wasn't much left to say and we went back our separate ways, like a couple of failed gun-fighters.

In the early morning, before the gold had entered the day, everything glistened bright and cold and the city was like any other, no longer on holiday and no longer predominantly dark.

We signed out of the hostel together and walked towards the station through streets already succumbing to the loud approach of the rush-hour. I had forgotten how heavy my rucksack was and I shifted it uncomfortably on my shoulders as we walked. She had been asleep when I got back last night, or pretended to be, and I had slept in my own room.

'He didn't hit me,' I said.

'Good. Did you really think he was a thief?'

'I don't know. I was a bit drunk. His father is rich, it never occurred to me that he might be.' It didn't fit the image.

'He's in the Embassy, isn't he.' It wasn't a question.

'How did you know?'

She paused. 'He mentioned it.'

'I suppose I only heard about half of what went on last night.'

The station was like the one in Budapest, a great grey building with a huge expanse of floor space. A man was sweeping with a broom that looked as wide as it was long. Three of the small, decorative flags dangled on a line over the edge of a bin. It was nearly seven and the first commuters were already arriving.

We had our passes stamped and checked the times of our trains – Helen's was first and I walked on to the platform with her. As the train came in we kissed, encumbered by the rucksacks, and I held her tight. Her eyes shone, I was touched.

'Wait,' she said.

I waited and watched through the window as she took off her rucksack and reached up, straining, to put it on the luggage-rack.

She opened the window and leaned out, her bare, still-untanned arms white against the dirty glass. Looking at me she sighed and spoke slowly.

'Loomis came to the hostel yesterday afternoon. We made love.'

It was well-timed because the train started to move out almost immediately.

'Just like a scene from *Brief Encounter*.'

I don't know if she heard, on the whole I'd rather she didn't know what I said to her, she would imagine something better than anything I could think of. I stood the way they do in films, watching the train disappear, and I only moved when I knew I had to, moved through growing crowds to catch my train, not the narrator but a minor character in a story I didn't understand.

Maybe she was right, maybe I was just jealous all along.

THIEPVAL

Ruth McCracken

He was hungry, and yet he had only just eaten. It was the food they gave you here – after a while you sort of rebelled against daily doses of bully beef and biscuits. He supposed his body had become immune to whatever nutritional value they had. He thought of his mother's home cooking: that was plain and simple cooking now, it was not as if they lived in the lap of luxury and had meat every day. But it was good food, it fair filled you up and left you bursting at the seams. Now and then Joe and himself would get up early on a Sunday morning before going to church, and go out to see if they could catch a rabbit using a couple of ferrets borrowed from Old Tom from down the road. He liked autumn mornings best, when the trees were all colours of gold and rust and yellow, when the sun filtered through the morning haze, and yet it was not warm but nippy. Sometimes, closer to winter, there would be a touch of frost in the air and crusts of frost on the grass and bracken, and their breath would be visible like smoke.

Or they would go fishing, him and Joe. Of course sometimes the old man would come too, but lately as often as not he did not, for he was getting on in years now and not really fit for it any more. Fishing was better done in the summer when the weather was better and it did not matter so much if you spent a lot of time up to your knees in water. Joe always seemed to do remarkably well at the fishing, catching more fish than you thought would be in the river in the first place. He would keep them all alive in a net and then at the end of the session select the biggest and throw the rest back 'for another day, you stupid fish, don't think you're getting away with it that easy – okay?', as he would say.

Then there was Christmas, when the hen the old woman had been feeding up would be killed and cooked for the festive table. 'That bloody thing's been better looked after than meself,' his Da would moan as he sharpened the knife to carve it, 'and I'm going to enjoy every damn bit of eating it.'

'How's it going, our Billy?'

The unmistakable cheeky voice and grin of his brother interrupted his thoughts.

'Hi, Joe,' he said, 'still fighting fit?'

'Course I am, I'm the young and healthy one of the family, remember?'

'Watch your tongue you cheeky wee brat, or I'll give you a cuff round the ear, so I will.'

There was only eighteen months between them, but the joke ran that Billy was in some way an old decrepit creature, whereas Joe was still a baby. In some ways it was true, for Billy had always been the more serious one, the one to take on his responsibilities with more care and attention. Joe, on the other hand, was forever getting into trouble, both at home and at the linen mill, the main source of income for most of the town. Yet with one of those impish grins, and a roguish remark that only he could get away with, he always landed on his feet. Somehow. 'There's a wee bit of the devil in that youngster,' his mother said.

Billy had never had such a great responsibility thrust upon him as on the evening before they were due to leave for England to train. His Dad came up to talk to him as he was out in the yard collecting wood for the fire.

'We'll miss you both,' he had said, 'and we'll pray for you, that you might come back safe and sound to us. But . . . Billy, I know you're a good sensible lad and you'll keep your head, but you know what Joe's like, he looses the bap so easy. He'll find himself in trouble if he doesn't watch it, real trouble mind, so just keep an eye on him, will you?'

Billy had nodded his head in silence, and ever since had tried to see to it that his brother controlled himself a bit more. Discreetly, of course, otherwise he would have borne the brunt of that quick temper.

'Did you know that tomorrow's the anniversary of the start of the battle of the Boyne?' asked Joe.

'Of course I did,' answered Billy, 'and if one more person says anything about King Billy . . .'

Joe began to recite, and then to run as Billy made to clout him: 'King Billy had an orange cat, it sat upon the fender, and everytime it saw a mouse, it shouted No Surrender!'

Then he yelled back: 'The U.V.F. are the boys to show Fritz how to fight!'

Billy shook his head, half laughing, half in despair.

He poked the mirror attached to the end of his bayonet over the parapet of the trench and, sure that no one was charging their way, went back to the dug-out. A few of his companions were there, playing cards, reading the Bible, writing home. So far the infantry had not seen much action: the odd peek over the parapet, the odd patrol at dusk — that was it really. They were to wait for the bombardment of enemy lines to cease before they had their chance.

Billy sat down in the dug-out and started to write a letter home. He found it difficult to describe how things were at the front without frightening the old woman, for even if he had just put 'accidentally scratched my finger' he was sure she would fear the worst and imagine him lying in hospital somewhere with his whole arm amputated. So, he just contained himself by writing that things were okay, that Joe was okay, that the food and the conditions were okay, and to asking how things were at home. Joe reckoned that even with that very neutral epistle the old woman was bound to think they were not being properly looked after, and send the Da up the walls with her worrying.

How nice it would be to be at home, thought Billy and not for the first time. 'No more sniper bullets whistling above your head and thudding into the trees behind for a start,' he said, half to himself and half to the world in general.

'What's that, Billy?' he was asked.

It was Young Tom, Old Tom from down the road's son. Everyone called him 'Young' Tom, even Billy who was younger still.

'Och, I'm just talking to meself,' he replied, laughing, and lapsed into silence again to think more thoughts.

As if the whole thing was not bad enough anyway, they had had to suffer a very severe winter with heavy snow at some points. Billy remembered a story that had gone round about one poor sod in a different division further down the line who had been frozen to death one night whilst on sentry duty. And now the weather was playing the dirty on them again, making the sun blaze down. The heat was stifling; it was almost impossible to breathe.

He gave up trying to write home and went to sleep instead.

He woke up when they were called to get ready to go out on patrol, the first one that evening. Afterwards they would try and sleep a while before the big day tomorrow: their first taste of real action. Everyone was in cheerful mood, chatting and laughing before going out into the devastated woods and falling silent. As they marched along, Billy could see the back of Joe's head bobbing about, and for some reason it made him smile.

They had nearly reached the lines when it happened. A shell landed in the middle of the patrol. There was a large roar, a huge gush of earth, and limbs and bodies were flung high into the air. A crater was gouged out in the mud. Billy had somehow been left unscathed by the shell and could hardly take it all in. The explosion had ripped most of the rest of the men apart. The wounded were screaming in agony or just lay whimpering like new-born babies. Then there was the hushed anguish of the dead, their bodies twisted in grotesque positions.

Billy looked for Joe. A few minutes earlier he had seen his younger brother alive and well. Now he lay in a spurting pool of bright blood. He had lost his arms and his legs; his back was arched across the remains of some tree. Dead. Dead eyes staring open and seeing nothing.

Billy felt sure he too had died. He felt that the horror that met his eyes was not real, not of this world. It could not be. He too stared deep into space, as Joe did. 'So this is what it's like to be dead,' he muttered.

He felt someone grab at his arm, and turned to face one of his comrades, eyes wild with panic and fright.

'Billy, Billy, come on, for Christ's sake. Don't just stand there, man. Let's get out of here and get some help for these poor souls.'

Billy shook his head. So he was not dead after all. Pity. He ran after his companion.

Later, at the dressing station, he half-heard reports of there only being two fit men from the patrol left, the rest being either seriously wounded or killed. He did not pay much attention — almost as if he was not really there at all. He spoke to no one and no one had the heart to speak to him. He did not even notice how he was shaking. All the time he saw before him a face staring: staring and seeing nothing. Eyes looking and looking and never finding what they sought. He should have gone back. He should have.

'I should have gone back and closed his eyes,' he whispered, and buried his head in his hands.

* * *

She had hardly slept all night. Not a wink. And how could she for lying there thinking about her two fine young sons and them away at the front fighting?

'How can I sleep, tell me that?'

'Lying there worrying isn't going to do them a bit of good,' he answered, 'for if they knew how you were fretting and getting on and nearly making yourself ill, they'd be none too pleased about it. And they're right, for not one bit of good is it doing anyone, you not getting any rest at night.'

So it went on every morning. He would wake and find her restless beside him, sometimes even fully dressed. He would gently reproach her for not looking after herself properly, but she never heeded him. They had been married nearly thirty years now, and it was the first time that Billy and Joe, their two sons, had been so long away from home. Of course it was only natural that they should be missed anyway, but under the circumstances . . . well, they were missed even more. There was a war on; the uncertainty of ever seeing them again was always present.

They both took it in different ways. The father was seemingly indifferent to the situation, going on with his life as if nothing extraordinary was happening. With the old woman it was never too far away from her thoughts: everything she did seemed to lead her back to the same thing. In reality, both attitudes were manifestations of the same emotion: the fear of losing their children.

'You better be getting up,' she said, 'or you'll never make it to the mill in time for the start of the shift.'

She left him to get ready and went downstairs. She herself had been up for ages, just sitting on the edge of the bed, listening to the regular breathing and snoring of her husband; listening to the slow steady tick of the old clock in the hall counting away the hours;

sighing as dawn broke and birds sang oblivious to the prayers that rose from her lips. She almost expected to hear the creaking of floorboards from next door that told her that the boys were already awake and getting dressed for work. The disappointment of that expectation hung heavy on her.

She went out into the back garden to the run where the hens were kept and found some fresh eggs for their breakfast. By the time she re-entered the house he had the kettle sitting on the range for tea and was shaving while it boiled.

She busied herself finishing all that had to be done and soon they sat down to eat. They did so mainly in silence: not the awkward silence of strangers when politeness strains the mind in search of the obligatory pleasantry, but the mutual and enjoyable silence of good friends who know they do not have to force the conversation, but rather let it wander where it has the good sense to go, like a mountain sheep.

She remarked on how good a morning it was, sunny and with a slight breeze – she would get good drying for her washing. He told her what a good cup of tea she made – 'not weak like your mother's, like water that is. This is decent stuff. No shamrock tea here, eh!'

She laughed. He always referred to weak tea as 'shamrock tea', meaning it was brewed with only three leaves.

Finally he took out his watch and said that he had better be off. She helped him on with his jacket and then stood at the front door, watching him walk down the road to the mill. The whole street, it seemed, went too: all the other men too old or unfit to have gone away, and all the young women with no family to look after. Everyone knew everyone else, and everyone inquired after all those absent.

There was not a house in the whole street that did not have a father or a son or a brother or a friend that was not away at the front. Except for the house at the end whose son, it was rumoured, was in Dublin.

He turned round when he reached the corner, as he always did, and waved at her. She returned his wave and went back into the house when he had disappeared from view. She stoked up the range with wood and put the kettle back on to heat water for the dishes. Then she went out to the pump in the street to fill the tin bath and put it on to heat for the washing. She sang softly to herself, but never once did she stop thinking of her family.

* * *

They all knew each other well in the battalion, coming as they did from the same district. Many of them had been to school together, many were neighbours. So it was throughout the whole division: men were forged together not just because of a shared nationality, nor because of a fierce conviction that their duty was to defend all things British, but because they had known each other a lifetime. It made, in some ways, for an easier life: they did not have to try as hard to get on or to adjust to each other's different temperament. Which was just as well since the conditions did not make the going all that easy. Only a few weeks ago there had been a cloudburst and as they had little shelter, and the trenches were a devil to keep drained anyhow, everyone had been soaked to the skin and had had to endure the extreme discomfort of having no dry clothes. Only recently had they been able to feel comfortable in their uniform, safe in the knowledge that they would not suffer painful chafing round their legs, their arms and their necks.

Half an hour before dawn every morning the troops on duty in the trenches would 'stand-to' in case of a surprise attack. Usually the bombardment would flare up again then and continue without mercy throughout the whole day. It had been going on for a few weeks now, on both sides. The forest at Thiepval, which had seemed such a quiet and tranquil spot when they had first arrived, now rang with the boom of shells which flung mushrooms of soil into the air and brought crashing down in flames great old trees. The whole place had been changed into one big pockmark. But they had grown used to the noise of shells and grenades, just as the noise of the mill did not seem so bad or loud after you worked there a while.

This morning was different: the shelling was to cease about seven, and that was the signal for them to go over the top and attack. They were tense, but not with fear. For all they had been through they had not been too dampened in spirit. They were all raring to go, to see some real action, confident that they would not let the division, nor Ulster, down. They were assured, full of faith, certain that no harm could come to them now. If they were tense, they were tense with expectation, with the restraint of having to wait even for a second longer.

Billy did not really know how he felt; he was too tired and numb. The full impact of what had happened or was about to happen had yet to take effect. He turned his face up to the sun that had begun to shine and cause the stifling heat to blast down again. The beauty of the summer air somehow made it all the more difficult to believe, especially when he glanced over to what remained of the forest. Floating magically like from another world he heard the tiny sound of birdsong struggling to reach the heavens. 'It's a nightingale,' Billy heard someone say in disbelief, 'it's a bloody nightingale.' They were unable to listen to its innocent tune for very long for soon the whine and boom of shells started up again. 'I don't know what that bird has to sing about anyway,' thought Billy.

He felt sure that he and all the others were going to die. In fact, the idea of death appealed to him at that moment – it would bring to an end all his problems and worries. Then once more he glanced out at the forest and heard the shells bursting and strained to hear again the sweet song of the nightingale, singing alone in the few bare branches left to it, and he felt a sudden anger. Why was he there? Why did he have to endure so much suffering? Why, for God's sake, why did his brother have to die?

He knew the answer: 'Damn you, Fritz, you bloody murderer. Fritz, I'm going to get you.'

When it turned quiet again and it was time to go, he waited his turn and watched the others quietly form into lines, one behind the other, and calmly step out in order, almost as if they were on parade. His anger took strength from their lack of fear. He burned with hate.

Those in charge had reckoned that, between the bombardment ceasing and the advance of the infantry, the Germans would have no time to adjust to the new attack, for it was only a matter of minutes. It was time enough. The first few lines of troops had already reached across No Man's Land and were into enemy trenches, but reinforcements were never to get through.

Machine-guns. Gunfire rattling relentlessly on, worse than heavy rain on a tin roof. The bullets mowed down the troops: men were falling and shouting and screaming all over the place. Yet the others marched on and still more fell and the rest kept on and the machine-guns never quit their firing.

Billy kept walking, though by now he again felt as if he was in another world far away and this chaos was not really happening to him. More bewildered than angry now, but he kept going. He saw the wounded crawling back to the lines; he saw bodies flung into the air, bodies contorted on the ground, and everywhere he saw those eyes staring. Staring. 'Please don't stare at me any more!'

* * *

When he arrived back for his dinner she was testing the potatoes with a knife. The fire on the range was merry enough, too hot maybe for this summer's day, but he noticed the wood in the scuttle was low so he volunteered to go out and bring in some more.

While he was out she mashed the potatoes and added the necessary butter, milk and scallions to make the champ. She dished out the food on the warmed plates and poured out two glasses of water. Then she went out the back to call him in but he was already at the door, a pile of small logs clasped in his arms.

Again they ate in almost total silence. He told her old Fred was back at work again after his 'wee turn', and seemed rightly enough. She told him she had been talking to Mrs. Smith from two doors down while she had been hanging out her washing, and that she was putting a brave face on it, poor woman, but you could see the death of her husband was still hitting her hard. And her only young too, poor soul. Thank God she had not been left with any young children, for that would have made it harder on her still, wouldn't it.

They lapsed into silence again, both wondering what they would do if the news came through, but it was impossible to know how they would react. At least they had each other, one would carry the other through. It would be worse if you were on your own. If it happened. They prayed that it did not.

It was time for him to go back to work. He helped her to clear up then took his jacket and left. Once again she looked out to wait for her wave before coming in to do the dishes. This time she could not settle. The conversation with Mrs. Smith had stirred within her a vague feeling of fear, worry and hopelessness. This coupled with her lack of sleep conspired against her and made her incapable of putting her mind to doing anything. She wandered about the house, trying to fight off this, by now, familiar ache, but finally, on entering the front room and seeing the cricket trophies her sons had won, she could contain herself no more. She sat down and let the tears flow.

A few hours later and he was glad to be going home, his work finished for the day. It was tough enough going at the mill, with the sound of the shuttles and the looms and everything rattling away in his ears. He liked the quietness and the peace he found in his own house and in the garden. Except of course for the noise the two boys made when they were fighting and arguing with each other, as invariably all brothers do. He smiled at some of the things they would pick at each other over; who had the most food, for instance, seemed a constant source of concern for them. But it was only a bit of fun between them, nothing serious, and they would never suffer the old woman to give them anything off her own plate.

'Come off it, Ma, you need that for yourself,' one would say.

'Aye, take a hold of yourself, woman,' the other would add. 'It's only this wee imp causing trouble again.'

And the old woman would tut as if she was all annoyed, but secretly she too was enjoying the fun.

He thought all this, and he smiled at the memory, then he coughed, then he paused to wipe his eyes before going into the house.

The table was all ready, laid with bread and butter, a bit of jam and a lump of cheese. She was standing beside the range with her arms folded waiting for the kettle to boil.

'A watched kettle never boils,' he said.

She turned round to him and smiled. 'Ah, there you are,' she said. 'This will be ready in a minute.'

He pretended to grumble as he hung his jacket up. 'Bad service in this place, desperate bad. Is there no such thing left these days as a decent place where a man who's been working hard all day can get a bite to eat when he comes in?'

'Get away on out of that, you old fool,' was her only reply.

'Maybe Sunday,' he remarked later as he put jam on his bread, 'maybe Sunday, before church, if it's a good morning, I'll go out and see if I can get a rabbit would make a nice bit of stew.'

'That would be nice, we've not had rabbit stew for a few weeks now,' she replied. 'I wonder if there will be any berries ready yet for the jam.'

'I'll take a wee look see when I'm out — if I go of course.'

Many a time he had thought to go out early to catch rabbits, but when it came to the bit he had just been too tired and had thought better of it. Things had been different when the boys had been home, for one or other of them had always been away early on a Sunday morning.

After he had helped her to do the dishes, he sat down in an easy chair with the paper and his pipe. She brought in the clothes she had washed that morning from the line, and gathered them into a heap, ready for ironing. 'Told you there was good drying today,' she said as she tested the iron to see if it was hot enough by spitting on it. Seeing that it was not, she settled it back on the range to heat through for another while.

He read out to her all the latest news from the war, and mentioned a few names from the district listed as wounded or missing. Thankfully today no one was reported killed. As he read she shook her head or murmured 'dear dear'.

'You know,' he said, 'they call it a glorious war, and sure there's nothing really all that glorious about it. If only the whole bloody thing had never been started.'

* * *

Up until then he had thought that the greatest pain he had ever endured was when as a small boy he had had a terrible toothache for a week before he managed to twist the offending tooth out and leave it in the hope that the fairies would give him a farthing. He was wrong. The shearing pain of the bullet that grazed his chest and ripped into his left arm left him in agony and gasping for breath. He lay on the ground a while, eyes shut, wondering what the hell he was supposed to do now. When he opened his eyes, the noise of gunfire and screaming still resounded around him. He found himself looking up into the grim and harrowed face of a stretcher-bearer who was patching him up the best he could. Billy's throat was parched and full of grit. He asked for a drink.

The stretcher-bearer produced a bottle and tipped it up to wet the cork. He took the cork out and passed it over Billy's lips.

'Sorry, Billy boy, that's all you're getting,' he said. He went on, 'Will you be able to make it back to the lines yourself, Billy, only we have our work cut out for us here and there's many the one's too bad to go back unaided.'

Billy looked again at the face. 'Och, Alec,' he said. They had been to school together and the scrapes Alec had got him in were countless.

'Are you fit, Billy? Will you make it okay?' he insisted.

'Aye, Alec, aye. I'm not dead yet.'

He watched Alec race off into the thick of it again, having given Billy an encouraging pat on the back. Billy tried to struggle to his feet, but without success, for he was too weak and shaky to pull himself up and walk. Yet he knew he was not finished for he could feel blood slowly trickling down his legs. He reckoned that, if he could feel something still, then that meant he was strong enough to go back to the lines by himself.

On the way back, with his belly pressed to the mud and the blood, ears alive to screams of guns and men, eyes blinded by smoke and tears of pain, he noticed his bandages unwinding. Still, Alec must have done the best he could. 'Thank you, wee Alec,' he whispered, 'thanks for not leaving me for dead.'

Funny how when you are alive and fit you sometimes long for death, and when that spectre finally stares you in the face you look on it with disdain and struggle against it with all your instinct for survival.

He was only a few hundred yards away from the lines and the safety of the dressing station when the shelling started worse than ever, with most of the shells, it seemed to him, being fired in his direction. He gave up trying to crawl on through that onslaught and made his way instead to a large crater left by a previous attack.

Down in its hollow it was relatively peaceful. The roar and yelling of the battle became muffled. He suddenly realised how tired he was, for he had slept precious little the night before. His whole body ached and cried out for rest, his wounds throbbed and, worse still, his mind was tortured by a never-ending series of thoughts and images and fears and longings.

With his good arm he began to scrape a hole in the side of the crater. He dug it just wide and deep enough for him to lie in. He became unaware of anything else, obsessed with one thought only: sleep; his chance to forget just for a while. He curled up inside the hole and closed his eyes.

When he awoke it took him a while to understand why he was lying in a bank of muck with a dull throb in his chest and a stiff arm. When he remembered, he groaned and then stretched himself up into a sitting position. He rubbed his head and then his eyes, thinking how much better he felt, despite being hit, and how he ought to try reaching the lines again.

He looked round the crater. He did not know how he had managed to miss him when he first came to the spot. Directly opposite was the corpse of a young German soldier. He was slumped as if profoundly asleep, but his mouth was open, his eyes were open and his hands were clutched tightly to his stomach. He's obviously been killed after the crater's been formed, thought Billy; he was in too good a shape to have been blown up with it.

Severe rigor mortis had set in, giving the lad a strange appearance; everything was clenched intensely, every muscle strained and stretched, as if in a last desperate attempt to keep a hold on life.

Billy stared in horror, and in reluctant fascination. He was probably the same age as Joe; maybe he even had the same temperament. Maybe he even had an elder brother who had tried to look after him and who now mourned him. Most certainly he had a mother and a father to cry over the loss of his innocent youth. Billy thought of Joe as he had last seen him: dead; with no limbs; destroyed beyond recognition almost. Then he studied the German soldier again. Joe would be in his state now. Perhaps even worse — perhaps he had begun to rot.

Billy cursed himself. He cursed himself for having felt hatred towards the enemy, for having thought that they were different somehow. Dammit! Every soldier was the same: dreamed the same dreams; suffered the same hell; died the same death. 'Billy boy,' he said to himself, 'there is no difference between men, give or take the odd name or two.' He felt pity for himself, for the Germans, for everybody. He stood up and went to take his leave of the soldier. 'Cheerio, Joe,' he whispered as he walked over to the corpse.

Closing its eyes he murmured: 'You can rest now, little brother.'

He managed the last few yards to the lines without mishap, for the shelling had died down somewhat. It was early evening by this time though it seemed later because smoke hung dark in the sky. Billy never wanted to have to go through another twenty-four hours like that again. As he sat in the dressing station, supping the rum he had been given, waiting to be taken to the field ambulance and so start the long journey to England, he heard whispers of terrific losses on both sides. He longed for home, for comfort, for contentment, even for a long day at the mill. Then he thought how empty it would all be without Joe.

He lay back. There came into his mind the image of two young boys racing home from school, and being met at the door by a woman gently telling them not to be impatient for dinner for it was nowhere near time for their father to be home from work.

He curled up into a ball like a little child afraid of the dark, and began to cry.

* * *

She was upstairs undressing, ready for bed but not ready for sleep. She could hear him downstairs, making everything safe, locking the doors. Sighing, she went over to the window and gazed out at a wonderfully clear sky, scattered with stars. She had often wondered as a child how anything so far away could seem so close. Now she thought the same about her family.

She heard her husband climbing the stairs, softly whistling to himself, and before he could enter she turned her face up towards the heavens and pleaded: 'Please God, see them home safe.' He had come in in time to hear her and, gently putting his hand on her shoulder, whispered, 'Amen.'

MADNESS

David Rogers

He had moved into his brother's apartment three months ago, and was living there alone. It was a four-room affair at the top of a house in a long, gaunt Victorian terrace. Straight-backed in a corset of dirty windows, steep-roofed, and built to last, the terrace fragmented with the Empire. The sheen on the arseniced top-hats of Bradford millionaires lingers only on the feathers of the skinny black crows nesting under the eaves. In an overflowing of creative energy these eaves had been adorned with seraphims and suns, a horn of plenty, and a dolphin swimming in sad Victorian gaslight. Hard times at the hands of the local heavy industry followed. The whole town was coated with a sticky corrosive black tar, similar to the one which clogged the lungs of its inhabitants, but slower-acting. This had caused a gradual metamorphosis in the carvings: the angel had fallen, becoming a spirit of decay, the sun had withdrawn into a lightless ball of hard matter, the cornucopia had been eaten, while the dolphin flapped half submerged in an oil slick. The remains found a grim unity in their resemblance to a blackened, jaw-less skull.

The apartment was full of expensive, uncomfortable furniture, bookcases, X-ray photographs, and snapshots of Katerina Szasz. Katerina Szasz was his brother's wife — they had met almost two years ago at a factory fire. They had held hands as they watched the old mill burning to the ground. Marriage had followed as inevitably as day follows night, and so had Katerina Szasz's death, from lung cancer, a year to the day after her wedding night. His brother had preserved all of her X-ray photographs which he had obtained by deception from the hospital, and they were framed and hanging around the walls of their bedroom. Apart from these, all that remained of pretty, unlucky Katerina Szasz were her snaps, which preserved Katerina under a mantle of non-reflective glass, for all eternity. The one which disturbed him the most showed her in a short black dress walking in the formal gardens of a nearby stately home. Her hair was thinning from the chemotherapy, and her expression explained that she was distinctly pissed-off with everything, and no, she didn't think she could really manage a smile right now.

It was on his ninth day in the flat that he received his first letter from Katerina Szasz.

Egg-yolk-yellow early morning sunlight slatted by Venetian blinds falls across the unmade bed, the table with the dinner plate serving thirteen cigarette butts, the open volume of Petrarch's sonnets. The man is lying in his daily bath, and falling asleep. Following the dark water down through limestone mountains, he eventually reaches the underground lake.

And now he is twitching sketchy sleep under a cooling quilt of green water, upon which placid surface the reflection of a strip light lies, and shudders in time to the slow drip of a tap.

The man is having a prose dream. He has many such dreams, which take the form of sub-verbal passages of prose — although not all are prose. Some take the form of very bleak, minimal poetry. These dreams have no visual component, but if they did, it might be in the form of a stream of white text pouring upwards on the screen of a visual display unit, or the image of static you get on an untuned television.

Strangely enough, during his conscious hours he suffers from a sort of optical tinnitus, which always takes the form of a two- or three-minute view of a landscape. The landscapes are limited in number: there are five — the walled garden, the chicken shed, the empty air force base, the frozen lake and the black river. At first he thought that these landscapes reflected his mental — or more accurately spiritual — states, a tarot of the soul. However, he has recently come to the conclusion that more than his own, personal tragedy is being referred to, but also the tragedy of his society, past, present and future.

He does not know the precise significance of each landscape, in fact he believes that their significance is diffuse, but he nevertheless regards them as being valuable insights into the nature of things. The only scene he regards as wholly personal is the black river. This is the rarest and the shortest of all the visions, and the one he feels most curious about. He is beginning to guess that it represents his death.

The man believes that he is going insane.

Oranges and lemons say the bells of St. Clement's.

His eyes could make no sense of the diagram on the floor
where once limbs intersected there was just a healing sore
His eyes could make no sense of the diagram on the floor
where once limbs in tersected there was just a healing sore
His eyes could make nosense of the diagram on the floor
where on cel imbs i n t e r — sected there wasj usta h eal in g sore
His e, yes cou, ld, make, no s, sense, of the

He has turned over in the bath onto his most favoured sleeping position, and has inhaled some bathwater. Simultaneously, in the hall, a phone begins to ring. He flounders out of the bath, ignoring the burning asthmatic constriction running the length of his windpipe, down which insufficient oxygen is passing to support life, stumbles naked and limps trembling to the phone. After the pips stop, he hears a woman's voice — the white earth — then the dial tone. He drips back into the bathroom to find a towel. He is trying to decide whether the voice on the phone belonged to Katerina Szasz, and decides that it did not. He walks into the bedroom and lies on the bed, sunshine igniting strips of skin. In the inner darkness Katerina's lungs shine like white phosphorus, blackening with the fungal growth of pulmonary cancer which eventually reached out a hand and quietly stopped her heart. He takes a long drag at his cigarette, watching the white paper crisp and flare, the tiny percussive hiss as clumps of tobacco catch, the chimney of grey ash forming. A flake separates, floats down, and is sucked up into his nose. He remembers a dream, from the days when he had normal dreams: he is in a hospital ward, in a paper nightgown, with a growth of black ivy in his lungs. Katerina is there too, her dark hair pulled back, her face very white. Two men enter, SS privates from some future Nazi régime. They want to take Katerina away for a shower, she doesn't want to go, looks to him for help. He climbs out of his bed and approaches one of the men, who explains to him in a civilised fashion that really he was silly to worry, these things happen to everyone here, purely routine, nothing to become concerned about . . . As they take her out of the door, he realises that he will never see her again. Slowly, gracefully, fat flakes of ash drift down onto the counterpane of his bed . . .

You owe me five farthings say the bells of St. Martin's

My Love,

You must wait for me, I am coming for you. Last night I reached the first landing on the staircase before I lost my shape. Tonight I will climb higher. You must be patient.

Katerina.

In the lunchtime press of secretaries, students, businessmen, housewives, down-and-outs and jobless youths he drifts down the pavement and into a cheap café, where he orders a coffee and sits at a white formica table. Salt grains have been swept by a quick cloth into cryptic lines. The plastic ashtray is choked with cigarette butts, and the cellophane wrappings of fresh packets. His attention finally snags on the sinister orchid of varicose veins on the calf of a fat old woman in a beige overcoat on the table in front of him. She is talking with her friend, another old woman. The smoke from *their* cigarettes floats upwards and condenses on the insides of their eyes, turning them into chips of coloured stone at the bottom of a canal. He feels an involuntary relaxing of his cillary muscles, and the world slides out of focus . . .

Along the grey shed, following the black wire strung with 100 watt lightbulbs, through a high window showing a square of white sky and into the compound. Then past the diggers, the cutters and the crushers, the black barrels of chemicals, and outside to the

Catching my coffee in this way, the light shows four little globules of grease circling in my cup. And here is some ash from my cigarette. Those women, talking about their arthritis, their children, last night's telly, are on hands and knees crawling around the white earth where nothing can grow. It is warm, the white mud steams, and the grey road of tank tracks fades off wetly into the distance.

wreckage of their lives — alternative pasts, alternative presents, impossible futures just the choking feeling they get looking at the family albums.

The park is gently bathed by clear November sunlight. The long shadows of the skeletal black beech trees cut long trenches in the bright green and yellow grass where the starlings were hunting for worms. People walking along the tarmac paths wear coronets around their heads. A slow wind stirs the bony trees, a jet flies overhead. A girl in a short black skirt walks by wheeling a pram. He stares at her through the smoke from his cigarette. Her sheepskin coat is open, and her breasts, unsupported, move through her red pullover. He feels a slow wind in his skeletal loins, just enough to make him feel cold. Again, he feels his eyes lose their grip . . .

This is Laura's garden. Pressed flat between heartbeats on a summer afternoon. Yew trees, birdless, circle the black grass of the ponds; lilies nod, scentless. The breathless air lies as heavy as dead flesh, embalmed in golden sunlight. The high garden wall, dark with ivy, and gateless, enwreathes all.

The most remarkable thing about the Victorian terrace is the staircase leading up to his flat. The house had been the residence of the son of a former ambassador to Italy. Pater supplied his offspring with a goodly amount of finest Italian marble from the Toppolinos' stoneyard from which Michaelangelo carved the tomb of Lorenzo de' Medici. To harmonise the past with the present, the banisters were made out of Coalbrookdale black iron. The whole found a satisfying synthesis in the form of the golden mean: the internal proportion of the banister, the stairwell, the landings were all based on the golden mean, as were the flights of stairs themselves, if viewed from above.

He spent some time at the optimal viewing point, half way along the landing outside his apartment, staring down the receding perspective of shadow, line and plane. It seemed to him like a long corridor leading to another place. He could walk down it —

through it — with the ghostly tinkling of the Moonlight Sonata in his ears. It was a gateway. And then the staircase attacked him. The long swan's throat of white marble writhed. The tape playing the Moonlight Sonata stopped and then began playing at different speeds, distorting horribly. His head filled up with blood, the staircase began revolving like a spiral with its ends lost in the dark. He stepped back from the banister, and the spinning stopped, but when he went back to the stairs, he found that he had lost his sense of perspective: he was no longer sure of any surface, line or shadow. The staircase was now a doorway for menacing possibilities . . .

The mask, turning, slipped from convex to concave . . .

As I was walking up the stairs,
I met a man who wasn't there
When will you pay me, say the bells of Old Bailey

Spectral, corpse-white, long black nightgown brushing the ground, face appearing and disappearing inside the soft cage of her long straight hair, the flesh of the late Katerina Szasz walked towards him out of the unintelligible staircase . . .

When I am rich, say the bells of Shoreditch

and in her hand she had a long pointed butcher's knife . . .

He wasn't there again today
Oh, how I wish he'd go away

He looked again. The staircase wavered like disturbed water, and the gateway folded out into the view of white marble stairs and black iron banister seen from above.

In the bookcase: *The Wasteland* by T. S. Eliot, *The Divine Invasion* by Philip K. Dick, *Lillith* by George Macdonald, Peake's *Gormenghast* trilogy, *Cities of the Red Night* by William Burroughs, Conrad's *Heart of Darkness*, Kafka's *Letters to Felice*, C. S. Lewis's *The Lion, the Witch, and the Wardrobe*, and Emily Brontë's *Wuthering Heights.*

*　　*　　*

He is jotting notes down in a Tesco notebook. Declining autumnal sunlight fills the sitting room. On the table beside him, a copy of the *Guardian* lies open. Its main stories cover the crackdown on Campaign for Nuclear Disarmament ringleaders, the razing of the Catholic areas of Belfast by the 'Action Groups' battalions of the British Army, the growth in the number of open exponents of ritual magic, and the imminent collapse of the world banking system. He is writing about his insanity: he is balancing on the one hand the fear of riding in a never-ending, meaningless roller coaster, with the growing conviction that he is gaining an insight into the metaphysics of human reality. He thinks the two cannot be reconciled, but adds that part of the nature of madness is that it fragments superficial unities, and recognises that contradictory and inconsistent facts may exist together with no problems. He thinks that most personalities subsume contradictory drives. He thinks that man was created to suffer. He believes that he was created to suffer in total isolation. He reads what he has written and tears it up.

He lies back in his chair, thinking about Katerina Szasz, with a paralysed, congested ache in his chest which will not transfer itself to his groin. He remains an hour in the same position looking at a photograph of her face, smiling, gesturing excitedly with one hand, the spring light minutely etching the smoke from its cigarette. The photograph is buried beneath glass, and their eyes cannot meet.

This is Laura's garden. Pressed flat between heartbeats on a summer afternoon. Yew trees, birdless, circle the black glass of the ponds; lilies nod, scentless. The breathless air lies as heavy as dead flesh, embalmed in golden sunlight. The high garden wall, dark with ivy, and gateless, enwreathes all.

A girl in white linen with long purple flowers in her hands is walking round the garden, head bowed amongst the copulating statues.

When will that be, say the bells of Stepney

Outside, in the street, a Boys' Brigade marching band is passing, police cars flanking slowing the traffic to a crawl. Rule Britannia.

Across the road, a Pentangle Bookseller is handing out copies of the Book, a dwarf in Punchinello costume and a fire dancer accompany him. Britannia rules the waves. From the hospital opposite geriatric patients stare through the window. Britons never never never. Mental patients in the windows below stare. They look shit-scared. Shall be. Nurses in brown uniforms pull them away. Slaves.

The base is empty. The guard-house, the black, bleak Nissen huts with their National Service tin mugs of char still lukewarm on the lockers, the airstrip, the military police land-rovers, the quartermaster's stores, the vehicle hangars, the controllers' tower. . . . In the sky, a diffuse skeleton of cloud separates, melts, disappears.

A cold wind blows off the airstrip, carries the smell of oil and tarmac, and a distorted after-image of the Battle of Britain. Beneath this is a smell of burning . . .

After the band had passed, the police began a sweep. Among the blue uniforms of the locals, there was a sprinkling of black. The Political Branch, the successor to the old Special Branch are here. Quotas to fill, nothing personal . . . a day, two at the most. . . . The Pierrot Police Clowns distributed red, white and blue carnations to the detainees . . .

One building exerts a strange fascination for him: it looks like a small hospital, or perhaps a technical college building. Upon closer examination, it becomes clear that the building has no entrance, and that the windows are, in fact, mirrors. He looks yellowed, unshaven, thin, disreputable. He walks around the building, and eventually finds a service hatch. He opens it, goes through, and finds himself in a large dark space. He switches a light and a light comes on.

Blue police vans are arriving. Citizens whose I.D. cards are in some way suspect are escorted aboard. Loudspeakers play 'Oranges and Lemons'.

Inside the building, there is only the sleeping machine. It looks like a huge transformer, squatting in the darkness. Or an altar. Moving closer, the hairs on the back of his neck stand up. He finds he has an erection. His mouth is dry. He moves within touching distance. The machine is decorated — circuit diagrams, magical symbols. . . . Railway lines lead to a circular door four feet up the sleek flank of the machine. He strokes the door, feeling a tingle of pleasure run down his spine. He opens the door as though he were gently opening his lover's legs. It is an oven door.

There can be no division between the public and the private lives of individuals. Just as all citizens together constitute the state, and constitute it at all times, whatever they are doing, the state must make it its concern to control the private activities of citizens in order to ensure its purity. We must therefore at . . .

He turns the television over to catch the six o'clock news. Outside, the autumn sunshine had long since gone, and a violent storm had developed and the room was adrift in it. X-ray flashes of lightning hitting skeletal trees, flesh curling back, sweating violet fat in the licking flames.

S.A.S. artists provoke abstract scrap steel revolutions, destabilising the unexpressed fears of selected social groups. Mental collapse precipitated in key targets. Moderate elements purged in press releases of cancer imagery. Dissident groups sectioned off in football stadiums. Heroin police used in infiltration programme instigated by the Central Control Authority. . . .

Report from Ian Hollister on Captain G.'s possible assassination mission. Contacted in afterburn of Californian morning, in the forecourt of the Federal Scanning Facility, between the primary mirror sculptures,

He walked out of the base, looking for the Manchester road. Darkness gathered. Winter stubble and the frozen white earth. Powdery snow on the wind. He still felt the tidal pull in his loins, washed bones stranded on the beach. And then the sky was taken away by a vast aeroplane. The shadow filled the valley, but did not pass over. It was a Second World War bomber, a United States Air Force Flying Fortress. The roar of its engines filled the valley.

It was partially skeletal, with metal ribs poking through the starving fuselage. The plane was black. Swamp black. He had a vision of the raising of

agent zeroing vectors onto the remembered smell of burning hair. Capsule implanted using invasion techniques first developed in the Auschwitz *vernichtenslager,* to be released later by means of psychoactive short wave radio waves.
Books into downtown motel, plays video of acausal scenes generated from *Waiting for Godot* to nullify C.I.A. precogs, paints mandala on his chest and phases out to the year 1932 (technical note: body inversion techniques first perfected in the I.G. Farben labs employ latent hindbrain psi powers to map a three-dimensional set from one time-plane to another) Munich was

this enormous plane. He could see the yellow machines, articulated like insects, swarming around the leviathan, hauling it out of the black swamp. Black mud stuffed in its gun bays. Dockyard cranes, massive government tractors straining in the flat plane of Passchendale mud against the suck of the black swamp. Scientists in their shiny white suits, shouting excitedly above the clicking of their geiger-counters, smelling burned flesh through their filter masks. Let's get this show on the road . . .
Staring at the tailplane twenty feet above them

He turns the television off, walks over to the window and stares out of it. The avenue is empty now of everyone. The streetlight nearest him flickers. It is just enough to illuminate the white smoke pouring out of the chimney of the hospital furnace. Through the curtainless windows, he can see the institutional yellow of the ward walls. Above the hospital the sky has cleared after the storm, and the stars are shining hard and bright in the sky. His eyes focus on infinity.

This is the white lake beneath the white sky, cold and pure, filled with clear light. The white lake and the white sky, and between them the black trees. The flat black trees on the window glass, inverted on the retina. Move. The black trees move slowly to the invisible tide of thin winter wind beneath the white sky above the frozen white lake. Nothing stirs, there is no sound, just the black trees at the lake edge.

There are bodies in the ice. People, embedded in the ice. Faces. Stare. Faces stare upwards, out of the ice, at the black trees moving

at the end of the lake, before the endless white sky begins.
This is the place Christ's blood froze solid.

The face, falling, finds the hands, waiting.

I do not know says the Great Bell of Bow . . .

My love,

Every night my need becomes sharper. The flesh they burned off me in the crematorium still aches. The wind has carried me all over the earth, I am lying supine in the lungs of so many people now. But I reassemble myself every night, in my black nightgown, with a butcher's knife in my hands. Tonight I will reach your door, turn the handle, and glide over to where you are sleeping. Please wait for me. And be sure to be asleep. Or you'll spoil my surprise!

All my love, always,

Katerina S.

Here comes the candle to light you to bed . . .

Staring out of the window, it seems to him that snow begins to fall out of the clear sky. Great fat flakes drift down out of the dark, land on his hair and eyelashes. He catches one on his tongue, and tastes ash. Flakes of ash are falling from the chimney of the hospital furnace. This is the place where they burned away Katerina Szasz's lungs. For some reason they also gave her a hysterectomy in the operating theatre, and her womb, too, went into the fire. He remembers the thin dying sterile body of his only love gasping in the oxygen tent, and he remembers the oven.

Here comes the chopper to chop off your head . . .

He feels the first pull of sleep on his limbs. He feels the ice whiten around him. He lights his fourteenth cigarette, tasting the fur of the previous thirteen on his teeth. Then the pain in his chest. All around him, ash is falling. Katerina Szasz is coming with her hot paper-pale skin, and white flecks on her finger nails, and ashes matted in her hair, in his eyes . . .

This is the frozen lake, where the bodies locked in the ice stare at each other. A thin winter wind. Bloody kleenex tissue, dry stiff as wedding carnations, scatter themselves over the ice. Because we lost faith. Because we lost our shape. Because we forgot the shape of God. The men and women digging in the white mud where nothing can grow, endlessly burying and re-burying charred limbs, minds filled by the engine roar of the plane of death. Every morning after waking, the knowledge of what was happening fell over the bedroom like the endless folds of white silk from a failed parachute, covering the room in clean white light, in which everything was clear. Katerina would begin coughing around about half past six, and continue until he brought her the cup of cheap, bitter coffee she could not begin the day without (grey translucent form drinking the first and shuddering colour into thawing flesh). He would rise around ten o'clock, eat his breakfast, empty the ashtrays, and read the paper in the front room where the furniture smelled of stale smoke. When he found out about Katerina's illness he took a sabbatical from his job in the senior management of a small firm making chemical filters for the Army's new Crusher class main battle tank. To look after her.

From somewhere in the distance, he hears the sound of distant clicking, like dry bone tapping dry bone. Or high heels on marble. Katerina is wearing her shiny high-heeled shoes . . .

Katerina would be properly awake around noon, sitting up in bed alternating oxygenator with cigarette. He would sit with her, feeling numb. Making plans. Sweeping the bloody tissue papers out from under the bed. He thinks of a photograph he remembered seeing as a boy. A young girl inside a huge iron lung, looking up at a mirror angled in front of her. He remembers how much the iron lung looked like an oven. When he first began having wet dreams, one of the most persistently recurring images was the girl in the iron lung, with the temperature slowly increasing, she would begin rotating, naked, inside the machine. And Katerina Szasz, in transit from the womb to the oven, would look at him as his head reappeared from under the bed with her vast grey eyes . . . north sea eyes, lined with white spray . . .

From the landing outside his door, the clicking becomes louder.

From somewhere off in the distance, he hears the Moonlight Sonata. The windows are opaque with ashes.

A dying member of a dying species, Katerina lay in the big double bed and stared upwards towards the shadows of the black trees moving on the white ceiling. Or at the mirrors behind her eyes. I'm half sick of shadows, she would say, looking at him over her knitting and smiling. As the days passed, it became harder and harder to smile back. Towards the end of her sickness, she began knitting baby clothes: pink and blue woollen bootees, caps and mittens. He feels his pulse beginning to accelerate, and a light tingling in his right arm. He lights a cigarette.

The footsteps slow, and then stop outside his door.

We are the dead.

I have a plan, she said, and giggled. We move to the Shetland Islands and buy up the spring water rights. When they finally fuck it all up well and truly we can grow rich on our clean water empire. Thirty pence a glass, free from all artificial flavourings, preservatives, isotopes . . .

The door swings slowly open . . .

When they are all digging in the white earth under the sunless sky, turning over the charred limbs and shitting in the hope of fertility . . . extinction of a non-viable species . . .

. . . and Katerina Szasz walks in, dressed in short black skirt and black stockings. Her white thighs appear over the top. Her face is made up, painted thickly with stark black, red and white. Ashes are matted in her hair. She has the butcher's knife firmly grasped in one fist.

He stands still and waits. She walks up to him and tenderly inserts the knife into his heart. He holds the knife, guides its entry as she used to guide him into her when they fucked. He feels a real spurt of pleasure, the first for half a year, and falls back onto the bed. Katerina gently kisses his forehead and strokes his hair. The ashes fall around them like silent, sacred rain. Katerina dissolves into wedding confetti, blowing on the thin wind over the endless fields of winter stubble. The world bends over him, holds her dark cup a little closer. He bends to drink from it. The stars are shining as bright and hard as coffin nails. The garden wall cracks and the agony floods in like a black tide.

This is the landscape now:

Young, soft English rock, still shrugging off the Ice Age. A spring day, green fields of barley and rye stretch beneath the blue sky, and the drifting shadows of cumulus clouds. Cutting down through the rock, in incised meanders, is the black river.

He is floating down the black river. The little space between the lightless water and the bright air is where he breathes.

Standing along the bank of the river are figures wearing long white veils over their bodies. He can tell that their skin is dark. They look African. As he floats past them they begin to sing, wordlessly, the melody gets lost in the wind. Finally he reaches a wide, shallow stretch. The people are in a line across the river, and they catch him as he floats up to them.

One of the figures cups her hands and dips it in the black water. She holds her hands out to him. He drinks some of the black water from her cupped hands, and remembers no more.

TOMORROW IS OUR PERMANENT ADDRESS

Diane Rowe

Thursday

I went to the hairdresser's today. Took the morning off. Thank God for dear old PMT – if it can get some clever bitch off a murder charge, it can get me off the never-ending shelving of Mills and Boon. Not to mention all that battered psychedalia, looking like the cross between a flower-child's near-side door and armistice day, all in glorious technicolor, I might add. Oh, I wax quite lyrical on the subject, I can tell you. 'Any nice romances, dear,' they puff like a load of old radiators – same hot air, fag smoke and menthol. Husbands' ailments, their ailments – they've got stomachs slipping into their lungs, half of them have, or fish-paste jars of gall-stones in their handbags. And the underhand tone of it all – you'd think it was hardcore, not some 'Buck' prancing around in thermal underwear. They probably like them 'cos they wrap up warm, like they've told their husbands to do all their married lives to stop them from catching the rheumatism and sciatica that they've now already got. Anyhow, the nearest I'll ever get to a buck is a bucks fizz and I don't mean the pop group, either.

Steve moaned at the condition of my hair, as per usual – 'Too much henna and gel,' he says. 'Ruins the condition,' he says. 'Oh, eff the condition, I want style,' I think, but don't say. Not amongst all those plastic palms. Nor the mirrors. I wouldn't like to see myself swear. Not in twelve-licate, or whatever you'd call it. Just as bad as in Miss Selfridge where I saw myself twelve times in a black and white dress (too small) looking for all the world like a startled zebra in a David Attenborough retake. There's no glamour in that place — it's all plasticised mesh and neon — the nearest I've seen to that in the outside world is a dishrack-drainer. Mind you, that's the world where those things will be seen.

'I've got a new dress, Kev.'

'Really.'

'Well, look at it, then.'

'That must have cost a packet.'

'Only fifteen ninety-nine, down Miss Selfridge. To go with me black jacket.'

'And your elephant's backside.'

I can hear Kev and Debbie at it now. Then she'd be in my room half the night, after she's left pinching herself and staring at herself and vowing never to eye another Mars Bar again and nicking my aerobics book and giving up sugar for the umpteenth time and swearing to devote the rest of her life to exercise and hard-boiled eggs.

'I don't know why I stick him. Fat arse. *He's* the one with the fat arse. I don't need him making comments.'

Thank God for liberation. Et cetera. Et cetera.

Still, I won't be trapped like her. Or be selling insurance. She dreams about him, no doubt, on the A1 in between trying to flog life assurance to unsuspecting academic innocents. Then stops for coffee and compares overdrafts with the wise ones.

But I mustn't talk about Debbie. This is my diary. If she wants to talk about her life, she must write her own. I was merely using her as an example of what I will not be like when I'm twenty-one. No way. No, no, no.

Freedom's the important thing. I suppose I am free in the library — no one cares what I say, what I do, what I wear (though the brilliant pink stretch '50 pants combined with two-tone mock-croc stilettoes with pom-poms of gen-u-ine mink with added day-glolime green silky socks caused a bit of a stir with the Head Librarian, I must confess). Still on the whole the atmosphere is liberal, verging on the apathetic. I've got my own pay packet, which is more than I'd have if I'd stayed on at school like they'd said. They wrote a snotty little sentence at the bottom of my reference saying that I was wasting my considerable academic potential by entering employment in this early, not to say crucial, stage of my development and that I ought to buy a new sixth-form uniform, graduate with my ciggies from the cloakroom to the plusher comforts of the sixth-form loos with their Parker-Knoll-style reclining sanitary-towel disposal-unit seating and continue to assimilate useless facts. That sentence took a lot of explaining away at the library interview, I can tell you. It almost lost me my job. Thank God the Head Librarian had a nodding acquaintance with the concept of Liberty. She went by train around Europe once and had it off with a Yugoslav defector whom she had found concealed without a passport on the luggage rack of a third-class compartment, behind a shabby canvas bag which she happened to own. She still sends him a card at Christmas, I believe – some bilingual offering from UNICEF that preached international unity. But I digress. I was talking about Freedom, I believe, and the lack of it at school, where my tendency to warble on was seldom prized. Home wasn't much better, so I left. This is just for the record; when I'm old and grey I might forget my motivation for moving to a bottle-green papered flat with cold and cold running water which has the distinct appearance of a mid-western free-standing letter-box. The flat, I mean, not the water. To Hell with precision, this is only a diary.

Yes, Steve and I agreed on the importance of Freedom all right. We were talking about the General Election and all that crap. Some political bloke had just emerged from under the driers and inspired Steve to wax lyrical on that rather crucial point. He said, with his all-American smile, that, if he was ethically sound, in my position of liberty that he would vote marxist. I looked vaguely puzzled and said that I would vote SDP because I didn't want any changes, thank you very much. I had my fair share when Dad went off with Nikki, who was into everything that anyone ought to be into, including martial arts and geisha arts, and had everything that ought to be had, according to the local fashions of the time, including my father and a methane-operated Swedish sausage-stuffer.

Saturday

Debbie's away this weekend, so I've got the flat to myself. I had a lovely lazy morning – it not being my library day – breakfasted on Tesco's croissants, black cherry jam and calorie-controlled margarine and left crumbs on the sheets. Going to the laundrette today, so who cares. Had Louis Armstrong on full blast until neighbours bashed on ceiling, then changed disc to rock and roll — more suitable. They've got no taste. Had a vigorous solo dance work out, marred by interference of bedside table. Mail arrived. Several agencies could be run by Katrina Hawkins (Miss) if she happened to be over eighteen and fancied selling Snoopy necklaces or boxed sets of last year's hit singles.

Went to flea market and came back with a fox fur wrap with a rabid glare, a skirt stiffener and, best of all, a valve radio with a sunburst all over the loud-speaker. Sounded weird with Radio One coming out of it. I put it by my palette-shaped table beneath the plaques of ducks and teddy girls' heads.

'Why do you buy all that crappy old junk?'

I can hear Debbie saying it now. Still, I don't care. Individualists are never popular, but *I'm* going to set my own trends. Right here in a grotty flat and a Local and District library, Katrina D. Hawkins will hit the world.

That looks a bit childish, now I come to think of it. You can think all those kind of things but not say them, it seems to me. All the stars must think they're God's gift but they keep damn quiet about it in public. Even in their diaries. You just think of it — they'd be telling their life story to some po-faced old guy with a tape-recorder, reading from their old diaries, on automatic pilot as it were when, wham bang: 'I really feel God's biorhythms were on the up and up when he made me, dear diary . . .' Good God, it doesn't bear thinking about; that facet of their super-star image that's anti-drugs, anti-porn, loves seals and directs old ladies through heavy traffic would be in for instant liquidation on the front page of the *Sun,* the *Mail*, the *Star*, or whatever. Even *The Times* or the *Guardian* might get a whiff of it somewhere. Under the obituaries, perhaps.

So that's enough of the proposed fame of Katrina D. Hawkins (Ms). The 'D' stands for Demelza, by the way. My mother, who had never been nearer to Cornwall than a caravan at Weston-super-Mare, also had a weakness for thermal-clad gents, provided the said were genuine eighteenth-century. Ross Poldark was her man — hence my middle name. I'd have preferred Marlene (Mum's middle name) after Marlene Dietrich. More my sort of fantasy — all gloves, rocks, gowns, furs, cigarette-holders and satin sheets.

Blindfold the band and cha cha 'till dawn, that sort of thing. Only that was later.

Talking of which, there's a black-and-white Saturday matinee on BBC 2. Much more fun than writing diaries.

Sunday Lunchtime

I feel bloody awful. Haven't drunk that much in a long while. Walked back from the Wine Bar with Hazel singing 'Basin Street Blues'. Jazz band fantastic. Cocktails better than usual. Thank God for this evening job; my overdraft is putting on weight. Manager stood me a drink as I'll be 'Staff' next week, as it were.

The 'phone woke me up. It was Debbie from some University JCR. She'd been propositioned by another Oxbridge reject and had the pleasure of telling him to piss off. In addition to which, Kev has proposed again and she's been stupid enough to accept. Hello, Milton Keynes. I'd have thought that she'd have had sense enough to leave things as they were.

Sunday, Later

So, Debbie'll soon be off in a flurry of orange blossom. I've been getting used to the prospect of all-change. It'll be strange having another flat-mate who lives here all the time. It'll be Eighties inside, not Forties-Fifties. And the potted palm in the sitting-room'll be for the chop. No doubt my room will be surprised by a coup from Interflora when the palm leaves get too dense. Maybe I could donate it to the library.

I'll have to take the bloody female out for a drink, I suppose. More expense. Friday perhaps. There's jazz every night, of a sort, but it's live Fridays and Saturdays. On Wednesdays the band's in a pub back room. I go there too. It's really great. But the Wine Bar's the best by far. The cellar: chocolate brown with sofas all puffy and tucked like cornish pasties, except they're in glazed cotton — gold shooting stars or blue and pink bucket roses. And there's stars on the lampshade too, except they're pacifists. They don't shoot, they just sit there on this milk glass saucer thing and look like something from an Odeon lounge. And everyone hangs about in groups, all dressed up; the real poseurs hang over the staircase smoking French fags and looking cool. It's really loud — those sax notes get you and just pin you to the wall and the bass sound seems to frisk you and kick to death all that's not jazz music and you see heavy, treacle-black rivers, wrought iron and shuttered rooms; there are blokes in a hot back kitchen that stinks of gin and drains, who don't care a shit that they're trapped and repressed, filthy dirty, dead sick, 'cos they're playing jazz music. Then you lose all that – I mean, who wants words and pictures when they've got real music? It takes you and fills you and you want to laugh and cry and scream and dance all at the same time and you can't stand its heat and you think you'll float, or faint, or die, be torn apart by the music.

An Hour Later

I think this last note is right. And it's important that it's right. Just for the record. Debbie says I go and listen 'cos I want to get laid. I told her what to do with her theory, in no uncertain terms. To be fair, diary, that music turns me on, but it takes more than that. More than marriage. More than love. I don't believe in love. Not 'till I get something real out of it. You can trip over an Oscar or a pink Cadillac when you get out of bed in the morning and I'm sure they'd give you a darn sight more fun than love.

Wednesday

I wonder whether I'll keep this thing going. There doesn't seem to be anything to say and yet it's remarkable the amount of time you can spend talking about nothing. Library today, same as ever. Packed lunch upstairs as couldn't afford to eat elsewhere. Propped a biography against my Totally Tropical Passionfruit, Pecan Nut and Guava Yoghurt (this month's new flavour). Foul muck. Give me chocolate yoghurt anyday. Or just straight chocolate. But, anyway, I was reading this book so Mrs McCluskie wouldn't talk to me about her daughter who's on the verge of failing all her exams. I don't like to listen because I feel sorry for daughter McCluskie who's nobody's fool and probably battling between her image and a sense of despair at the big trap we've got ourselves into. 'There's no point in working,' I tell her in the little chats that we have in my head, 'They'll get you to spend more and more of your time swallowing all that academic stuff, then when you've had enough time to conform and lose your pride, they'll pick and pick and give you more and more and say that you ought to be grateful to be torn apart and given next to no praise, 'cos you're doing it all for self-improvement. Well, I don't need to self-improve,' I tell her (that is, daughter McCluskie), 'I know *I'm* bright — I could do it all if I didn't want to be a slave.' And a slave is what you are if you're a 'good girl'.

Mind you, we're all slaves. The boredom of this place is slavery. But there were some slaves that worked until they dropped, mind and body, and some just did what they had to to get by and they played jazz and I'm one of those slaves. And so, I believe, is daughter McCluskie. But I don't want to hear about her today. I want to read about this bloke Nijinsky.

It's amazing how many books I've read to avoid having to talk. Real people, I've discovered, do have interesting lives, but they're part of a minority group, to say the least. It's faces that interest me, thanks to my artistic nature. I've got his face in front of me now, neatly clipped out of the book with toe-nail scissors. It's beautiful. You can't say it's beautiful for a man, because he doesn't look like one. You can just say he looks beautiful as Nijinsky. That makes him dangerously un-Cadillac-ish and abstract, a sense that's increased by the fact that he's dead. Fortunately his non-existence makes it easier to ignore his undoubted charm.

Wednesday 3.12 a.m.

Tom cat yowling in the dustbins again. Sounds like either Bob or Mr. Tumnus.

It occurred to me to wonder why I want to be free and individual and yet am frightened of someone else who succeeded in the same game (i.e. Nijinsky).

I am agonizing again and I must stop. It stops me from sleeping and I heard on Debbie's portable that you must sleep well to ensure a good chance of survival over the age of sixty-five.

Wednesday 3.32 a.m.

Cat still at it, worse luck. I'd stone it if I had the energy. I am, in the immortal words of Mrs McCluskie, more talk than do, and, I might add, more think than talk.

Returning to the subject of Nijinsky, am I a hypocrite?

Thursday

Today I saw a French film: flat land with poplar trees, cellars of pickled vegetables (probably onions) in little farm houses set back from the road and the hero as a boy fishing very quietly with his friend's family in a boat on a sunlit lake. She had very fat, pale grey plaits (probably meant to be blonde). Then he grew up and fell in love with his friend, yet proceeded to have an affair with her brother. And her mother had seduced him years before. Then everything became very complicated.

At lunchtime the jazz band were busking in the square. Of course crowds of people were listening. The whole town felt alive because they were playing and I sat and listened and clapped. I thought I'd got blisters, but I hadn't. And they played my favourite songs — the ones that make me think, my God, they've captured Life; instead of all my thoughts tearing around inside my head, just crashing about and getting everything all mucked up, they're pinned down by some song until they're not frightening any more, like a raging bull turned into a sandwich.

I got a notelet from Mum through the post today. She says, will I come up to London for Karen's confirmation? Karen's got a lovely new saint's name and the Priest asked if I would be coming. The weather in London is close for the time of year, Mum's blood pressure is as good as can be expected and the tortoise is well.

Stuff it.

My confirmation was an utter disaster area. Mum had asked me what I wanted for a present and I said I'd like the carving that Dad did of the hare. Mum said 'No' because she'd lost Dad by this time and didn't want to lose his bunny into the bargain. She said there had been something special between her and Dad which I couldn't share and that the hare had been part of this, so I couldn't have it and would have to put up with a silver St. Christopher instead. In reply to which I said to myself: 'Well, if I can't bloody have it, no one else will,' and smashed the wretched thing, and that put paid to both the St. Christopher and the Special Treat to Battersea Fun Fair.

All in all today was a day of non-action. Weather very close here, as well as in London. Atmosphere like a duvet. Flowering cherries flowering in the pavements. Went to see Mike at the Wine Bar to discuss terms; library won't be pleased when they hear I'm holding down two jobs. Had to cross a part of town where nothing flowers. Wine Bar similarly bleak; thank God we only talked upstairs, not down in the cellar – I couldn't bear to see my favourite place silent, swabbed down and empty. Work sounds monotonous and hard. I went home wondering, for the umpteenth time, whether anything will ever happen to me. I remember Debbie telling me that at the grand old age of twenty-one she has given up asking that question. Personally, I am not surprised – the answer would get her down.

* * *

I have not written this diary for some weeks. I have been working a lot at the Wine Bar and I think to myself as I wash up out the back, surrounded by rancid corks and fly-blown cheesecake, how funny it is that it is the musician that has the skill, yet he couldn't be famous without his instrument.

When I have not been getting dish-pan hands, I've been getting to know the band, especially Nick and John (Sax and Bass respectively). Free wine and cheesecake were vital in this respect, at first, but are no longer entirely necessary. In fact I stay on drying up because of the time I keep spending remarking to myself how Nick looks more like Nijinsky than anyone else could, except the true, and dead, original.

It's easy to talk to Nick. We agree about everything, particularly his talent.

These days all-American Steve could wander in wearing nothing but a three-piece tattoo without lighting the warning light in my blood pressure. I wouldn't be trampled to death in the rush, I'd just be making my ten per cent selling brandy for the wounded. I've got better things to do with my time. I'm very dedicated these days, I've discovered, darling diary, vowing myself to the study of Nick's technique, watching him making love to his sax and wishing that I was his instrument.

Monday

The little bleepy pen thing at the library broke. Had to use the rubber stamp and it sounded like soft, soft lips and all the readers' eyes were his eyes.

I didn't feel quite real coming home. It was that drained, coming-out-of-a-weepie-matinee-on-a-Saturday-afternoon, eye-aching feeling.

It all seemed inflated and the shops gently swayed when the lorries passed, like the back-cloth of an old movie.

Perhaps at some point during the day I have died and been re-incarnated one step nearer to that extra-terrestrial orgasm (what I assume to be the Buddhist's idea of heaven).

Spilt Instant Whip all down myself at tea. Debbie said I was a pathetic moonstruck moron who'd be a darn sight better off when the whole silly packet fell through, as it was bound to do according to the laws of nature – laws which Debbie thinks she knows quite well thanks to a D in Biology O Level. She said she knew that I was going to the seaside with the band on Saturday but that was only busking (which is begging jazzed up) and was hardly a thousand-pound honeymoon trip to Honolulu even if I was just going with the one I wanted, but if I was going with the whole crowd of them it was bloody stupid and a waste of money. I couldn't go out with all of them at once and what were the rest of them going to do on Saturday, if it wasn't a rude question, play the bloody background music? Not that there would be any need for it, she said, pummelling her teabag. That Nick was a dead loss, if I knew what she meant. If I had to behave in my present moronic fashion over anyone it could at least be over someone sensible.

The trouble with Debbie is that she's prejudiced – some people hate Parkis, some people hate women . . . and Debbie hates Nick. God knows why.

Tuesday

By the frozen food counter I thought: 'One day, I'd like a kitchen with curly wrought-iron bar stools and lacquered walls. Pillar-box red. And a black bathroom with mirrors and ferns, overlooking a London park. I'd buy my fish from Harrods, fresh from the ice. And Nick would perform at a club with a revolving stage and I would sit, spotlit, in a slick black number with contrasting pink hair, pink champagne.

Stayed in all evening to set hair.

Saturday

Murky day, so the place's ice-cream-sucking, pinball-playing, bingo-blaring image was rather muted. Dog walkers everywhere with sticks and sandy turn-ups. They probably double up as flashers in their spare time, when they're not trying to kid their spaniels to dash into the sea after stones.

Place fading around the edges. Amusement arcade has a fairground's surface – slick optimism. It's the outskirts that are dying – the rockeries, the cliff walks, the Thirties open-air dance floors and beach huts – fading blues and greens under rotting sunbursts.

I said to Nick: 'Don't they know there's a revival on?'

'Revivals are just for evenings. People don't take them seriously.' Usual little cough as he lit up.

'But I take them seriously.'

'More fool you. I used to. John used to. It was bad, so negative. We didn't build anything, living in the past. You ought to *build* . . .'

I said I didn't want to build. I knew what I wanted for the future but how was I to get it. You can only dream one day you'll wake up and it'll all be better. How could I *build* all the things I wanted?

'Want less.'

'I *can't*, I'm not defeatist. Don't be stupid.'

He told me not to sulk. It would spoil my face. It was a calm sort of remark, in the tone he used to John about my profile the other week, when he moved my head like an ornament on a stand. The thrill I had expected never came; I felt I hadn't been touched by him at all.

Saturday Night? Sunday Morning?

Went straight out to a party with Debbie. Two-up, two-down, stereo screaming, plastic cups and baked potatoes everywhere. Atmosphere like a sex-starved sardine can: inhabitants pickled yet struggling. The bedroom had filled up long ago – armchairs bulged with moaning, laddered, plastered inhabitants.

I almost threw up at the thought of another night of going through the whole goddam routine on some coats, in the bog, on the sofa, in the corner.

The front door was swinging (the last one at the party dancing) and I fought my way outside. It was cool. Clear. Smattering of stars. The last bus had gone. All the dogs had been walked. All the drunks had sung themselves to sleep. I must be getting soft in my old age or I would have stayed. Indian take-away on the Ring Road open. Stayed there for an hour before going home, eating a curry, and I wish I could have watched the telly. I would even have watched the testcards; I know that girl's face by heart now. I wonder who she loves.

Definitely Sunday Morning

I wrote 'love' in this book last night. I make myself sick. I must snap out of this or it will all end up in complications and messes. Think of Mum or of French films. They end up in crime passionel, drowning like flies in what seems to be a particularly sticky-sounding foreign pudding.

Maybe if I live with Nick (in a purely realistic and practical manner) and he gets famous, I'll come off the pill. Even if he did chuck me, pregnancy in such a position would be a kind of autograph.

What happened last night shook me. I can't be as grown-up as I thought. People in the library, pampered people my age, look like, act like kids. I'm no kid, but there's something inside, like a baby, only it's me. Me as I was, bobbing about inside like my own baby. Sometimes it looks out of my eyes and uses my brain, then everything looks weird and big and important and scary. And every time I'm mauled and sucked and chewed and worried it gets squashed and cries, especially when some bloody great prick shoots up and jabs it. I used to ignore it, hope it would go away. Thought it was something about me that was sick and pathetic and didn't want to be made good by experience. Now I reckon that, if I don't disturb it, it'll fall asleep and sleep so long that it never wakes up. Nick doesn't disturb it. Blues rock it to sleep.

Tuesday

Very gentle evening. Sky ice-cream sundae pink — I remember it clearly several hours later — it keeps leering before me when I try to think of something else. Yes, a sky of ice-cream sundae rose, pink as the tinned salmon, pink as the strawberry jam, pink as the packet of fondant fancies that were spread out on the lawn before them at John's house. It was a nice house. There was a road of houses just like it with thin gardens, wire fences and roses and tubs. The odd mangled fruit tree, old car. Plenty of kids riding bikes. Just an average road, in fact. Nothing ought to have happened there. I ought not to have opened the gate, rung the bell, got no answer, gone to the back garden gate because it was sunny in a dying sort of way and they might have been outside. I ought not to have seen it. Why didn't Nick say?

My personal belief is it ought not to have happened. It was wrong, perverted, filthy, intense and tranquil, exclusive, *unfair*. And then to have the cheek to invite me in for coffee. Proper coffee, not even instant granules shaken into a mug by a diseased and guilty hand. 'Love a Cat,' the mug proclaimed. Well, I might as well. Why not indulge in a little tea-time bestiality — everyone else was sinning. Only the cat as likely wouldn't take me — I would wander in and see it in the arms of another woman.

They'll teach me the sax, though. I'll get that much out of them. One step on the stairs.

Nick didn't like playing in the Wine Bar. He was looking forward to going to London to a serious club that would appreciate good music. They would buy a house.

On the way home the sky was bloody, clammy. There was an unpleasant proliferation of lovers, probably brought out by the lovely weather. Bloody lovely. Bloody, bloody, bloody . . . nice, round words. Nice simple words. Nothing complicated, nothing complicated that makes you feel like that French film's mixed-up hero's girlfriend.

Stopped off at the church on the way home for the first time and prayed for hours. I'll go to Mass every Sunday from now on. I'll haunt the confessionals. I even lit a candle. I wondered how my sister's confirmation went. Maybe I ought to go back home to London. Why's everyone making close relationships (even Karen and God) and me left on my own with the priest and the church and sodding, burning, praying candles.

Life seems very empty now. So cool, so very cool. So cool that it's almost hot, like very cold hands beneath a cold running tap. There's nothing to get up for so I stayed in bed all day until I got a headache. Got up and smoked, drank endless black coffees and finished up the cooking sherry. I've got through twenty-one and a half tissues in one and a half days, yet have no cold. Is this a record?

A FREEBORN MAN

Philippa Tyson

Michael Fleck. Born: November 23, 1924, Cushendall, County Antrim. In the North of Ireland; not the Republic, no; British citizen Michael Fleck, who fought no British wars.

Why should he? He would like to know. The '50s decade of his life was always asking, and for why? Because he spent those years in Dublin, romancing and working when he could, which seemed to be that much more sensible to be sure. And why should he let himself be shot at because the English did not understand the Nazi need for domination, when they themselves — God knew it — were a powerful lot worse. They talked about the Jews now. Still talked about them. What about the Irish then? And what about Lord Cromwell, that hero of the people, who slaughtered as Lord Hitler did without the gas? That was what Michael Fleck would like to know.

Sometimes.

When he thought about it.

The rain fell steadily from a grey sky. Michael's room was green with damp and the window leaked, so that the monotonous drip onto the floorboards had the sound of drops in puddles. Michael lay on his mattress which was fairly dry. He kept it away from the walls and window. The large Regency window, rotten and warped, through which he could see the Anglican Cathedral and see the Huns attend their nationalised services.

Everything in England was bloody nationalised, even their damn religion, may Holy Mary and All The Saints forgive them.

Michael had watched the rain since dawn. His overcoat collar was turned up against the cold which hugged his face and fingers.

He had nothing to burn in his grate: the day's collection had yet to be made; and, anyway, the rain was coming down the chimney; nothing would burn there in a while.

Michael's face was hard. His eyes were blank, as if hypnotised and without instruction. He was still; had learned that movement in the rain only got a body wetter, and if he concentrated he did not feel the cold.

Although it would be worse outside, rain down his collar and nowhere to shelter, Michael knew he must go out. His first movement was a sigh. The dank air of his room filtered his lungs and made him cough. His second movement. Next he shivered and swung his legs over onto the floor.

He stayed in this position for a while looking at the wall, his eyes roving across the peeled wallpaper, the fungus patches and the lichen which grew there. Sometimes he felt this room a cave, when the bats above the wardrobe drifted in and out of his window on heavy summer evenings.

There was nothing in the room apart from the mattress, an old sack, the grate and the empty wardrobe. There had been a chair once, but Michael had needed a fire more, his leg being bad and all. The wardrobe was saved for another such occasion.

'How long you lived 'ere then?' had asked a native of Liverpool who had moved into another room the other week.

Michael had frowned. 'I don't rightly know,' his ageing voice had lilted, 'To be sure, it's been a while.' The sound of the Glens stayed with Mr. Michael Fleck and for that he was grateful.

How long? he mused now, staring at his wall. It would be running into years since he came to work in the docklands which were now Pierhead and a museum. Years and years. 'Late Sixties, was it, Michael?' he asked himself, his Irish blue eyes dark as speedwell staring beyond the wall. Come only for a wee while, time enough for a skeedle and two biscuits, he had thought: and now he was still here, a ferry ride from Belfast.

He had thought about moving on when the council cut the water off, until he had found a way to track down the stop-tap and turn it all back on. Water was God's drink, and Michael could not see why a body had to pay for something that fell from the heavens. If the council wished to poison it, to be sure Michael Fleck saw no call for him to pay to make it clean again. And no one came to the house again. More water was lost in the leaking mains than the men of Michael's house could ever use.

'If we showered and bathed all day,' murmured Michael, as he turned to watch the rain fall through his window.

Perhaps it was time to move on. There were better houses left forlorn in this God-forsaken city; houses where the back-doors hung on rotting frames and where to enter was to break nothing that nature had not spoiled already.

There were times when he thought of returning to the Antrim Coast, to the peace and tranquillity of an Ireland north of the Troubles and south of geological tourists; where the hills of the Glens rose high behind the sea. The Irish Sea.

But the same water flowed past Liverpool, and although the English city was far from being home, Michael Fleck had only vague yearnings to cut short his visit.

Michael sighed again. The shock was not so great this time and he got up. For a man in late middle age Michael was older. His shoulders were broad and still strong from his labouring days, when he had worked the harbours of Belfast and Dublin, spent time in Larne and climbed the hills above Carnlough to the High Lakes, as people named the bogland mires. But in their strength they bent slightly, from the weight of misspent pride.

'Ah, Michael Fleck,' his mother had said, as some mothers will, 'whatever will become of your wilful ways, son?'

Nothing had come of them.

Michael flung the sack into the puddle by the window and watched its edges darken. Then he turned to his door, which rested slightly open, and began his slow walk out, down the stairs, through the side-door and into the steady torrent.

On the street he met a fellow dweller. There was a loathing of names among his people; Michael himself was known only as The Irishman, a title which lacked the familiarity of Brass, or Knocker, or Rudolph — as some dwellers were known — and which pleased Michael. Now. It had taken a while to get used to his distinct nationality.

'Hello there,' said Michael, without enthusiasm. 'Any luck?'

The fellow dweller was a Liverpudlian who had lost all his front teeth at an early age, and who spat slightly with any word he uttered. Not that that mattered in the rain.

'Luck? Well it depends what yous call luck really, doesn' i'?'
'I suppose so, lad, aye,' replied Michael.
'I suppose you'll be wantin' stuff to burn yeh?' the toothless dweller went on.
'That was the general intention,' Michael answered. His hand went to his chest in reply to a sudden pain.
'You'll have to be watchin' that chest, mate,' said his friend, 'yous don't want to be stuck another winter, now do yous?'
'Indeed not, lad, indeed not,' Michael's voice struggled against the pain.
'Are yous okay?' The friend put out his hand and laid it carefully on Michael's shoulder. 'I can get your gear for you, man, if you're not feeling so good.'
Michael appreciated the help, but was not in great need right then: 'It's all right, lad,' he said, 'I'll be just grand in a minute. You go on ahead there before you have to wring yourself out.'
'I'll be gettin' on then, if you're sure I can do nothing. Watch yourself all-ri'?' The toothless dweller went on his way through the rain.
Michael did not move. The pain in his chest burned. The same pain as the last time, and that ended up as pneumonia, God help him. 'Ach 'tis just fear, Michael Fleck,' he said aloud, 'fear is all it will be. Pain is a terrible thing, terrible.' His eyes closed against the terrible thing for a moment. Then he forced himself to straighten against his fear, turned his head away from the Anglican Cathedral so that the Hun would have no cause to blight him, and walked on.
Instead of going down to the office blocks where the building and demolition work guaranteed something for a fire, Michael carried on down Hope Street to the modern Cathedral. It had shocked him at first that such a thing of concrete could hold the flame and a chapel to the Blessed Virgin. For years he had refused to go up the steps. And, when he had gone in, he had kept his eyes tight shut for fear of a monstrous conspiracy of ugliness to drown his faith.
But the light through the windows was a Christian blue and such a sight as Michael sat down on the back row and marvelled. The great wheel of the Church pivoted around the central altar, towards which Michael had bent a stiff knee and blessed himself before leaving. He had sat an hour in the peace of the place, maybe

more. And when he had come out, that first time, the world had been beautiful.

This time however he was not expecting such enlightenment. He had got friendly with one of the ladies in the tea-shop who was not above slipping him the odd cup and bun. Michael felt the need of a place bright and warm. Perhaps he could slip his coat off if there were to be enough room. In the winter months the dwellers did not wash at all, and Michael was enough of a gentleman to know that amid the hygiene of Cathedral visitors such realities would be likely to put folk off their teas.

He was drenched by the time he walked through the double doors and down the stairs to the basement. Mary Dougan was there with her flaming red hair and her rough red hands.

'So there you are, Michael Fleck,' she said to him quietly, but with her eyes flaring, 'and there was me wondering whether you'd died in the last fortnight.'

'I've been busy, Mary, wile busy I have,' said Michael, his eyes twinkling at her mock anger.

'And what have you to be busy with, Michael Fleck? That's what I'd like to know. Angels and Saints preserve us, keeping alive, I shouldn't wonder. You not even signing on the brew either. It's a fair wonder the Good Lord doesna take you from us as I speak.'

'And hows about a hot skeedle o' tae, Mary Dougan, before your words make the Good Lord wonder,' said Michael, quieting the woman, because for sure she made him restless with her talking.

Mary Dougan made a clicking noise with her tongue, rolled her eyes to heaven and went off to find something for this contrary loafer, in the name of Christian charity. She often wondered why she did not just let him starve, she surely did not.

Michael decided it was best to keep his coat on. The water brought out the natural smell on a man better than anything, except perhaps heat. The two together, Michael knew, would be too much for even Mary Dougan to bear. The coat from Help the Aged was thick enough to exude mainly its own odour. And Mary was wont to say that that was quite enough.

So Michael sat in the far corner of the tea-room away from heat or people or draughts and watched folk come and go and never notice the old Irishman tucked away. He sat there some time, watching. In the daytime they were mostly women with small children; sometimes there were men who were fed-up with their old haunts and who had long since given up the idea of a job. They were people with homes and families: Michael could pick out a home and family from two hundred paces.

Mary kept him supplied with tea and sugar and the trimmed left-overs from other people's plates. Michael was quite happy. It would mean he did not have to go to the charitable ladies with their soup and questions for at least another day. Mary was a good woman.

A group of students came in. Michael knew they were students from the way they draped their scarves and laughed a taint too loudly. They would be gone from the city in a year or so, gone and out. Was always the same; the young ones always left. And why should they stay? Had not he, Michael, done exactly the same thing when he left Ireland?

Not the same, no. They was British wars being fought in Belfast then: the Troubles were just British wars and Michael Fleck wanted no part of that. Not the smallest part. Ireland would always be his home, across the water — 'Going across the water then, Michael-boy?' he remembered the voices asking. Across the water aye he had come. No one asked the Irishman now whether he would go back: no dweller could go back. No. Across the water Michael Fleck would remain.

Michael's eyes had narrowed and he hardly saw the group. Quite suddenly he focussed on one of their number, a young girl with bright hair and dancing eyes. Michael bent forward against the pain which struck his lungs. The vision swam. He was surely to pass out. He struggled to focus again. To see clearly. Terrified that the lass would leave before he could. 'Holy Mary Mother of God,' he murmured.

He sat up slowly. The girl was still there, laughing with her friends. Steam rose from her cup and Michael felt he could almost warm his hands on it. He was quite bewildered by her face. It was almost twenty years since he had seen a face like that, and then on a wee lass half his age.

What loving they had had in that summer twenty years before. And how Michael Fleck had wanted the young woman for his bride as well as bed. And how he had never told her.

Michael felt a rush of warmth through his whole body and memories, put away for decades, tumbled through his mind. Not that his face showed anything: Irishmen never show their loving, no, not even from a reborn remembering.

But he felt it.

Remembered swinging his fair Lorna high when the beaches were empty and only the gulls were watching. Remembered waking beside her in the dove-grey dawn and watching her leave before any man was wake enough to see her. Remembered climbing the roads before Ballycastle to the forests there and tumbling with young Lorna like a puppy – and he a man of forty summers.

She had gone. Upped and left without a smile, or the briefest of farewells. Michael had never looked for her, nor ever seemed to miss her. His mother was not surprised, and was privately pleased that her son had been released from the wench: he had enough sisters to look after him when she passed on and God knew it was hard enough to keep her Michael from the paths of sin without cluttering his way with women.

Michael had watched for Lorna for many months, privately and completely unobtrusively: he would probably not have admitted it to himself, that he was doing anything of the kind. But every curly, chestnut mane made him frown slightly and any lassie with a spring in her step made him stop a minute and look back. Such was the love of Michael Fleck.

'But it was no love,' he insisted now, in the tea-room of Liverpool Cathedral. To love Lorna would mean he had lost Lorna, and Michael had not been close to anything in his life enough to lose it. Mislay it maybe. He viciously chortled at the pun when attached to Lorna. No. She had gone and good luck to her. His life was easier without the shackles of those temptresses. He muttered heavenly thanks and blessed himself.

But his eyes would still wilfully watch the young girl with Lorna's laugh, and Lorna's hair. He could not help thinking that the child must be around nineteen.

Child. So Lorna had been a child too, had she? Michael, you were a wicked man. Old enough to be her daddy so you were when you took that wee one in your arms and held her tight. Michael smiled the smile of a father as he thought. Mary Dougan was surprised by his eyes when she brought his tea.

'And what will you be lookin' at, Michael Fleck?' she asked brusquely. 'You with the look of a woman on your face the like of which I'm ashamed to see on a grown man.'

'Hush your noise, Mary Dougan,' said Michael softly. 'Have I the look of a woman then? So I have. A bonny wee thing I knew a long time ago.'

Mary Dougan decided he was just suffering one of his turns and left him be. Getting to the age of rambling was Michael Fleck: not that he talked much, she could say that for him. Not like some of the old ones as came in here, no: talk the ears off a lugged jug they would in a hurry. But not Michael. Good man was Michael underneath all that gruffness: the Irishman. She shook her head in her what-will-the-world-come-to way and went back to her duties.

The girl had gone. Michael still stared at the space where she had been and felt stranger than he had done for many years. He did not feel homesick. Heaven knew he did not know for sure whether many of his sisters were alive or dead. He cared, but preferred not to know. Once a year, at Christmas, he would give Beatrice a call on Mary Dougan's telephone, and sure she would tell him if the clan survived. He regarded this Christmas as a possible shock: so far he had only been told of births and marriages, but God knew even a Fleck could not last forever.

Michael coughed. His chest was still hurting and there was no living Lorna to keep him from thinking on the pain. He could not untangle how he was feeling in himself, so he let it be and did not fret about it. That had worked before. Holy Mary, it would be sure to work again.

He wondered where the wee lass studied. Ach, it was more than his time was worth to go chasing after that pretty thing; he would probably get arrested for persecuting her.

That night his room was cold. He had got the rubbish to burn after he had left the Cathedral, but it had been too wet to catch; had only smoked and sputtered. His mattress too was damp: the puddle had quite saturated the sack; water travelled across the floor and climbed into Michael Fleck's bed, a trespass he did not forgive.

Most nights when the fire would not burn Michael slept straight away, whether his bed was wet or no. It made no difference. Quickest way of getting comfortable was to sleep, any dweller knew that. Sleep with your boots on and sleep damn well if you were half a man.

Was Michael half a man? In the light from the street-lamp he surveyed his hands, all cut and dry they were, filthy and blistered. They had seen too many winters. Michael thought about the time when they were tanned and leathered by sea air and sun; when they were the bravest hands in Dublin and he the handsome young protester from the North. He had broken a few hearts then and never thought twice about it.

The same hands now were broken, and he had not thought twice about that either until today. What, he wondered, would Lorna think of these paws? Would she let them touch her now? Now, when his whole body was so lived in it smelt of . . . smelt of a body? Had that been the reason she had left him?

No. He had not been half a man then. She had had no reason. Women's whims and wiles; Blessed Virgin, even she had had some.

Michael breathed slowly. He was not agitated, only saddened. He looked at his field of wall, at the patterns which changed as the overgrowth grew, and tried to recall his world where he owed nothing, paid nothing and relied on no man.

But it was hard when child Lorna would dance in his head.

He would go down to the university in the morning. Not that he expected anything, Heaven keep him, no. It had been a while since he had been there, and it did not do well to dwell in one place for too long. People he had not seen in a while were said to be down there these days, Old Toby and Todd to name two. And a body must see people to keep going. And the bushes would be dry there in some shelter: he could not go two days without a fire.

He stretched and curled. Tomorrow was decided then. He was not going to be seeing Mary Dougan, which was a good thing; the woman looked ready to be questioning him and that Michael Fleck would not bear. Another good reason to be going to the university. He might learn something.

Michael smiled at his joke.

And slept.

Washing in winter, Michael reflected, as he shook the water from his face, was a bad idea. The basement was cold, dark and cold with a smell of wet dust. Without soap Michael's ablutions were hardly satisfactory, but he had made the effort and felt virtuous.

He found his hair was thinning alarmingly: it straggled where once it had fallen in thick locks. The charitable ladies occasionally took their scissors to it, but otherwise it was left to the wind and any combing insects that might be passing. The charitable ladies could definitely keep their scissors to themselves in future.

He looked down at his clothes. Without his coat he did not look his best to be sure. He would go down to the clothes heap and look out some new trousers: a man could not go through his life with one pair of trousers now. Where is your pride, Michael Fleck? And his shirt. The collar had frayed away completely and the cuffs had rubbed his wrists raw. Ach, Michael, look at the state of you.

He straightened himself as best he could, which was not very well: 'If you were a pathway, Michael Fleck,' he told himself, 'you'd be weaving and winding all over the place.' Indeed he would. He brushed his coat down and was surprised by the persistence of the muck that clung to it. 'Never mind there,' he told himself, 'for sure you'll not be seeing the Queen on your travels.' Not that she would be much of a reason for Michael to be de-mucking himself.

Anyhow, he gathered himself together and set his shoulders for his walking out. It might have been a bright day, but it was not and the rain fell as grey as it ever did and as steady. 'Was hardly worth it,' muttered Michael, with private reference to his toilet.

The university was only a pace away. The buildings had the well-kept air of affluence which Michael reckoned was once the whole city of Liverpool; for to be sure it was a beautiful city when the sun was shining. It was a terrible shame what the English had done to it. But then look at Belfast . . . Michael realised he had not looked at Belfast for a good many years: not much left of it by all accounts.

He found himself a place on a low wall beside a concrete building he did not like much but which stood between him and the worst of the rain. He should go and look out Old Toby and the other fellah, old tramps that they were, but that could wait until his wall was uncomfortable.

It was not early, and the student population came and went, gathered and dispersed as regular as breathing. There were so many of them; Michael had never noticed before. The faces were young and all thought themselves older; Michael smiled broadly as he watched them pass. One or two offered him money, which he declined: he was no beggar, nor a wile man for the drink, so what would he want with money? The word would go round and dwellers he had not seen for weeks would come and pester him in his privacy.

What people wanted with money he could not understand: it was no wonder some of them tried so hard to get rid of it. 'No thank you, son,' he would reply firmly, 'very kind, very kind, but no thank you.' And for why did people offer him their coppers? Just because he was sitting on a wall did not mean that . . . but he had other things on his mind than anger, so he did not waste his time.

It was well past mid-day when he saw her again. She ran down the pavement, her hair flying and her papers flapping. Michael saw her only for a moment. A precious moment. And she was gone.

Lorna had never run like that, never had legs so swift or hair so fine. Ah, were Michael Fleck a younger man he would truly love that child.

An hour later she emerged again, looking persecuted. She was with a friend and they stopped just a little way from Michael.

'I absolutely loathe that man,' his wee Lorna was saying, 'hate him, hate him, hate him. Whatever I do he makes me feel that small.' She indicated her thumbnail. 'What the bloody hell does he want from us?' Her language grew more liberated as she waxed lyrical on her theme.

And Michael wanted to say, 'Child, child, don't bother yourself about the man. A wee lass like you should not know those words, should not even dream them.' His sisters had not, he was sure, and God above knew they were none of them as pretty as this lassie with the English tongue whose voice brought back no memories.

But then she would have been raised here across the water. What could Michael expect?

She was upset, Michael could see that. Education was a powerful thing and sometimes it could destroy a body. Perhaps wee Lorna was studying too hard. He remembered his sister Martha getting so thin when she was doing her school certificate; brains of the family was Martha. Michael himself could never get much from book-learning, but he had great respect for those who could. That was why he had missed Martha most of all when he first went south. So little Lorna was studying too hard. Michael was proud.

'Where are you going tonight then?' Lorna's friend was asking when Michael next turned his ear to them.

'Down to Fletcher's then on to the Everyman: Jonathan got two tickets for us weeks ago.'

'Not off to the party?' The two had begun to walk on past Michael, on up to the bus-stop.

'We'll probably come on later,' said Lorna, 'if we don't have anything better to do.' And the girls laughed their knowing laughs, leaving Michael to his wall and the rain.

He raised his eyebrows slightly. Busy life his Lorna had and her just a strip of a lass. Must do her studying during the day, or perhaps the rest of the week. 'Anything better to do': he had more than an idea what that could mean. Get a lass into a powerful lot of trouble that kind of talk. But it was none of his business.

He collected bits and pieces for his fire, which that night burned strongly for a while before glowing to ashes. Michael boiled water in a borrowed pan and drank it with sugar. It was a good warmth he slept with, on a bed almost dry.

It was a week before he wandered to the university again. He was content knowing his wee Lorna would be there, somewhere. He did not want to know the better things she found to do. And anyway his chest was bad and the weather worse. Old Rolly brought his kindling and Jake with one eye got him sugar and two carrots. Michael watched the Hun Cathedral change colour in the fleeting sunlight and lay as still as he could. It would pass if he did not fight it; that too he had learned.

Mary Dougan was waiting for him when four days later he was back in her care. 'And what do you think you were doing, Michael Fleck, sitting in the rain all day gathering water like a bucket? Gracious God in Heaven and you with a pair of lungs as wouldn't serve as bellows to a gnat fire. What were you thinking of, man?'

Michael murmured apologies.

'And why should you be sorrying to me when you should be upstairs on your knees to the Blessed Virgin asking her forgiveness for your thickheadedness. Ah, Michael Fleck, if I worried for you I'd be in my grave by now. What'll you have?'

Michael would be having tea as usual thanking you.

Mary strode away to find a few crumbs, not that he deserved them but he did look sick. Michael was not sick at all, it was just that his chest was bad. The sun would shine on Wednesday and he would step on out again to see his Lorna. Michael smiled a quiet smile. His room had been so warm this week despite the rain, how could a man be ill?

'Are you sickening for something, Michael Fleck?' said Mary harshly when she returned with a half round of toast and Michael's sweet tea. 'For I surely have never seen your eyes so bright.'

'Sickening for nothing, Mary, but your bonny smile.' Michael drew charm from an old source.

Mary was quite taken aback. 'Get along with you,' she said, and even forgot to dig his ribs as she normally did when her men said airy things. Something was not right with Michael Fleck. She thought about it for a while and then just took him more tea. He was just going through one of his turns; none of them was getting any younger. Although if that was going to be the way of Michael's aging he had better watch himself, may all the Angels and Saints do likewise.

That afternoon Michael took his walk down to the clothes heap. It was in the basement where the charitable ladies lurked.

'Oh, Mr. Fleck,' said one with faintly purple hair, 'we haven't seen you for a while, have we? How are you keeping? What can we do for you?'

Michael smiled an awkward smile. 'Well, madame,' he said carefully, 'it's trousers I am wanting, and a shirt.'

'Yes indeed, Mr. Fleck,' another lady emerged, 'we are in a bit of a state, aren't we?'

Michael mumbled assent and allowed his choice to be guided by their good taste and judgement: 'Those would be a little large, Mr. Fleck, don't you think? Try these. They're much more your colour.'

'And what about that hair, Mr. Fleck? Would you care for a trim?'

Michael said he would rather not, scooped up his clothing and left hurriedly.

Mary noticed the next day and shook her head. What was the

world coming to? New clothes in winter and Michael a dweller. If she had a mind to do anything of the kind she would worry.

The chest pains eased. Michael woke and washed again. Twice in a week, the Lord God preserve his skin. Michael was not at all sure that this new leaf was one that wanted to be turned: sure the world looked no different with a freezing face, and there was nothing he could do about his teeth: the sugar water often told him that they had all rotted black years ago. What was the use of Michael Fleck having a morning face and coal-black smile? It was the last time he would apply water to any part of him in quite a while and that was his oath.

Mid-day saw him on his wall in pale sunshine, watching the world go by. There were not as many people around: it was a week later into the term and the late nights were beginning to take their toll. Michael did not worry about the fewer faces: students came and went like travelling people and Michael saw no reason why there should be any method in their movement.

The wall was dry, Michael noticed: Mary Dougan would have nothing to complain on this week, poor woman. It was awful hard for him to sit still and keep watching: a dweller must stay in corners or someone would move him on.

She came, walking this time, with the same girl as the week before. They were talking, but were too far away for Michael to place their words. He just looked hard at her face and saw the curves of Lorna's mouth, the tilt of Lorna's eyes. He almost laughed aloud. It was a beautiful day to be sure.

They disappeared into the building. Michael suddenly thought that wee Lorna was carrying nothing. Well, learning was only heavy on the mind; he was sure Lorna would have with her all she would need.

She emerged minutes later, her face red and fists clenched. She leant against the glass doors, her eyes shut and tears lacing their edges.

Michael was heartbroken. He could not move for pity. He just watched her suffer. When he found the man he would do him harm, he surely would; with narrowed eyes and flint fists he would show what Michael Fleck would do in private wars.

His Lorna had pulled herself together and forced herself forward.

Her head was down. Her eyes would not meet Michael's in their shame. He reached out and touched her arm. 'Don't fret lass,' he said softly as she turned.

With a look of sheer panic. 'Get your hands off me, you old tramp,' she flared.

Michael took his hand away as from a live flame. 'I'm sorry, Miss, I . . .' His voice stumbled and the offending hand passed across his eyes before resting on his chest. 'Forgive an old man,' he said more clearly.

The girl had not run away: she was angry and humiliated and was going to let loose on someone. 'I could have you arrested,' she said in triumphant spite.

Michael hung his head. He had been in the cells before: they held no fear for him. But her threat feared him more than the pain.

'How dare you lay a finger on me,' her voice was clear and cold.

As was her face when Michael raised his eyes to meet it. 'Tell me one thing before you go, lass,' Michael controlled his words precisely, 'would your mother be Irish?' His face tilted to look directly into the girl's frozen eyes. Eyes which kindled with contempt. 'Irish?' she almost spat. 'Irish? My mother? You must be mad.'

The interview was over. She twisted herself from Michael's gaze and stalked off to her bus.

Michael sat in the sunshine, rocking gently; his arms folded across his chest, hands tucked away. He felt nothing, thought nothing, saw no man.

The day passed in a haze of clear November lines. Liverpool was a harsh city, Michael Fleck: no place to dwell; no place to breathe. The sea smelt different here, here where the English Mersey swamped the salt. Where are your feet taking you, Michael? To the water? To the Pier? To your working days, Michael Fleck, when the chains clanked and ropes took skin from the hardest hands?

Michael walked the day away.

It was near midnight when he rested on the railings looking out over the river. He was humming Irish folk songs and wondering whether Beatrice still baked bread. The sky was clear, so clear and full of stars. Michael could not find the moon.

He would go to Mary Dougan in the morning and get some food

inside him, for he was awful hungry. And his room would be an ice-box. 'You are a wile stupid man, Michael Fleck,' he murmured into the starlit dark. 'No lass is worth the forgetting of firewood.'

He turned from the water and began the walk back. Of course her mother would not be Irish. A wile stupid man with your dreaming, Michael Fleck, wile stupid with your crazy Irish dreams.